SHAD

Other novels by Erman Sands

Spirit of the Wolf
Battle of Whiskey Valley

To see more books by Erman Sands visit
www.wc-books.com/authors/erman-sands/

SHAD

A Novel

By

Erman Sands

Walnut Creek Publishing
Tuskahoma, Oklahoma

SHAD

ISBN: 978-1-942869-10-8
Second Edition, Paperback
Published 2015 by Walnut Creek Publishing
10 9 8 7 6 5 4 3 2
African American Historical Fiction

Books may be purchased in quantity and/or special sales by
contacting the publisher;
Walnut Creek Publishing
PO Box 820
Talihina, OK 74571
www.wc-books.com

ERMAN SANDS

To my wife, who never lost faith, and to my wonderful, whacky, loving family and friends, without whom this book would never have been possible. I love you all.

CHAPTER 1

"Conrad!" Ingrid screamed as her eyes picked out the still form at the base of the oak. Dropping the basket of food, she ran stumbling over the old cornstalks. Falling, she rose and ran again. Crashing to her knees beside the still form, she stared in shocked disbelief. Gently grasping a shoulder, Ingrid rolled Conrad onto his back. There could be no doubt, Conrad was dead.

"No! No!" Ingrid screamed, pulling Conrad's shoulders onto her lap and clasping his bloody head to her bosom. Her screams died off to great racking sobs as she sat rocking to and fro.

Ingrid stared in disbelief. *It isn't possible,* she thought. Just hours ago, she cooked his breakfast. Conrad deviled her the whole time. Her world was complete when he rose from the table.

"I'm going to tackle the big oak today," he said as he kissed Ingrid's smooth cheek. "Danged if I'm going to plow around it all next year."

Tall and slender, she pushed an errant strand of blonde hair into place, whisked the breakfast dishes off the table and smiled at his back as he went through the door.

Conrad sniffed the crisp fall air. There was just the hint of frost in it. The black gums mixed their mantles of red with the golden yellow of the maple and the old gold of the oaks. The mountains calmly accepted their coat of many colors.

"Yes, sir." Conrad told the mules as he hitched them to a homemade double tree. "With that hand mill and baking powder, we'll have biscuits like that every morning."

Both mules nodded their heads. They didn't understand the words, but the tone was reassuring and they knew all was well.

Gathering the chain in callused hands, Conrad bunched the muscles in his thick shoulders and leaned his five-foot eleven, one hundred and seventy pound frame back against it. When the double tree cleared the ground, he spoke softly to the mules and guided them toward the cornfield.

A large oak stood in the center of the field. For almost two centuries, it had spread its branches over the soil, furnishing acorns, buds and other food to whatever animal or bird that chose the shelter of its large canopy. Mulch, created by the annual leaf fall, was in part responsible for the good crop of corn Conrad harvested this year. Last year, Conrad hadn't had time to cut and remove this monarch of the forest.

After removing all the brush and smaller trees in the vicinity, he chopped the bark off a wide band around the oak's trunk. Its lifeline severed the oak withered, dropped its leaves for the last time, and died. Now, decay showing in the branches it occasionally dropped, the oak stood in the way of progress.

Conrad tied the mules to a sapling on the edge of the field. They were far enough away the oak could not hit them regardless of which direction it fell.

Retrieving a saw and an ax from the hollow log where he stored them yesterday, Conrad slowly circled the huge trunk determining which way the tree leaned and which side had the largest branches. He stuck a finger in his mouth and pointed it upward in order to gauge wind speed and direction. Each of these factors had to be considered when deciding which direction the tree would fall.

Conrad leaned the ax against the backside of the oak and began swiping the one-man saw back and forth across the bark less section of the trunk. Singing a merry tune, the saw threw sawdust to and fro with each powerful thrust of Conrad's strong arms. After the saw sang its way into the heart of the tree, Conrad removed it from the cut and placed it against the other side of the tree. Examining the cut, Conrad grunted his satisfaction and reached for the ax.

Callused hands and thick shoulders, young and strong, drove the ax in great arching blurs as the blade bit deep and true into the wood. Large, thick chips flew from the tree as the ax formed the notch that would guide the tree to the ground. The impact felt good and seeing the ax deliver chip after chip to the growing pile, gave Conrad a deep sense of satisfaction.

The first blow of the ax shivered and shook branches far up in the top of the old oak. As the crescendo of blows fell in a steady cadence, the shudder of the branches became more violent. With a grinding crunch a branch, perhaps twenty-feet long and six-inches thick, broke loose and plunged downward. With a solid crunch, the branch struck Conrad's head, knocking him onto his back. Slowly a leg drew up and pushed his body over. The broken neck let the head fall at a grotesque angle. Sightless eyes stared at the blood-spattered trunk.

After Conrad's peck on the cheek and departure toward the barn, Ingrid washed the breakfast dishes and began the process of converting wild grapes to jelly. She enjoyed the peace and solitude of the farm. Slender, supple and strong, she actually enjoyed the long hours of work.

Just think, she mused to herself, *at the tender age of twenty-five, she and Conrad owned more land than her entire family in her native Sweden. Furthermore, no greedy tax collector was going to confiscate half or more of the year's produce. No press gang was going to shanghai Conrad into military service.*

While dinner cooked, Ingrid plaited the long blonde hair across her head in the traditional Swedish fashion. Delivering lunch to Conrad in the field was the high point of her day.

Checking herself in the small mirror, she packed the wicker basket and departed for the field.

Ingrid was puzzled as she approached the field. She usually heard sounds of activity. Creaking harness, the snort of a mule, Conrad's softly spoken gee or haw always gave her an idea of what was going on before she came in sight. Today, the only sound she heard was the screaming of a jay and a fox squirrel scolding him for being such a noisy neighbor.

The mules flipped their ears forward and pulled at the sapling as she passed them. Large amounts of droppings and deeply trampled earth told her they had been tied there for some time.

"Conrad," she called tentatively. The screaming jay ceased his tirade and the squirrel raced for the safety of the treetops.

Then she found him. It couldn't be. It just couldn't be. She held the bloody proof in her arms, but her brain could not accept it as fact. He had been so alive and vital. It didn't seem possible for him to be struck down this way.

Ingrid would never be sure how she did it, but she took the mules back to the barn and hooked them to the wagon. Getting help never entered Ingrid's mind. There was no one closer than Tendrilhoff plantation and it was five miles down river. Neither Conrad nor Ingrid had the time or inclination to visit a large plantation. She didn't know anyone there.

Upon her return with the wagon, Ingrid was so distraught she failed to see the black boy sitting a few feet from the oak. Impassive and quiet, he sat with a long rifle lying across his lap. The boy, about ten years old, held a rifle longer than he was tall. His shirt was a homespun butternut gray, the tail of which hung loose just below his waist. About the waist, there was a wide belt. Mounted on this belt hung two large scabbards, each scabbard contained a razor sharp hunting knife. The hair above his remarkably fine-featured face was cropped short. His lean body and supple limbs promised grace, speed, and endurance. The only parts of him that moved were the intelligent brown eyes.

Shad was in the process of stalking a large buck on the ridge to the south when Ingrid found Conrad's body. Her anguished screams attracted his attention and piqued his curiosity.

Shad's father had pointed out the farm on previous hunting trips and always cautioned him to stay away from white folk.

At this time in the South, it was instant death for a slave caught carrying a firearm. In spite of this, old Mister George liked wild game on his table and gave Shad's father the job of hunting for the plantation table.

One reason Mister George sold the plantation in Virginia and moved southwest to the wild country was because he chafed under too many laws. Out here in the wilderness, his word was law.

Most plantation owners disagreed with Mister George's handling of slaves anyway. He was too lenient. Everyone worked. That was the times. If a man didn't work, he didn't eat. But, the crack of the whip was never heard on Tendrilhoff plantation.

Breaking off from the buck, Shad eased down the ridge and stalked the commotion as he would have stalked a wild animal. Using all the woods craft his father taught him, Shad fearfully moved from cover to cover. When he arrived at the edge of the field, he leaned against the trunk of a large beech tree to break up his outline. From this cover, Shad watched the woman unhook the heavy double tree and drive the mules toward the barn.

After Ingrid departed, Shad cautiously entered the field, ready to flee at the slightest sign of danger. The smell of death was strong on the morning air. He was standing beside Conrad's body when he heard the wagon returning. Taking a few running steps toward the forest, he stopped. He had an inquiring mind and a thirst for knowledge. He learned something from most situations. Picking a hole in the brush to escape through and a tree to dart behind if necessary, he turned and sat down.

Ramrod stiff, barely breathing, Shad watched the woman drag Conrad's body to the tailgate of the wagon. He continued to watch as Ingrid struggled to lift the heavy, lifeless body into the wagon. Rising slowly, always ready to flee, he moved quietly toward Ingrid.

Placing the rifle gently on the ground, Shad helped Ingrid slide the body into the wagon. Ingrid stared at him through swollen, tear-stained eyes, then climbed silently to the wagon seat. Without a backward glance, she slapped the check lines on the mules' backs and headed them toward the house.

Shad retrieved the rifle and stood, uncertain. He was remembering the funeral of his father, two weeks earlier. Considering he was a plantation slave, his father's funeral had been an elaborate affair. All the other slaves thought Shad's father was a medicine man, a man who could bring good luck to them with a smile, or cause great pain and suffering by a scowl. It was believed he could converse with the other world; casts spells, or have the demons and haints at a man's heels every night. All the black folk were sure the hunter would be back and walk the plantation at will.

Shad never put much stock in such stories, but Shad's father had taught him certain chants, charging him with the responsibility of never forgetting them. At this time, his father also gave him a hat and cloak made of finely worked leopard skin and a bag of something resembling ground herbs, admonishing him to let no one know of their existence.

The gift shocked and honored Shad. Although only four at the time, Shad vividly remembered his father turning the skin rough side out and rolling the potion in it. Working it into his loincloth as a belt, he smuggled it through without question from slave catcher or shipmaster.

All the white folk on the plantation, those from the big house, the overseers, and the blacksmith had been present at the funeral. Wild horses could not have kept the black population away.

The death of his father left a great empty hole in Shad's life that he was sure would never be filled. Now he was witnessing the grief of another.

After a few minutes of pondering, Shad gave a wave of resignation with his left hand and followed the wagon tracks toward the house.

When he arrived at the house, he found the wagon parked on a small rise behind the garden. Ingrid was digging alongside it. She dug furiously, stabbing and tearing at the unyielding earth. Moving up beside her, Shad took the shovel. Ingrid stared at him. An uncomprehending look clouded her eyes. After a moment, she reluctantly yielded the shovel. Then gathering her skirt up in one hand, she raced to a large old sycamore tree. Once there, she collapsed into uncontrollable sobs.

Later, they lowered Conrad's body into the grave and Ingrid said a few words over him. Picking up his rifle, Shad disappeared in the forest. His going was as silent and swift as a ghost. Ingrid wondered if indeed he had been there or if she imagined him.

CHAPTER 2

"What am I going to do?" Ingrid asked herself for the hundredth time in the past two weeks. She sat curled up in a willow branch rocking chair Conrad made. One of the two books she managed to bring south with her, lay on the floor beside the rocker.

By placing the rocker on the end of the porch, she could see the grave. She could also see the yard gate. The day after Conrad's funeral, a dressed turkey had been hanging on the gate. At regular intervals a swamp rabbit, a brace of quail, and other woods offerings appeared.

Her thoughts returned to the old country. Her folks had a rough time there. They finally said enough and sailed for America. She fought back tears as her mind recalled their burial at sea. Neither of them lived to see the America they had pinned their hopes on.

If she loaded the wagon with grain and drove it to civilization, she could sell the whole works. They wouldn't bring enough money for passage to the old country, even if she wanted to go. With a shudder, Ingrid remembered her arrival in America. A young girl with no friends, and she couldn't speak the language. She remembered the days of wandering the city, starving.

Unbidden came the mental image of the sweatshop owner's leering face as thoughts of long hours, dreary days, and months of sewing until her fingers were so callused, she no longer needed a thimble to push a needle through the fabric.

The sweaty face, roving hands, and immoral suggestions of the foreman came to her as clear as if it happened yesterday.

Later the laughing, fun loving young German arrived with his dream of a farm in the wilderness. Ingrid spent her honeymoon in a wagon rolling south, searching for this utopia. A grant of land, a lot of hard work, they almost made it.

Ingrid sat bolt upright in her chair. Almost made it? She would make it! She had food for a year. She now owned all they accumulated. She would learn to plow and plant. It would be better than... a movement at the gate caught her attention. A black boy was tying something on the gate.

"Wait a moment," Ingrid called.

The figure jumped, ran a few steps and stopped. "Please wait, I want to thank you." Ingrid instinctively knew not to move.

Shad's eyes were taking in everything. Fear rose in his throat. The rifle on his arm became a real weight. His father's warning about getting caught carrying a firearm came to mind. Still, the unmoving woman on the porch didn't seem too much of a threat. Slowly his fear subsided. Wariness replaced the fear.

"Please, come in I want to talk to you. I need to talk to someone." The hurt and loneliness was clear in Ingrid's voice.

Slowly Shad opened the gate and took a few steps toward the porch. His eyes instinctively searched the door, windows, and corners of the house. They were seeing everything and concentrating on nothing. Stopping two steps short of the porch, Shad stood with the rifle dangling in one hand and a back strap of venison hanging from the other.

"What is your name?" Ingrid asked after a moment of silence.

"Shad." His eyes were still searching everywhere for some hidden danger.

"Shad what? What is your last name?" Ingrid added when she saw him hesitate.

"Just Shad, ma'am. I'm a slave at Tendrilhoff Plantation."

"You're a slave and they let you wander around?" Ingrid

moved for the first time, placing her hands on the chair arms.

"No, ma'am. I'm the hunter." Shad relaxed a little, this woman was no threat to him.

"You don't talk like a slave." Ingrid was still trying to place him in her mind.

"Mister George insists all his people speak passable English." Shad's eyes made another sweep of the area, and then settled on Ingrid again.

"Well anyway, I want to thank you for the food, the meat I mean." As she spoke, Ingrid rose and moved to the edge of the porch. Her toe bumped the book and it fell to the ground. Landing on its back the book lay open. A breeze fluttered the pages.

Shad didn't answer. He stood, staring at the book. It fascinated him. Never had he held a book in his hands. He had seen them in the library at the big house, but never actually held one in his hands. Without taking his eyes off the book, Shad placed the rifle on the ground, handed the strip of venison to Ingrid and picked up the book. Tenderly, in great wonder, he ran his finger over the printed page. The finger circled as if trying to feel the words.

"Are these words?" Shad never took his eyes off the page.

"Yes."

"What do they say?"

"Well, they tell a story." Ingrid stepped from the porch and taking the book from Shad's hands turned it right side up and handed it back to him.

"I've heard words before, but I've never seen words. Are they your words?" Shad continued to try to feel the words with his fingers.

"No, those words were written by a man named James Fenimore Cooper." Ingrid tried to suppress a smile as she watched him.

"These are his words and he ain't even here?" This was arousing Shad's curiosity even more. He pried his eyes from the book and looked her in the eye, searching for the truth.

"No, and he has never been here. He lived up north. It is a story about people, settlers, Indians, and hunters like your self." A thought was born in the back of her mind. "Would you like to learn to read?"

"A slave can't read." Shad turned back to the book.

"Pshaw!" Ingrid snorted. "A slave can learn to read same as anybody. I can teach you."

The thought startled Shad to the toe of his boots. Could he learn to read? Then there was Mister George. Since Shad was four-years old, he had belonged to Mister George and during that time, he never did anything contrary to Mister George's wishes.

"It's against the law for a slave to learn to read. It's also against the law to teach a slave to read." Shad handed the book back to her.

Ingrid took a slow, exaggerated look around. Then, standing on tiptoe, she looked over Shad's head. "I don't see any law," she said at last.

Taking the book, Ingrid opened it and pointed to a letter. "This is an A, this is a B. You will have to learn all the letters. There are twenty-six. Picking up a piece of slate rock Ingrid pulled a hunting knife from Shad's belt. She scratched an A on the rock with the point. "That is the way you make it."

Handing the knife back, Ingrid stared at him for a long moment. "I would like the company." Then she corrected herself. "I need the company."

Shad often stopped by Ingrid's in his coming and going.

He spent hours around his campfires scratching letters on rocks, then tossing them into the fire. First, it was just letters, then simple words. Finally, the day came when Ingrid loaned him the precious book. This was the high point in his life.

Placing the book in his hunting jacket, Shad raced over the mountain to the edge of a secluded meadow. Placing his rifle on the ground beside him, Shad settled against a tree and began laboriously reading the book.

Warm sun used the bare treetops to cast crisscross shadows on the ground around him. He could hear the whirr and flutter of bird's wings as they flitted to and fro through tree tops. A soft breeze rustled brown frost-kissed grass.

Breezes carried the damp smell of the river and a hint of spring rode their gentle breasts. The meadow was a small window of the world at peace and rest. Shad's head began to nod. His chin settled on his chest.

It began as a pricking at the back of his neck. Instinct jerked and tugged at him until it finally pulled him wide-awake. Something or someone was staring intently at him. Looking up, he saw a tall man dressed in a long black coat slowly walking toward him. A flat crowned, wide brimmed, black hat sat squarely on the man's head.

Terror seized Shad. What to do? This man saw him reading! Bile rose in his throat, choking him with the bitter taste. Why did he get so engrossed in the book that someone could walk up on him? Run? Shoot the man? Thoughts raced through his mind as the man drew closer and closer. Indecision held him motionless with the damning evidence in his hand. Evidence that could get him shot or hung on the spot!

A sad smile played about the mouth and eyes of the man. He recognized Shad's terror. Never breaking stride, he pulled two books from his pocket as he passed Shad, one old and worn, the other almost new. Hesitating, the man looked at both books, came to a decision, dropped the new one into Shad's lap, and walked on. Just as he passed into the timber, the itinerant preacher began singing "Amazing Grace."

Slowly the terror passed. A copper taste was still in his mouth. Shad spit into the pine needles, laid his book down and picked up the one the man dropped into his lap.

Turning it over, he read Holy Bible across the front of it.

Even after his scare, Shad could not resist. Looking across the meadow, he sat stock-still. A red bird flew up onto a bush, then dropped back to the ground and began stirring the leaves. A busy fox squirrel hopped into the meadow and scampered out of a doe's way as she led a yearling onto the remaining grass. Both stood for a while, testing the air, and finally began nibbling at the grass and herbs.

They would nibble for a moment, raise their heads, test the air, turn their big ears this way and that. One or the other was on guard almost constantly.

Satisfied the deer would warn him of any approaching danger, Shad opened the Bible and began to read. He kept sight of both deer in the corner of his eye.

A warning snort from the doe and they bounded into a thicket. Dropping the books into his shirt, Shad picked up his rifle and faded silently into the brush.

Lying on his stomach, Shad peered between two rocks. On the trail below the meadow there was a flash of movement. Two men entered the meadow. One was tall and lean, the other broad and muscular. Both were dressed in buckskin shirts and doeskin pants. Small packs hung on their backs. Each carried a long rifle and moved with the long easy strides of woodsmen accustomed to traveling beyond the far horizon.

Long hunters, Shad thought. They were a fiercely independent troublesome bunch at the best and fight to finish battlers at their worst. Shad kept his chin in contact with the ground.

He moved nothing but his eyes. The rocks and brush broke up his silhouette. His butternut clothing blended in perfectly with the surrounding rocks and brush.

Even though their strides never changed, both men began taking long looks at the surrounding terrain. They could feel Shad's eyes upon them. The tall man swung his rifle up and held it in both hands. Muscle man held his by the grip and laid the barrel in the crook of his left arm.

Shad lay still until the men passed through a gap at the far end of the meadow and disappeared. Brushing cobwebs from his hair, Shad eased to a sitting position. Fishing the Bible from his shirt, he began reading again.

It was a long word. It was a pesky word. No matter how hard he tried, how many ways he broke it down, it didn't make sense.

After struggling with the word for some time, he decided to ask Ingrid. He wanted to show her his new possession anyway. It was the first thing he'd ever owned. The clothes he wore, the rifle he carried, his boots, his very person, everything belonged to the plantation.

Coming down the mountain near Ingrid's cabin, he heard strange sounds, voices where there should be silence. They were quarrelsome voices. He couldn't understand the words, but the tones carried a message even at this distance.

Circling around in order to keep the barn between him and the voices, Shad cautiously approached. At the corner of the barn, Shad dropped to the ground and peeked around the end of the logs.

The long hunters were there. The tall, lean one stood in front of Ingrid. The other leaned, with crossed arms, on his long rifle a few feet away. The voices were louder, but still indistinguishable.

Circling back to keep as much cover as possible, Shad crawled in behind a bush at the edge of the yard. He never looked directly at either man. Both focused full attention on Ingrid, who stood her full five-feet seven and glared at the taller man.

"Now dimples, you wouldn't pull ol' Fess's leg would you?" The leer on his face was obvious. Weight on the balls of his feet, head tilted and leaning forward, he looked like a diamondback rattler about to strike.

"Husband, husband hell, I've been standing here talking to you for near onto half hour and I ain't seen hide nor hair of no man. I don't think he's going to walk in here and if he does ol' Ferd or me'll kill him. What do you think Ferd?"

"No husband." Ferd rested his chin on arms crossed on the rifle barrel and smiled in anticipation.

Fess's arm shot out, his fingers grasped Ingrid's dress at the throat. Giving a mighty yank, he tore most of the front out of it. She went for his eyes. Stepping back with an oath, Fess back-handed her hard across the face. Stunned, Ingrid stumbled backward a couple of steps. Before she could get her balance, Fess lunged forward and backhanded her again.

Ingrid fell on her back, then tried to rise. Fess's boot made a solid thud when it connected with her ribs. She fell back again, writhing in pain.

"That's better." Fess wiped blood from the scratch marks around his eyes and stooped to pull the rest of the dress from her body.

Without a thought, Shad's rifle leaped to his shoulder and when the sights settled on the top of Fess's ear, he pulled the trigger. The heavy bullet, designed to kill deer, bear, and other large game, exploded Fess's skull. His brains erupted over a large area.

Eyes shining with battle lust, Shad charged Ferd. Startled, Ferd stared at Fess for a horrified unbelieving moment, then tried to bring his rifle into line with a charging Shad. Swinging his rifle with his left hand, Shad knocked Ferd's rifle barrel up and to the left, sending Ferd's shot harmlessly skyward. Whipping the knife from his belt, Shad drove in low and loosed a powerful upward thrust toward Ferd's lower body. Ferd grew up rough and tumble. Like a cat, he leaped to the side, pulled his stomach in and let the knife pass harmlessly through his jacket.

Taking Shad by the arm, Ferd pulled him on past and drove a smashing elbow to the side of his head. Darkness then bright spots, then more darkness alternated through Shad's head. The knife dropped from his hand. Flipping Shad to the ground, Ferd delivered a powerful kick to the side of his head, hesitated a moment and kicked him again. Shad twitched, then lay still.

Ferd glanced at Ingrid struggling to get out from under Fess's body, pulled his jacket out and examined the long cut Shad's knife made in it.

"Young rooster's sure full of fight," Ferd muttered to himself. "Wonder if he would be as full of fight as a capon."

Picking up Shad's knife, Ferd ran an exploratory finger along the razor sharp blade. A sadistic gleam kindled in his eyes. Ferd's lips drew back. His long yellow teeth gleamed.

Yes, sir! He was going to have some fun! It had been some time since the young Indian girl strayed into his waiting arms. Unconsciously Ferd's hand moved to his belt, making sure her scalp was still there.

He sat around many campfires toying with the scalp, remembering her screams. Yes, sir, Old Ferd had made an Indian scream.

"Your scalp is too short and wooly." Ferd leaned forward. "But those ears will look right handsome on either side of this scalp. Don't die on me now boy; Old Ferd wants to hear some music."

Shad stirred. Kicking Shad viciously in the ribs, Ferd hesitated to see the results. Yanking Shad's head up by the hair, he placed the knife blade on top of Shad's ear, laughing in anticipation. Motionless, Ferd waited for Shad's eyes to open.

A resounding boom and Ferd straightened, his face wore a puzzled look as he fell backward to reveal Ingrid holding Fess's smoking rifle.

Dropping the rifle, Ingrid knelt beside Shad. "Are you alright? Shad!" She yelled. "Can you hear me?"

"Yes, ma'am." Shad slowly pushed himself to a sitting position. Shad held his hands out trying to focus his eyes on them.

"Are you badly hurt, Shad?"

"Don't know," Shad mumbled.

Ingrid looked down at her bare breasts. They were spattered with Fess's brains. She screamed hysterically. Desperately she tried to wipe off the offending matter. The more she wiped the more the sticky, greasy brains smeared. Snatching up pieces of the torn dress, Ingrid raced for the house.

Later, a scrubbed clean, fully clothed, composed Ingrid appeared in the doorway. She glanced down the porch to where Shad sat with his head in his hands.

"Shad," she called softly. "Are you hurt?"

"Make no difference if I was," Shad mumbled.

"Of course it makes a difference!" Ingrid was perplexed. "At least it makes a difference to me."

Rising, Shad looked her in the eye. "Miss Ingrid, I done killed a white man. They are going to hang me."

"Those aren't men." She gestured toward the bodies in the yard. "They were animals. They were going to kill me." Ingrid leaned against a porch post. "They were going to kill me real slow. If... if you hadn't come along." Her voice trailed off.

"Makes no difference," Shad insisted. "If a slave kills a white man, the slave hangs. There is no acceptable reason for a slave to kill a white man."

Ingrid stood in silence, digesting the truth of his statement. "Shad, nobody knows they were here. I doubt anyone even knows or cares where they are. We will bury them and their belongings down by the creek and nobody except you and me... will ever know."

Ingrid sat down on the edge of the porch silent until she figured Shad was getting settled down.

"We better get on with the burying. I'll harness the mule and get the sled. You go through their packs and pockets. See if we can figure out who they are or where they come from."

Shad went through the pockets and packs without finding a clue. Surprisingly, he did find two heavy bags of gold coins, one in each pack. He gave both bags to Ingrid. Ingrid counted each bag into a neat pile. "That's strange; there is the same amount of gold in each bag. They must have stolen it or robbed someone and split the take evenly," she speculated. "We will bury everything but the gold. Here you take it." Ingrid dumped all the gold into one bag.

"What use does a slave have for gold?" Shad walked away in disgust.

Shad and Ingrid buried the bodies in a single grave, which Shad dug extra deep. He tossed the rifles in on top of the bodies. Ingrid shuddered as she lowered the packs into the grave. Never again, she vowed, would anyone catch her unprepared, unarmed, and helpless.

CHAPTER 3

Ingrid leaned on the porch support, then surveyed the yard and surrounding area as the new day slowly arrived. Two months had come and gone since Fess and Ferd's visit. The nervousness and fear finally subsided, but the vigilance it brought would last a lifetime. Inside her aprons, a new pocket had been sewn and Conrad's smallest pistol had taken permanent residence there.

Studying new buds beginning to form on the red oak in the corner of the yard, Ingrid stirred restlessly. It will soon be planting time, she thought. I better start breaking ground today.

The mules were rambunctious and intractable as she caught them and harnessed them. Except for an occasional foray after firewood, they had done nothing since last fall, but graze and eat grain. Being veterans on the farm, the mules sensed that work time was here.

Ingrid harnessed Jack first. She put his bridle on and turned to harness Jake. Jack trotted off and ducked into his stall. After getting Jake's harness buckled in place and his bridle on, she tied him to the top rail of the corral. Dragging the reluctant Jack from his stall, she snapped the ends of both check lines onto the bits. Harness jangling a merry little tune, the team pranced from the lot as if they were walking on eggshells.

When Ingrid swung them around in front of the turning plow, both mules snorted. Pretending the plow was a booger, they swung their rumps around so they were facing each other. Hooking the inside trace chains Ingrid pulled, shoved, and grunted until they relented and let her hook the outside chains.

Dragging the heavy plow into the garden, Ingrid set it up. She tied the check lines together, then placed them over one shoulder and under the other arm as she had seen Conrad do so many times. Taking a deep breath, she lifted on the plow handles and spoke to the mules. Obediently they moved forward. The plow point bit into the rich black earth and began rolling it over.

"I'm plowing!" Ingrid cried jubilantly to the mules. The plow continued to sink deeper and deeper into the earth. The mules strained mightily to keep it moving. Desperately, Ingrid quit lifting on the handles and began pushing down to bring the plow back to proper depth. As the plow rose through the soil, the point hit a rock. Like a living thing, the plow leaped from the earth. The left plow handle delivered a smashing blow to Ingrid's ribs knocking her sideways. The wing came to earth and flipped the plow in the other direction. The right handle came back like a club and hit the hammer of the pistol in her apron pocket. A loud boom and the ball ripped through cloth and entered the newly turned earth. The mules bolted, jerking a staggering Ingrid down, and dragged her with the check lines. Her weight on the reins quickly brought them to a stop.

Shaken and gasping, Ingrid struggled out of the check lines and staggered a few feet. Both mules stood quietly, long ears forward, heads turned. They stared at her inquiringly.

"Better quit picking on me!" Ingrid shook a small fist at them. Leaning forward, she placed one hand on her offended ribs and the other on her bruised hip. "I'm the only one who can open the door to the corn crib," She threatened.

Circling the mules, Ingrid set the plow back into the furrow. The plow had a mind of its own. Struggle as she might it ran deep, ran shallow, or leaped from the ground. About the time she thought it was running right, it would hang a root and the crossbar would smack her in the stomach. The handles pounded her mercilessly. She would not quit. She dared not quit. She told herself over and over.

At the end of the day, Ingrid leaned on the plow handles depressed and dispirited. Here and there, she saw bare spots of unbroken ground, and here and there were great piles of earth too deeply turned. Never had she been so bruised, battered, and tired. Looking back across the garden, she lowered her head to the plow handles and let loose with gut-wrenching sobs.

"We will do it again tomorrow." She promised the mules as she drove them toward the barn.

Unharnessing the mules, Ingrid slowly limped to the crib and carried them an extra ration of grain. Then she walked straight to her bed and fell into it. She was too sore and tired to wash up, change clothes, or think of a meal.

The next morning, Ingrid awoke aching. She tried to think of some part of her body that didn't hurt. She tried to rise, groaned, and fell back on the bed. Rolling off the bed onto the floor, she pushed herself to her feet.

Raiding her small hoard of precious coffee, Ingrid drank a cup and limped to the barn. Harnessing the mules, a chore at any time, took an hour this morning. She got to enjoy the pain of lifting the heavy harness several times. It took several attempts before she could lift the harness high enough to slide it onto the mule's back.

As she turned the mules into the garden, her aches were diminishing. There was still fire in her ribs with every breath, but the rest was beginning to work out. Swinging the mules toward the plow, she stopped, staring unbelievingly.

The garden was plowed. Furrows straight and neat, the earth turned evenly all the way across the garden.

"Ok mules, there is the big field to go." Ingrid said as she hooked them onto the big plow.

The plow had not learned a thing, Ingrid thought as she wrestled it down one side of the field. It still had a mind of its own. When she made the turn at the end of the field, a black hand took the handle alongside hers.

"Turn loose," Shad ordered.

The unruly plow immediately settled down. It cut and turned the rich dark earth with a steady swishing sound. After a complete round, Shad called a halt.

"You're working too hard at it," he informed her. "Hold it up straight and let it run itself. If you have it adjusted right at the bulkhead, it will run the right depth. Lean it to the left a bit and it will move a little to the right. Lean it to the right and it will run to the left. Walk a little farther back so if it hits a root or rock the handles don't whack you in the ribs."

"Now you tell me!" Ingrid exclaimed, and then she realized the fire was mostly gone from her ribs.

"Now, you take it for a round," Shad suggested. "Watch Jake, that old scoundrel will sneak out of the furrow to the right. He knows the plow won't bite as much land and will pull easier. When he does that yell haw at him and he will get back where he belongs."

Around they went, the plow minding its P's and Q's for the most part. Once it leaped from the ground, but the handles missed Ingrid. She couldn't keep from dodging and Shad couldn't keep from grinning. After two complete rounds, Shad called a halt.

"Enough for today," he announced.

"But I have this whole field to plow!" Ingrid protested.

"Yesterday, last night, this morning, the mules have earned a rest." Shad picked up his rifle. "A teacher for the teacher," he said. Then he was gone.

By this time, Shad was a very proficient and insatiable reader. Many times, he thought of the great volumes resting in the library at the big house and yearned for the knowledge they contained. Of the three books available to him, the Bible was by far his favorite. It not only contained the story of Jesus and all the miracles he performed, it contained stories of great men, great wars, and great deeds both good and evil. His favorite though, was of a race of people held slaves until God heard their groans and freed them. He read about their long flight to freedom, and their rise to great power and wealth beyond belief.

He spent hours thinking of the timid ones who cowered, held back, refused to believe in their destiny, and dragged the others down at times.

Today, after finishing his allotted chores, he took the Bible behind an empty tobacco barn and sat in the reflected heat of the early spring sun. After reading the book of Exodus again, he tipped his head back against the weathered wood, closed his eyes, and tried to get a mental image of Moses.

After a few unsuccessful minutes, he opened his eyes. There, right in front of him stood Mister George! Mister George had a mighty stern look on his face. Slowly, Shad folded the Bible back against his chest. He was terrified. He was too frightened to move or speak. He could only sit and stare.

Mister George crossed his arms on his chest and stared back. After a long moment, Mister George turned, walked to the crooked rail fence. Leaning on the top rail, he stared off across the fields.

"Shad, come here!" Master George came to a decision.

Shad was too petrified to answer or move.

"Shad! I told you to come here!" Impatience shaded Mister George's voice.

"Yes, sir," Shad finally stammered. Slowly, he managed to push himself up the wall, head hanging, shaking like a leaf, staggered to the fence.

"Can you read that Bible?" Mister George demanded.

Shad could only nod.

Mister George took the Bible. Closed it and looked at Shad. Opening the Bible, he handed it back to Shad. "Read that page," he ordered.

Shad took the Bible. At first, he stumbled and stammered. As his eyes ran over the familiar words, Shad's composure returned somewhat and he finished strong.

"I'm not going to ask where you learned to read." Mister George's stern face relaxed a little. "I've heard of the lady beyond the mountain and I notice you go and come from that direction."

Shad hung his head. Tears came to his eyes. Not only was he in trouble, he was bringing trouble to Ingrid.

"Can you do sums?" Mister George questioned.

"I can add, subtract, and multiply." Shad's fighting blood began to rise. No one could touch Ingrid. His hand moved to the knife in his belt. He looked at the old man. He'd... then it dawned on him, he couldn't attack this man, no more than he could have harmed his father. Since his younger days, Shad looked upon Mister George with a hero worship youngsters often develop. Mister George always responded as a favorite uncle would. His arms dropped and he hung his head in despair.

Mister George saw the flare in Shad's eyes at the mention of the lady. He saw the movement of the hand and the look of despair when Shad realized he couldn't do him any harm.

"Buck up, young man." Mister George took Shad by the arm. "Nobody is going to harm the lady. I want you in my office, first thing after supper." After a moment, Mister George strode purposefully around the barn.

Shad stood transfixed. *Mister George said no one would harm Ingrid. Did he hear the words right? Should he run? If he ran, where would he run to?* Since arriving from Africa as a small child, he had never been anywhere else or wanted to be anywhere else. *Leave?* The thought shook him to the core. Leaving had never entered his mind. This was home. He slowly sank to the ground and leaned against the fence.

Shad sat where he was, his mind in turmoil. He tried to imagine what it would be like to hang. To dance on the air, twisting and choking. His hand involuntarily moved to his throat.

The cook rang a triangle, announcing suppertime. Shad continued to sit by the fence. After a sufficient amount of time passed for the meal to end, he rose and stumbled woodenly toward the big house.

Darkness was rising from the river. The last of the light lingered along the ridge tops to the west. A whippoorwill began calling at the edge of the clearing. All this was lost on Shad as he moped along. At least his father wouldn't be there to see the end his son was coming to. His father... Shad stopped cold.

The big house was right in front of him. Where was everyone? When a slave was punished, all the slaves were called in to watch the punishment. Shad stood motionless. Carefully, he listened to the sounds around him. There were the usual evening sounds of chores being finished and the plantation settling down for the night. A single light burned by the door. It casts a weak glow across the veranda.

Shad tiptoed across the veranda and took hold of the bell rope, lost his nerve and retreated across the porch. He stopped on the steps, squared his shoulders, tromped back to the bell rope and gave it a resolute tug. Chimes sounded from somewhere back in the big house.

After a few moments, the big door swung open to reveal Hannibal. The old butler looked fresh and crisp in his tailored suit. His once curly black hair was now striking silver.

"Mister George is waiting for you. Come this way." Hannibal's manner suggested Shad was breaching some point of etiquette.

Hannibal led Shad down a hall and around the corner. At the corner, they met George Junior, a lad of twelve, not as tall as Shad, a permanent pout about his mouth. Junior was quite a figure in polished boots, tailored breeches, hunting jacket, and white ruffled shirt. He had striking blue eyes with shoulder length curly blond hair.

Junior stopped short. "What's he doing here?" He demanded of Hannibal.

"Mister George sent for him."

Tilting his nose up a little, Hannibal breezed on down the

hall and opened the wide doors to the library. "Office is in back of the library, the door in the corner."

Hannibal pulled the library doors shut and left Shad on his own. Shad crossed the room without a look at the bookshelves, pushed the next door open and entered.

Mister George sat behind a huge mahogany desk. Glancing up, he pointed to a chair sitting at the corner of his desk. "Be seated."

As soon as Shad sat down Mister George handed him a sheet of paper and a pencil. "Here are some math problems. Can you solve them?"

Stunned, Shad sat for a moment, looking at the pencil, then went to work. After completing the task and checking the answers, he silently handed the sheet back to Mister George. Mister George swiftly graded the paper, and grunted his satisfaction.

"I caught my bookkeeper stealing." Mister George turned his chair facing Shad. "The scoundrel was bleeding the plantation every week. I sacked him and I caned him thoroughly. I suppose I should have shot him, but I didn't. I sent him back down river."

Shad was silent. He couldn't see what this had to do with his own misdeeds.

"Bookkeepers are hard to get out here in the wilderness." Mister George continued. "And, if you do find one, the scoundrel wants an arm and leg to work this far from civilization."

Mister George leaned forward and laid a hand on the desk in front of Shad. "I'm going to teach you how to do account books."

Shad was stunned to absolute silence. He barely breathed.

"Oh, this is going to be our little secret." Mister George chuckled at the stricken look on Shad's face. "As far as anyone else is concerned, you come to this office to fetch and carry these heavy books for me."

Mister George picked up the book in front of him and placed it in front of Shad. "Open it," he ordered.

Shad took the cover of the book and opened an entirely new and different kind of life for himself. He knew money existed, but he never knew the value of it. He never owned any money. All his needs were taken care of by the plantation. Never had he purchased a single item. When he opened the ledger book, he stepped into a world totally foreign to him, the world of finance.

Eventually, he would be dealing with the entire financial operation of a large plantation. He would know the monetary value of every item the plantation used, right down to the price of a horseshoe nail. He would know the value of every hogs-head of tobacco, pound of cotton, and bushel of corn the plantation sent down river.

CHAPTER 4

5 Years Later

Shad threw a pine knot on the fire and leaned back against a tree. Damn! It felt good to be in the woods again. After that first night in Mister George's office five years ago, his time in the woods grew less and less. Mister George gave him the job of training another hunter two years ago and since then his duties at the plantation kept him busy from sunup to sundown.

He camped on top of a mountain beside a clear, cold spring he had developed some years before. The water boiled out of a crevice three or four feet below the surface, rushed up to leap the small retaining wall, and then fell with a gurgle of laughter at its escape. After this it whispered quietly to the rocks and pines as it hurried away to join the big river below.

The full moon was a great glowing ball in the sky. Its soft rays kissed and caressed the mountains and canyons until the dark night was transformed into a soft twilight. *I could climb the tallest tree and tickle the moon's tummy with my fingers,* Shad thought.

From where he sat, he could see ridge after tree-covered ridge as the country fell away to the South. Each one seemed to run away into infinity in the half-light of the moon. There was a great dark notch where the ridges met the big river. Over this was a long glowing line of light. The moon had not forgotten to illuminate the river fog.

The gentle spring breeze set the treetops to swaying and gossiping like two old maids at a pie social. The breeze also carried and scattered the fragrance of the wild flowers until it seemed the whole forest was a big flower garden.

Shad glared at a light on top of a mountain four miles or so away. The country is filling up with settlers and game is getting scarcer every day, he thought. Not that it matters much, he muttered darkly.

Mister George permitted him time to visit Ingrid and expand his education. This worked out well. Mister George was more than generous with his library and Shad was able to carry many quality books on his visits to Ingrid.

Ingrid didn't have much time to read. She was plowing, hoeing and harvesting, doing the work of two men. But, she always took time for Shad and the books were a comfort on long winter nights. The bond between them continued to blossom and grow. Shad rose to Ingrid's level of education and they continued exploring and teaching each other.

Shad had proven to be especially adept at mathematics. He could carry huge amounts of information in his head and was quick to work out a problem. His honesty was beyond question.

Mister George depended on him on more and more as time went by. He gave Shad a horse and freedom to roam the far reaches of the plantation. He could see or talk to anyone he chose.

Two years earlier, when the steamboats began running up river, Mister George put Shad in charge of the slave gang that loaded and unloaded them. No one paid the slaves any attention. They were just the muscle that put cargo on and took cargo off. But Shad, with his ability to carry figures in his head, was quick to spot unscrupulous boat captains that lined their pockets at the plantation's expense and report the same to Mister George. Shad's books were also quick to point out an overseer that tried the same. It soon became known that Mister George was a man who paid attention to detail. Don't try to cheat him.

Shad's abilities were the most guarded secret on Tendril-hoff. Mister George, Shad, and to some extent Ingrid were the only people who knew. Shad traveled under the guise of being Mister George's personal body servant and was respected by slave and overseer alike. They knew he had constant access to the old man.

One dark cloud hovered on Shad's horizon and it became darker as time passed. Mister George Junior. As with most young gentlemen of the time, schooling in the form of books and the like were beneath his dignity. He spent his time learning the graces. Dancing, parlor games, organized bird shooting, fencing, riding to the hounds, playing the piano and card games were more to his liking.

Junior had no time for such mundane things such as riding with his father to check on crops, visit sick slaves or come to know the overseers. He spent no time in the office deciding which crops to plant and when. He learned to sign his name to expense chits to be paid out of plantation coffers and decided he knew all about the operation of the plantation he wanted to know.

Junior's arrogance was both feared and hated by slave and overseer alike. In Junior's defense, it must be said that Shad's unique position may have been the reason Mister George didn't insist on his presence more often.

Junior wasn't too busy to notice the time Mister George spent with Shad. He noted the easy manner between the two and felt the slave was taking something from him. He wasn't quite sure what, but it was something. He resented the fact that Mister George spoke to Shad more like an equal than a master keeping a slave in his place.

At every opportunity, Junior assigned Shad to the dirtiest, most menial tasks he could think of. When Mister George assigned a horse to Shad, Junior wanted it, demanded it. Shad walked ten miles across the plantation and brought back another horse. Junior took it. Mister George led a horse in and placed the reins in Shad's hands. Junior stewed, but that horse was eating grain from a nose bag in Shad's camp.

Junior was spending some time in the clapboard settlement springing up around the steamboat landing. Most of the population consisted of river riffraff; pickpockets, cutthroats, professional gamblers, and a few honest workingmen.

Shad shook his head and picked up his Bible. The pine knot he threw on the fire was now blazing with enough light for him to read by. The Bible was becoming somewhat worn, frazzled and sweat stained from riding inside his shirt so much. He read about Joseph in the book of Genesis.

CHAPTER 5

Ennis strolled up the old dirt road that served as the main passageway along the river. It wasn't much of a road because all traffic of importance traveled by water. It sort of meandered around among the trunks of the virgin forest, dropped off into and crossed streams on whatever material nature happened to provide. The road came to be from the human habit of following in the tracks of anyone who had previously passed through. No one put any thought or labor into improving it. They struggled through the mud holes, over the bumps and across the creeks.

Ennis's black, bare feet kicked up little puffs of dust each time they came to earth. Grains of sand squashed up between his toes, not too hot, not too cold, it felt good.

Above the feet hung a good pair of trousers, but they were dirty, rumpled, and showed the wear and tear of being slept in many nights. The shirt and light jacket showed the same wear. On top of his head sat an old ragged hat. It had lost its shape long ago. The crown had holes scattered around it where someone blasted it with a shotgun. Ennis had found the hat in a dump several days ago.

Ennis's weather-beaten face and callused hands marked him as a man who had spent most of his thirty five years working outdoors. He belonged to Master Harcourt for twenty of his thirty-five years.

Harcourt farmed a small place and owned only one slave. Several years ago, typhoid had taken Mrs. Harcourt and her two infants to their eternal rest.

With the loss of his family the fire died in Harcourt. He was satisfied with eking out a bare living for himself and Ennis.

Two months ago, death carried Harcourt to join his family. When Harcourt realized his condition wasn't going to improve, he summoned Ennis to the deathbed.

"You have been a true and faithful servant Ennis, "Harcourt rasped. "I can't leave you the farm. They wouldn't let you keep it. I can give you your freedom. I had these papers drawn up. Take them and guard them with your life. I suggest you go north and look for work. Take anything you can carry, but leave before I die."

Ennis had not taken all of Harcourt's advice. He was holding Harcourt's hand when The Master called. He did have sense enough to depart before anyone laid claim to his person. Packing what food there was, he drifted toward that vague place called the North.

He had been challenged several times. After showing his papers, he had been allowed to continue on with a stiff warning to keep moving. A good whipping convinced him not to approach slaves to ask for food. A freed slave was not tolerated on the plantations.

Food became a major problem. He was walking along now with his stomach growling. He may have been too occupied with his stomach.

"Hey nigger, stand where you are!" The voice cut the air like a knife.

Ennis looked in the direction of the voice. A few yards off the road a small fire smoldered. Three young white men sat around the fire. The one in the middle held a large bottle of whiskey.

One clambered to his feet, bringing a rifle up with him.

"Yo nigger, com'ere," he ordered, pointing the rifle in Ennis's general direction. He was a tall young man with a prominent nose and a receding chin and forehead. His hair was long and almost as filthy as his ragged clothes. The cruel eyes were deep set. A thin, scraggly beard clung to his chin as if it were afraid to spread over the rest of his face.

"What do we have here?" The man with the rifle asked.

"A runaway slave," the man with the bottle chimed in.

"I's no runaway." Ennis reached for his papers. There was an ominous click as the rifle hammer was jerked back.

Ennis froze. "I's jest reaching for my papers."

"Bring that hand outta yore pocket real slow. An if'n they's anything but paper, yore one dead nigger." The cruel eyes were flat, cold.

Ennis slowly passed the papers over.

"I can't read," Cruel eyes said. "Here J.D."

The man with the bottle took the papers. "Can't read. Jim Bob,"He passed the papers on.

"Can't nobody read these papers, Alf." Jim Bob threw the papers onto the fire.

Ennis let out an involuntary scream and leaped toward the fire. Alf smashed Ennis in the face with the rifle barrel and brought the butt around to the back of his head in an arching blur. The force of the blow drove Ennis's face into the dirt. Stepping astride of Ennis, Alf shoved the rifle barrel against the base of Ennis's skull.

"Might as well kill 'em," J.D. said, taking a pull on the whisky bottle. "If what he said about being freed is true, there ain't no reward."

"Hold on a minute. Ain't no nigger ever told the truth until he was rightly warmed up," Jim Bob objected.

"Yeah, that's right." Alf liked the idea.

When Ennis regained consciousness, he was hanging on a tree limb. His hands had been pulled around the body of the tree and tied together above a limb about chest high. Groaning, he pushed himself to a standing position.

"Wal, look who's back with us." Alf rose from the fire and walked over to Ennis. "Tell us which plantation you run from nigger."

"I's a freeman. Ain't running."

Alf picked a thick switch from the pile they had laid by the tree. Rubbing the switch across the cut, he put the rifle barrel in Ennis's cheek, "Tell me now or tell me later." He crooned. Ennis flinched, but was silent.

Alf stepped back and brought the switch in a long whistling circle until it reached Ennis's back. The blow was like a hot iron across his back. The muscles acted involuntarily. They drew his head and shoulders back until his hands strained against their tie.

"No!" Ennis's wail drifted through the treetops.

"This nigger's got to learn his lesson the hard way." Jim Bob rose from the fire, picked a switch, swished it back and forth to test it, and stepped on the other side of Ennis. "Work that side, I'll work this 'un."

Both switches came at the same time. They crossed each other on Ennis's back.

"No!" Ennis rubbed his forehead on the bark until blood ran down his face.

They waited each time for Ennis's back to recover from the blow before. They wanted to deliver as much pain as possible. The beating went on and on. The only interruption was to pull on the whiskey bottle. "No use for now." Jim Bob eyed the unconscious form hanging from the limb.

"He'll be real sore for tomorrow. He's sure a hardheaded nigger." Alf slapped the bottle away from J.D.'s mouth.

"Whaa?" Squalled the startled J.D.

"We've done all the work so far." Jim Bob pulled the bottle out J.D.'s hand. "Yore going to watch him tonight."

Ennis would almost regain consciousness, then slip back. Finally, his eyes opened and the fog began to clear from his brain. He turned his head and located his tormentors. Alf and Jim Bob were sprawled on either side of the pile of glowing coals. They were both snoring. Alf still held the now empty whiskey bottle in his right hand. J.D. sat, with drooping head, between Ennis and the fire.

Ennis gathered his shaking legs under him and forced his body up the tree. The pain came in little prickles at first. Then hot searing waves of pain flowed across his back. Spots danced before his eyes. He locked his jaws and struggled mightily to keep from crying out. A small groan finally slipped between his clenched teeth.

As his hands slid up the tree he realized the leather strap they tied them with had stretched from his weight hanging on it. The loop around his right hand had stretched enough to let that hand slip through it. He began wiggling his fingers, trying to get some feeling back into them.

"Wal, wal, you back with us nigger?" J.D. moved up beside Ennis. "You ready to talk now?"

Ennis stood, silent and staring. Taking the tail of the shredded, blood soaked shirt, now dried and stuck to wounds on Ennis back, J.D. jerked outward on it. Fresh blood flowed down Ennis's back. Gathering all the clotted blood and saliva in his mouth, Ennis spit it into J.D.'s face. J.D. stood staring for a moment, then his face twisted and turned purple. His blood-shot eyes became ugly.

"You ain't ever seen a beatin' like you're gonna get!" With this he bent to select a switch from the pile.

When J.D. took his eyes off him, Ennis slipped his hand through the loose loop. Turning, he ran his left arm under J.D.'s throat and grabbed the loose end of the strap with his right hand, jerking J.D. upright. The strap strangled J.D.'s startled cry. Great waves of pain wracked Ennis's body. A curtain of red, then black, then bright spots passed before Ennis's eyes. A fury he had never before experienced rose in his pain wracked brain and he pulled the strap tighter. At this moment, the single purpose for his existence was to hold that strap tight. Each step J.D. took, each wiggle of his shoulders was a new agony for Ennis. A curtain of black settled over his eyes, but Ennis held the strap.

J.D. staggered toward the road clawing at the strap and carrying Ennis with him.

The curtain began clearing and the fury died. Ennis let go of the strap and rose from J.D.'s lifeless form. He had no idea how long it had been since he had looped the strap around J.D.'s neck.

Then he remembered Alf and Jim Bob. A glance at the fire reassured him, they were still snoring by the coals. He thought of finishing the job, but knew he couldn't accomplish it in his condition. Slowly he turned and limped off toward a mountain, he could see the sky lighted on the horizon. Like a wounded animal, he knew he must find shelter, a place to hole up and mend his wounds.

Next morning Alf kicked J.D.'s stiffening body soundly. "Stupid jackass got what he deserved. "That boy went this way." Jim Bob pointed toward the mountains.

"Ain't worth the trouble." Alf began throwing his gear together.

"If what he said about being a freedman was true, we could still take him south and sell him to a cotton planter. He ain't got them papers anymore."

"You should have thought of that before we worked him over. What do you think he'd bring now? Besides, we still got a job to do and that runaway from Henderson's plantation is worth a lot more money than he is."

CHAPTER 6

Shad awoke before the noise was close to his camp. The horse's raised head and pricked ears confirmed the sounds his ears were hearing. Taking his rifle he leaned against a tree and waited.

The form of a man staggered into his camp. The figure stopped, looked confusedly around, swayed and collapsed into a heap. The smell of blood was heavy on the air.

Shad stood still. Was it a trap? While Shad tested the forest by sight, sound and smell, the gray dawn arrived over the mountains to the east.

Satisfied the man was alone; Shad pulled the rifle hammer to full cock and approached the camp. The sight and smell of the man's back turned Shad's stomach. He moved around the man's feet in order to see his face.

Lowering the hammer, Shad placed the rifle on the ground. Taking a banged up saucepan and a frying pan he returned to the spring. Gathering the frilly leafed ferns growing by the spring he tossed them into the frying pan. Filling the saucepan with water, he returned to camp.

Tossing some wood onto the coals Shad poured a little water over the ferns and set them on the fire to cook. He warmed the rest of the water and set about soaking Ennis' shirt loose.

After the clean up job was finished, Shad took the bubbling

pan from the fire. Fishing the stems and solid parts of leaves out, he set the pan into the cold runoff water. As the liquid cooled, it jelled into a white salve. After Shad applied the salve, Ennis became semiconscious and began babbling about papers being burned.

Shad knew Ennis needed more help than he could give him. He debated on whether to take Ennis to Ingrid or to Tendrilhoff. Ingrid won.

With a little help from Ennis, Shad loaded him onto the horse. He then tied Ennis's feet underneath the horse and tied his hands to the saddle horn. After all was in order, Shad led the horse down the mountain.

Ingrid and the mules were already in the field. With five seasons behind her, Ingrid was an expert with the big turning plow. The rich black earth peeled off the plow in a steady roll. Glancing up, she pulled the mules to a stop with a gentle "whoa."

Shading her eyes with one hand, she studied the approaching situation.

"Who beat him?"

"I don't know. He staggered into my camp last night. He's been out ever since. He was babbling about some kind of papers. Something about somebody burning them."

"Is he a runaway slave"?

"I don't know."

A convulsion shook Ennis's slumping frame. Ingrid stepped forward and touched his arm.

"My God, he's burning up with fever. Bring him to the house." Ingrid unhitched the mules. They needed no urging to turn toward the barn.

Ingrid placed a piece of sealskin on the upper end of the bed in order to protect the corn husk mattress from the oozing wounds. It was about the only thing she had left of her crossing from Sweden to America.

"Go to the creek and get some willow bark. It will help with the fever."

"Ok, I've got some fern salve in my gear. I put some on this morning. Do you think he will make it?"

"Only God knows. It will probably depend on how much he wants to live." Ingrid was trying to adjust the pillow under Ennis's chest and head. "He's in a bad way right now, but he looks pretty healthy otherwise."

After making Ennis as comfortable as possible they walked out onto the porch.

"I don't like to leave you alone with him." Shad was concerned.

"That man is not going to be able to bother anyone for quite a while, if ever." Ingrid patted her apron pocket. "I can handle it, if necessary. Besides, you'll be back before he is able to get up. We can decide what to do with him then."

Shad hurried along. The day after he delivered Ennis to Ingrid, Mister George announced he was turning the day-to-day operation of the plantation over to Shad. Everyone would be informed Shad was a messenger carrying Mister George's orders to the various branches of the plantation. For fourteen days his duties kept him too busy to check on Ingrid.

When he came into sight of the house Ingrid was nowhere to be seen. Ennis was in the woodpile, trying to balance a stick of wood on the chop block so he could split it with a clumsy, short, one-handed blow of the ax. His forehead had healed to a red welt, but his back was still an ugly oozing mass.

"Where's Ingrid?" Shad demanded without preamble.

"The Angel?" Ennis managed a grin at Shad's concern. "Her an' them mules are in the field."

"The Angel?" Shad questioned.

"Yeah, when ol' Ennis felt that cool hand on his forehead and looked up into them blues eyes an' blonde hair, he just knowed he was dead, an' this's one of Saint Peter's Angels, carrying him home." Ennis shook his head. "Scared the devil outta ol' Ennis, I guarantee."

"What are you doing out of bed?"

"If that Angel can plow, ol' Ennis can surely cook dinner, can't he?"

A jangle of trace chains announced Ingrid's arrival.

"I saw you come over the hill," She called. "Come help me with the team."

Ennis painfully picked up a few sticks of wood for the cookstove and went into the house.

While they were unharnessing and feeding the mules, Ingrid filled Shad in on Ennis's story. "And I think I'll offer him a job here," she finished.

Shad was silent for a few minutes. There were several issues gnawing at him. Not the least of which was the fact that Ingrid had always been sort of his. And now, another person was intruding.

"Do you believe him?" Shad finally managed. "Yes, and it checks with what you said about him babbling over burning papers while he was out of his head. "I sure could use some help here," she added wistfully.

After the dinner was eaten and dishes washed, they sat back down at the table.

"Would you like a job here?" Ingrid asked Ennis

You mean stay here an' work?" Ennis was shocked.

"Yes, I mean stay here and help me work the farm." Ingrid repeated.

"I surely would, missy. I surely would like to stay."

"I don't have any money to pay you with."

"I'll work for my food," Ennis offered.

"No, I've been thinking about it. When they gave us the grant, I mean Conrad and I, they were very generous. They thought if we made it, we would draw other settlers to the area. We were granted this entire valley except the south end. Down to where the valley bends back east."

"The country is settling up. I'm afraid I can't hold it all unless I put it to some use. Here's what I can do. If you work for me four days a week for five years, I'll deed you the land between the big sycamore and the bend."

Shad sucked in his breath. That was some of the richest land in the valley.

"Just a minute. Just a minute. You're tellin' me if I stay here an' work, you will give me that land?" Ennis didn't believe his ears.

"No, I'm not going to give you a thing." Ingrid looked him steadily in the eye. "If you take this deal you will earn every inch of it. If you don't earn it, I will pay you for what you do and you can go your way."

Ennis was flabbergasted. Own land! The thought was so farfetched he had never thought about it, and such land as he was being offered.

After swallowing hard several times, Ennis held both hands up. "Missy, I reckon I'd work them fingers to the bone for that land." He said huskily. "What about them papers the slave catchers burned?"

"I'm sure Mr. Harcourt recorded them with the authorities. If need arises, we will find out where. Now, we will put a bed in the harness room. You can sleep there and take your meals here. On the days you don't work for me, you can build your cabin."

"Cabin? What cabin?" Things were moving too fast for Ennis.

"Your cabin." Ingrid smiled at him. "When that is finished, you can begin clearing your land. I want you to cut the logs for your cabin in the north end of the valley. I know it's a long way to move them. You can use the mules and wagon to haul them to where you decide to build. This way we can clear some land up in the north end and put all the land to some use. You think about it and give me your answer tomorrow."

Ingrid fell silent and after a few minutes, Ennis went to look after the mules. He needed to be alone and try to digest what had just transpired. After closing the door, he pinched himself to make sure he was awake.

"He would have worked a lot cheaper than that," Shad said after the door closed.

Ingrid glanced distastefully around the house, and then nodded at the bare shelves in the cupboard. "Maybe with his help I can put up some jelly again."

"What if he won't work?" Shad was having trouble becoming used to this idea, "What if he is just plain lazy?"

"If he was lazy, he'd be lying in bed right now. His hands say he has done a lot of work. They are well callused. He said that he and Harcourt ran a farm, just the two of them. I've talked to him quite a lot since he regained consciousness. I've asked a lot of questions. He knows farming, and I've not been able to catch him lying to me.

"Anyway, I don't have a lot to lose. As I just told him, if he gets that land, he will earn every inch of it. If he doesn't earn it, I'll pay him for what he has done and send him packing. I still have our money, mine and yours, squirreled away.

"We will need another team, some more plows and a milk cow. Do you know where I can get them?" Ingrid was planning ahead.

"What if Ennis is not smart enough to handle a farm? What if he sells the land?" Shad was not ready to let go.

"If he gets the land, he will have earned it. Hopefully, if he sells it, I'll be in a position to buy it. Quit worrying, I think Ennis and I can work to both our advantage. I have a feeling about the matter, how about the team and other things?"

"Mister George has bought the land for several miles up river. He's going to send for teams and other supplies. I'm sure he will bring in what you need for a fair price." Shad still wasn't too happy with the situation.

"Speaking of buying, a good-looking, well-dressed man rode a tall bay horse into the field where I was plowing, and announced he was my new neighbor. He bought the south end of this valley."

CHAPTER 7

When Shad loped his horse into Tendrilhoff, he was still occupied with thoughts Ingrid, Ennis, and the stranger. Several of the loose dogs ran with him barking at the horse's heels.

Shad could barely remember his mother. He had just turned four when the slave hunters hit his village. For the past five years, Ingrid had filled the void her absence left in his life. She was sort of a bastion, a person and place he could turn to. A place where he could air his innermost thoughts without fear of ridicule or reprisal. It had always been just Ingrid and himself. Now, another person would be dividing her attention.

Swinging from the saddle, he led the horse toward the tack room.

"Hey, boy! Where you been?" Junior's voice cut the air like a knife, a thunderbolt from the blue.

All Shad could do was stand and try to pull himself back into the present. He was so preoccupied, he had failed to see Junior and two slaves sitting on a bench in the shadow of the barn.

"Answer me boy or I'll flog you." Junior's mouth was drawn into a thin line. His eyes glared his dislike.

"Business," stammered Shad, still trying to collect his thoughts.

"I've got some questions I want answers to and I want them now." Junior strode up into Shad's face. Finding he had to look up in order to stare into Shad's eyes, infuriated him even more. Shad smelled the sour odor of whiskey on his breath.

"I want to know why you hang around my father all the time. What do you do in that office?"

"I do what Mister George tells me to do." Shad was gaining his composure.

"You will do what I tell you to do."

Shad nodded

"Sure you will. I brought Elias and Moses with me to see that you do what I tell you to do." Junior cast about as if looking for something to tell Shad to do. Elias and Moses looked very uncomfortable. They feared Junior as much as they liked Shad and knew he was close to Mister George. They weren't going to come out of this good any way it went.

"My boots need cleaning, boy. Wipe my boots off."

Shad slowly drew a handkerchief from his hip pocket.

"No. No, wait a minute." Junior turned, walked to some fresh horse droppings, and rubbed the toe of his boot in it. "Clean my boot, boy!" Shad hesitated. He stood twisting the handkerchief in His hands. He could see no way out.

"With your tongue boy, lick my boot!" Junior sneered. Shad's back stiffened. His nostrils flared.

"Elias, Moses, make him do it!" Junior ordered, his face reddening.

"Junior!" Mister George strode into the scene. He was visibly upset. "What's going on here? No, no, it can wait. There are two gentlemen at the house who want to see you."

Junior looked at the papers in Mister George's hand and turned white around the mouth and eyes. All the arrogance and animosity drained out of him.

"Come along Shad." Mister George said more from habit than anything else.

Alf and Jim Bob stood twisting their hat brims. They weren't sure how their gamble was going to turn out.

"Do you know these men?" Mister George pointed in the general direction of the nervous pair.

Junior gulped, nodded his head and looked at his boot toes.

"Did you sign these IOU's?" Mister George demanded.

"I... I... didn't want you to know I was gambling."

"Head for my office boy, you men go back to that den by the river. These notes will be paid."

Alf and Jim Bob scurried down the road grinning at each other. If they had known it was this easy, they would have done it a long time ago.

Mister George turned to Shad. "I should have done something about that devil's den long ago," He mumbled. Then he strode purposefully toward the house.

CHAPTER 8

It was about two hours after sundown when Shad followed Mister George up the muddy rut that served as Main Street in shanty town. It had been two months since Alf and Jim Bob visited Tendrilhoff plantation.

Mister George mentioned the shanty town several times. Once he sent a trusted overseer on a fast horse to deliver some letters to the Governor.

Mister George stopped his horse in front of the River Queen Saloon, he fished around in his vest-pocket and handed Shad a note and a gold coin. The note said, *"Need two rooms suitable for a gentleman and his servant,* signed, George Hoff Tendrilhoff Plantation."

"Take this to the hotel, give them to the clerk and wait for me there." Mister George swung down and climbed the saloon steps.

The clerk read the note and began to flutter around. He had never met George Hoff but everyone knew Mr. Hoff was the original settler here. He owned all the land around the collection of shacks that comprised the shanty town, not to mention he was the richest man for many miles around.

Yes siree, he sent a flunky running to the General store for two new sheets for the bed. Go find two chairs and a small table. Place them in the gentleman's room and don't forget to wash the windows.

When Mister George appeared in the saloon door, Jim Bob

was the first to spot him. Blanching, he half rose from his chair. Alf followed Jim Bob's eyes and hesitated in the act of raking in a pile of money on the table. Alf's hand dropped to make sure the pistol was still snug in the top of his tall boot.

"Sit back down, you dummy." Alf rasped.

"What's he doing here?" The fear was apparent in Jim Bob's voice.

"I don't know, but we're going to find out. He's coming over here."

Mister George politely picked his way across a floor where river boatmen were leading the saloon ladies in what might be called a dance in some circles. What the dance lacked in grace and finesse was made up for with stomping and yelling. With a hesitation here, sidestep there, a few "Pardon me's," all over the place, Mister George reached the table.

"Good evening, gentlemen. Is this chair taken?"

A moment of silence... shock. "No, sir. Pull that chair right up and sit in with us for a hand or two." Alf used the general stir of Mister George getting seated to switch an honest deck of cards for the marked deck on the table.

Mister George's pile of money increased slowly but steadily for the first two hours. He watched the consternation on Alf and Jim Bob's face and smiled. They should have known he had belonged to the best gentleman's club in Virginia and had some of the best teachers in the poker playing world.

After two hours, Mister George excused himself for a visit to the small building behind the saloon.

"What's he up to?" Jim Bob demanded as soon as Mister George was out of hearing.

"I don't know, but he sure can play poker." Alf eyed the pile of money Mister George left on the table.

"Most of that money is ours." Jim Bob's hand slid toward the pile of money.

"Don't be a fool Jim Bob. It may be a set up. Only a fool walks off and leaves his money on the table and I don't think he's too much of a fool."

"What are we going to do Alf, quit?"

"Quit and let him walk off with our money?" Alf cast a look of scorn at Jim Bob. "Wait a minute! Jim Bob, that's it."

"What are you talking about?"

"Walking off with our money, he's trying to win back what we took from the brat." Alf leaned forward in his chair. Excitement gleamed in his eyes. "Sure, that's it. He thinks he can outplay us."

"Jim Bob, we've got us a turkey to pick." Smiling evilly, Alf switched the deck of cards again.

Mister George lost steadily for the next two hours. Never a big loss, but his pile of money slowly shrank. He eventually got back to about the amount he sat down with.

"I must beg off now, gentlemen." Mister George tossed his cards onto the table.

"So soon?" Alf was genuinely disappointed to see him leave.

"Business, I have business early in the morning."

"Will you play tomorrow night?"

"Gentlemen, I've been out of touch so long. I'm going to play in the other two saloons tomorrow night. I'm going to try to meet some of the people. Maybe we can meet another time?"

"Another time, the pleasure will be ours."

"He'll be back." Alf prophesied as Mister George went out the door.

The clerk officiously escorted Mister George to his room. Shad's light was already out. Mister George hesitated, decided everything could wait for morning and turned in. The next morning they went to the only cafe in the shantytown. It was a hastily thrown together board and bat shack with huge cracks in the floor. The cracks in the floor were the kind green lumber always leaves when it dries and shrinks. The place seemed clean enough though and the man and woman who ran it wore clean aprons.

They ordered identical meals. Mister George ate his at a table. Shad ate his on the back doorstep.

After breakfast, Mister George and Shad picked their way

down the street. Stunted clumps of grass grew along the edge of the street and provided some relief from the mud.

The first building on the street was constructed in the usual board and bat manner. The lumber was shiny new, but the carpentry work was good and the four windows below the steep roof gave it a look of permanence. A sign hanging halfway across the porch proclaimed it to be "Mickey Doon's General Store." Under that in smaller print; "If we don't have it, you don't need it."

Shad followed Mister George up the steps. Both men scraped the mud from their boots on a board nailed upright to the edge of the porch, then wiped them on a handwoven grass mat provided for this purpose.

Inside, the store was bright and colorful. A counter ran full length of the building on the left side of the door. The first thing on the counter was a large jar of candy. Beyond that, various and sundry merchandise was stacked or hanging neatly.

Behind the counter, shelves reached from the floor to the high ceiling. A ladder had been carefully placed so as not to block the view of merchandise being offered for sale.

A barrel of horseshoes sat to the right of the door. Beyond the shoes was a low square box of sand in which a round, black sheet iron stove rested. Its long black pipe disappearing into the soot mottled ceiling. Around the sandbox were several different kinds of chairs occupied by the local spit and whittle crowd.

A burly figure rose from the group and moved to meet Shad and Mister George. The man was tall and lean with broad beefy shoulders. After that a body got mixed up as what to look at next. The broad face, the smiling mouth with large, strong teeth, or the big nose splashed cheek to cheek with freckles. No, maybe the red hair curled around his big ears. Finally, the lively green eyes with laugh tracks around them stopped anyone from going any further.

"Welcome to Mickey's, Mickey Doon, proprietor." A huge

hand with red hair on the back was extended to Mister George.

"George Hoff, Tendrilhoff Plantation." Mister George met the man's firm handshake.

"We were just discussing your visit, sir. News gets around fast in a small place." A wave of the hairy hand took in the place. "What can I do for you?"

While Mister George was making a few purchases, Shad roamed the store. He looked at this and fingered that.

The two men left Mickey's and slogged on down the street. They passed all three saloons, which looked empty and forlorn in the morning light. Well down the street, they passed a small but neat church. Behind the church, a group of men were busily constructing a parsonage. The sound of hammers and saws echoed off the other structures. The men ceased their activities and watched as the pair walked past. Beyond the parsonage was a collection of newly-constructed houses, shacks, lean-tos, and a few tents.

The last building on the street was of the familiar board and bat. The haste with which it was constructed was apparent. A sign on the wall, hand-painted across the board and bat, marked it as "Boughton's General store."

The steps were crusted with dried mud. The screen door hung on a slant, its bottom hinge broken or never fastened.

When they stepped through the door, both men stopped to let their eyes adjust to the dim interior and their noses get used to the odor. The smell of spoiled food, pickled fish, body odor, and smoke from a leaky stovepipe permeated the poorly vented place.

A short counter sat crossways, a few feet from the door. A sack of stock feed lay on one end. A pudgy, bald-headed man reclined on the sack, his muddy boots on the counter. Deep-set pig eyes glared at Shad.

"If I catch that boy stealing anything you are going to pay for it," Boughton growled at Mister George.

"If you catch him stealing, I'll pay ten times the price." Mister George's level eyes pulled the pig-eyes into his. "Ten times the price, sir!" An angry thump of the cane on the hollow sounding floor punctuated the statement.

The pig eyes couldn't hold Mister George's.

"I didn't mean..." Boughton swung the muddy boots over the edge of the counter and sat up. "I meant... well, if you find something you want just holler, you hear?" With that, he lay back and placed his muddy boots back on the counter.

Shad and Mister George walked a slow tour of the store. They didn't look at Boughton as they passed him on the way out.

Turning back up the street, they paused before the blacksmith shop. Staying on the tufts of grass as much as possible, they returned to the hotel.

"Well? What do you think?" Mister George asked after they were comfortably seated in his room.

"Mickey Doon has good merchandise at a fair price. Boughton has shoddy merchandise and his prices are little short of robbery," Shad stated.

"Boughton does a lot of credit business." Mister George stroked his chin. "I guess after someone trades with him for a while, they can't afford to go anywhere else."

"There are a lot of people moving into the area." Shad ventured.

"Good people and bad." Mister George turned his chair toward the window. This gave him full view of the street. "I'm going to the other saloons tonight. You stay here and have everything ready to leave tomorrow morning."

Mister George rested his boots on the windowsill and spent the rest of the day watching the comings and goings of the town's people. The three vertical creases in his forehead and the wrinkles around his eyes told Shad he was deep in thought.

Evening shadows were long before he stirred, ordered a bath, lay out a fresh suit, and began preparing for an evening in the saloons.

It was a neatly dressed, sweet smelling, Mister George that strolled through the *Green Eagle* saloon door. When he saw Alf,

Jim Bob and another man sitting at a table in the back of the room, he tucked the silver-headed cane under his arm and smiled.

"Gentlemen." Mister George nodded.

"Evening." Alf peered over the cards he was holding. "Mister Hoff, Mister Barclay, he owns the *Green Eagle.*

The game started slow and stayed slow. Every time it seemed on the verge of becoming a high stakes game, something happened to slow it down. Sometimes lady luck smiled on one and sometimes on another. Players came and went in the other seats, but Alf, Jim Bob and Barclay sat in every game. Under the guise of looking at his cards, Mister George studied the three men carefully.

After playing for two hours or so, Mister George rose and excused himself.

"You're not quitting so early?"

"Yes, like I told you, I'm going to play in the Steamboat down the street, just to get acquainted with some of the folks here."

"Will you be back tomorrow night?" Jim Bob asked hopefully.

"No, my business here is finished. I must return to the plantation, early tomorrow." Tucking the cane under his arm, Mister George strolled into the night.

"Some pigeon!" Barclay exploded as soon as Mister George was out hearing. "You said you had a fat pigeon that wanted to win his money back."

"We do. We do," Alf said soothingly. "He's just being a little more cagey than we thought."

Barclay picked up the coins on the table in front of him, studied them for a moment, then snorting derisively slammed them back on the table.

"He'll be back," Alf again predicted.

CHAPTER 9

Several pair of curious eyes watched as Shad and Mister George loaded their bags and the few purchases from Mickey Doon's on a packhorse and splashed out of Shanty Town at a slow trot. The ride back to Tendrilhoff was a quiet one. Both men were lost in their thoughts. The beauty of the old forest with its church like quietness and hanging moss was lost on them.

Mister George dismounted stiffly in front of the barn and turned to Shad. "Gather all the overseers. Have them at the big house day after tomorrow morning. Tell Billy to have a stand of rifles oiled and ready with plenty of ammunition for the rifles. Don't forget to bring in the horses. Tell the cooks to put tables in the yard by the veranda and have breakfast cooked for the men."

They came in twos and threes. It was a buzzing, curious bunch of men passing platters of fried eggs, ham, great bowls of potatoes and gravy. Golden biscuits, a bowl of butter and a jar of wild honey sat in the middle of every table.

Among the servants ferrying the food from the cookhouse to the tables was a young mulatto girl. She was about fifteen years old. Tall and willowy, she moved with an easy grace that belied her years. Her smile and lively brown eyes lit up a face that everyone looked at twice. Being better dressed than the rest of the servants, marked her as one of Miss Anna's personal servants.

She seemed to always be in the vicinity of Shad's table. Every time he took a shy peek, her smile seemed to brighten a little. In his activities at the big house, he had admired her from afar but could never work up enough courage to speak to her. Hannibal told him her name was Rebekah. Everyone called her Bekah.

Shad's contact with women was severely limited. His mother had been left behind in Africa when he was very small. His sole contact with the fairer sex was Ingrid.

Several times, he had considered bringing up the subject of Bekah with Ingrid but he always backed off because he was afraid he would make a fool of himself.

The buzz diminished, then died altogether, when Mister George walked out the door and leaned both hands on the veranda rail. All faces turned expectantly toward him.

"Gentlemen, I'm going to shanty town tonight and here is what I'm going to do." Moving slowly back and forth along the rail, he laid out his plan.

"I've spent a considerable amount of time and money investigating the shanty town growing at our steamboat landing and have come to the conclusion it presents a danger to Tendrilhoff. "There are some good people there but the gamblers, cutthroats, pickpockets, and other scum controls the town. Tonight we are going to take control of the town and throw the riffraff out. We'll save the town if possible, but if we can't save it, we'll burn it to the ground and eject every man back there.

"Now, there is a Gold Eagle for every man who rides with me. If you don't want to go with us, you can go home. No hard feelings. "If for any reason there is one among you who thinks of trying to warn shanty town, hear this. I will hang you without regrets." He stood silent for a moment, letting them think about this.

"All who are going with me, go to the barn and get a rifle and a horse if you need one. All of you who are going home, I suggest you stay in the yard and enjoy our hospitality through dinner before you leave. O.D. and John come to my office in thirty minutes," he ordered.

As a man, the group rose and walked toward the barn.

When Mister George walked back into the hallway, a shaken and pale junior, flanked by his mother, confronted him. "I'm not going!" Junior shouted. Mister George sighed, then looked Junior in the eye. "Yes, son, you are going."

"George, he's just a baby and there will most likely be a fight. He might get hurt."

Mister George's face took on the look "I'll brook no more interference". "He's not a baby anymore. He's a young man, old enough to consort with professional gamblers and no telling what else. He's going with me. In fact, he's not getting out of my sight until we leave," he gritted through clenched teeth. "Anna, the very existence of Tendrilhoff may rest on bringing this situation in hand, and shaping the future of this shanty town," her husband reasoned.

"George..." She pleaded.

"Didn't you hear what I said about hanging anyone who tried to warn shanty town? Come along Junior."

Junior cast a despairing look at his mother, hung his head, and followed his dad down the hall.

Shad turned in the saddle. It was a long line of silent, grim men who followed him up the river road. The only sound being made by the creak of saddle leather, thud of hooves, and an occasional snort of a horse. Looking back, he watched the ramrod straight, determined back of Mister George and the sullen, pouty slouch of Junior.

On the last rise at the edge of town, Mister George halted his horse and studied the layout while the group assembled behind him. Few lights glowed, most people having gone to bed. At this late hour, no traffic moved on the streets.

Nodding his satisfaction, Mister George turned to the group. "O.D. take your group to the *Green Eagle*. Bind Barclay and the bartender, disarm anyone else and bring them to Mickey's store. John you and your men take the Steamboat.

Don't harm anyone unless it becomes necessary, but if you have to shoot, shoot to kill. "You all know what is expected of you. We'll go in at a walk and hit all three places at the same time."

A smile lit Alf's face when Mister George entered the *River Queen.* "I told you our pigeon wouldn't fly the coop!" He growled triumphantly to Jim Bob.

The smile turned to puzzlement, then consternation when Shad and two armed men appeared behind Mister George. Alf's hand dropped toward his boot. The ominous click of a rifle hammer being drawn back at the window beside him stopped him in mid motion. Two more armed men stepped through the back door.

"Stand where you are and no one will get hurt." Mister George ordered as he leaned on his cane. "We mean most of you, no harm. Tie those two and bring them along. The taller one has a pistol in his right boot, a knife in the left, and a pistol in his waistband on the back. The other has a pistol in the back of his waistband and a knife hanging down the back of his neck. If they reach for either, kill them."

"You can't just come in here and..." Alf began.

"The only choice you have is to live or die," Mister George cut in. "Which is it going to be? Raise your hands and stand up slowly and carefully."

Alf looked at the window. A rifle barrel was pointed right at his chest. He could almost feel hot lead tearing into his chest smashing vital organs. His face went pale as he raised trembling hands above his head.

Mister George looked around the room. "There is going to be a town meeting in front of Doon's store in a few minutes," he announced. "Everyone is invited to attend."

Mister George was pleased and relieved as he strode toward Mickey Doon's store. Total surprise worked. Not a single shot fired. He could see the other groups approaching the store.

"Ring the fire bell and light the torches," he ordered.

Taking a hammer from his saddlebag, he climbed the steps and nailed three sheets of paper to the porch post of Doon's store.

While the strident clanging of the fire bell woke the sleeping residents, Mister George stood at the top of the steps flanked by a still sullen Junior on his right and Shad on his left.

Men and women were piling out of their houses in great haste. Some were still struggling to fasten their clothes as they ran. One fellow had one boot on and the other in his hand. He would run a few steps, stab the foot at the boot, miss, run a few more steps, and stab at the boot and miss again.

While the crowd was assembling, the overseers placed torches to illuminate the street in front of Doon's store and retired to strategic positions in the shadows.

The crowd was buzzing. "Where is the fire? What's going on? Who are those men?" Confusion was everywhere.

After most of the people were in the street, Mister George held his hands up and shouted for silence. After the buzz died down, he continued. "For those of you who don't know me, I'm George Hoff, owner of Tendrilhoff Plantation."

The crowd fell silent.

"Tonight we are cleaning some of the riffraff out of shanty town."

"What makes you think you have the right?" Boughton stepped to the fore.

"Mister Boughton I have posted three pieces of paper on this porch post. The first of which is a copy of the deed to the land on which this town is situated. I own this town. Indeed, this town is growing up around the steamboat landing I built to bring supplies into Tendrilhoff. In fact, all of you are tres-passers."

After a stunned silence, the crowd erupted. "That ain't true. This is open land. We'll fight."

"Hear me out!" Mister George raised both hands. "Hear my proposal."

The crowd settled somewhat and stopped to listen when Mister George began speaking again.

"The country needs this town. More settlers are arriving every day. They need a place to obtain supplies and market their goods."

"What makes you think we are going to listen to this loud-mouthed drivel anyway," Boughton cut in.

Mister George smiled at Boughton. "Because it is the voice of reason, Boughton, and because that rifleman by the corner of the store has a bead right between your eyes."

Boughton glanced at the corner, ran back into the crowd and ducked behind a woman holding a baby. The crowd roared with laughter. Mister George needed this. It broke the tension.

"I'm not proposing to destroy this town. I am proposing to straighten it out, make it a decent, safe place for everyone, including women and children. You honest merchants have nothing to lose and a lot to gain. If you will hold a town meeting, name this town, elect officials, and hire a police force, I am prepared to deed the land your business sits on to you. Anyone not prepared to do this better get ready to move."

While this was going on Alf regained his composure and was looking for a way out of his predicament. "Junior, I have always been your friend." Alf learned long ago to attack the weakest link.

Junior looked his dad in the eye. "He's right, he is my friend. Don't that count for something?"

Mister George held his son's eyes for a moment, then motioned the two men holding Alf to bring him forward. Reaching up Alf's shirtsleeve, he extracted several cards and handed them to Junior. Reaching into Alf's pocket, he extracted a deck of cards. Turning so the crowd could see, he shuffled the deck. Holding the deck face down in his hand, he looked at the back of the top card.

"Three of spades," he said loud enough for the crowd to hear. Peeling the card off, he showed it to Junior and tossed it into the crowd. After going through several of the cards, he handed the deck to Junior. "That's how he got all those IOU's from you."

Junior threw the cards he was holding at Alf's feet.

"You are a smart, tough old son of a bitch with my hands tied and an army at your back!" Alf was livid. "I should've killed you when I had the chance."

Mister George glanced at his son and then at the crowd. "Cut him loose."

One of the men holding Alf produced a knife and sliced the small rope binding Alf's hands.

"Stick a pistol into his waistband."

"Mister George!" One of the men protested.

"Do it!" Mister George ordered coldly, holding Alf's gaze.

The man put the pistol into place.

"You don't think I'm stupid enough to reach for that with fifteen rifles aimed at me, do you?"

"If this man is as lucky as he seems to think he is, let him walk out of here." Mister George spoke loud enough for everyone to hear.

Alf looked into the cold, blue eyes again. Suddenly it dawned on him. He wasn't looking at an old man on a cane anymore. This wasn't the polite old gentleman he and Jim Bob collected the IOU's from. This was the German army officer that led Prussia's lancers against the flower of Napoleon's French army at Jenna and Waterloo. These eyes had seen death and destruction on a scale Alf couldn't begin to imagine and then led his men back into the maelstrom for another round.

Frantically, desperately, Alf searched the eyes for a shadow of doubt, a flicker of fear, and found nothing but resolution and confidence. Alf was rattled to his shoe toes. Beads of sweat appeared on his forehead. His mouth went dry. He had beat and bullied his way for years. He took great pleasure in dealing out hurt and punishment to lesser or helpless individuals. Never had he faced the death he saw in these cold blue eyes. His mind cast this way and that for a way out. He cursed himself for going too far. There was no other way. Desperately his hand reached for the pistol butt.

The cane came in a whistling blur. Whack! It landed on

Alf's elbow. Alf's numb fingers let the almost drawn pistol fall to the boards. The cane came again. This time it came end first into Alf's chest, staggering him backward. The next arc came up between Alf's legs into his groin. Alf bent over, grabbed his stomach, and vomited on the porch. The next blow was on the back of Alf's head, just hard enough to put him on the floor.

"You can stay down and I'll flog you after I'm through with my business, or you can get up and I'll kill you."

Alf was silent.

"I didn't hear you!" Mister George raised the cane again.

"Flogging, I'll take the flogging." Alf soiled his clothes and fear shook him violently.

"Tie him to the hitching rail and bring me a whip." Mister George ordered.

Mickey Doon leaped to the bottom step and faced the crowd. "I think we should take George up on his proposition."

The crowd, silent and watchful while the struggle was playing out on the porch, erupted again. A babble of voices went through the crowd. Some were argumentative, some questioning, some trying to discuss the situation with a neighbor. Several voices joined Mickey's in urging acceptance.

Mister George held his hands up and shouted for silence. "Hear the rest of this before you make up your minds. The men we have on the porch are leaving town, tonight. The second list nailed on this porch post is a list of businesses that are closing regardless of what transpires. You will have two days in which to gather your stock and go." He continued.

"Mister Boughton, will you kindly join us on the porch? Your stock in the store will be divided among the people listed on your credit books. God knows they have already paid for it."

Boughton leaped out from behind the woman and child, opened his mouth to protest and looked into the cold blue eyes. His protest died before it was born and Boughton meekly climbed the steps and took his place beside Jim Bob.

"The third list is made up of people who are leaving by

tomorrow night. If there is anyone who thinks my information on him or her is in error, you may come discuss it at the meeting tomorrow night at the grove on the north edge of town. I will expect an answer to my proposal at that time."

Drawing another piece of paper from his vest, Mister George held it aloft. "To those of you who question the legality of my acts, this is a court order authorizing the removal of all squatters from Tendrilhoff lands. I'm posting it with the others."

Mister George took the whip an overseer held and stepped into the street. Alf began to squirm and whimper.

"Alf it may comfort you to know this whip has never drawn slave blood." Mister George flipped the whip out and sent the first snapping lash onto Alf's back. Alf screamed and passed out.

Mister George grimly kept on until ten lashes had bitten into the pale quivering flesh. Alf hung by the arms, head back, blood flowing from the mass of cuts on his back.

Disgustedly tossing the whip into the darkness, Mister George turned to the silent crowd. "To those persons on the 'leave' list, make no mistake. If you are caught on Tendrilhoff lands after the deadline, I will hang you. Good night, gentlemen."

The grove Mister George had chosen at the edge of town was a very defensible position. Located on top of a small knoll, the land, sloped in all directions clear of cover for at least a long rifle shot. With an alert sentry, there was little chance of surprise. Mister George posted a double guard and set the rest of the men digging a series of shallow foxholes around the perimeter of the grove.

About three the next afternoon, a group of townsmen approached and the meeting began. In short order, the people voted to accept Mister George's offer of land. They elected a town council and mayor, hired a city marshal and named the town Hoffman in honor of Mister George Hoff who was generous enough to donate the land.

On the way home, Mister George sagged tiredly in the saddle, eager to be home so he could rest. Shad rode in silence and tried to devise a way he could speak to Bekah. Junior rode along planning a way to get a boat and a slave to row him to the dives across the river. That wouldn't be much of a problem except he would need to sneak it past Mister George.

CHAPTER 10

Under Mister George's clear vision for the future and Shad's devoted insight and careful handling of day-to-day operations, Tendrilhoff prospered.

The time spent on shanty town put Shad behind in his work. Avoiding Junior as much as possible, he labored eighteen to twenty hours a day trying to catch up. He would have skipped most meals except for Hannibal.

The old butler guessed more about Shad's real job than anyone on the plantation. He made it his mission to see that Shad ate properly. Hannibal detested Junior and provided ways to help Shad avoid him. Hannibal also watched Shad's sidelong glances at Bekah with great amusement.

After he finished the last of the "have to be done immediately things on his list," Shad turned his horse toward Ingrid's farm.

When he came off the mountain at the north end of the valley, Shad pulled his horse to a stop. Before him lay a new clearing, small but plowed and planted in neat rows. Continuing on, he passed the field in which Conrad died. Corn was up and the ground well tilled.

Circling Ingrid's barn, he pulled the horse up again. A woman's laughter floated on the gentle breeze. Glancing around, he noted the new poles in the corral fence, the new palings in the yard fence, and some new shingles on the house and barn.

Shad eased his horse forward a step and looked at a long legged bay tied at the yard gate. One glance told him the horse was of good breeding and the gear it wore was of good make and well kept. He sat listening to the deep rumble of a man's voice and the higher pitch of Ingrid's answer.

Riding up beside the bay, Shad saw Ingrid and a man seated on the porch in deep cheerful conversation.

"Shad!" Ingrid crossed the porch and leaned on a post. "Come in."

Dismounting reluctantly, Shad shuffled toward the porch.

"Mr. White, come meet a dear friend of mine." Ingrid smiled at Shad's reluctance. "Without Shad, I never could have stayed here."

A slim, well-built, well-dressed man rose from a chair and crossed the porch. He stood at medium height, broad across the shoulders with short cropped black hair. A sparse tint of gray marked the temples. A thin black moustache turned up at the corners when he smiled. Lively brown eyes took in everything. He held a narrow brimmed funny looking hat in his hand.

"Shad, this is Albert White. This gentleman bought the south end of our valley. Mr. White, I adopted Shad as my son several years ago." Ingrid said as the two met at the edge of the porch.

Albert White nodded and extended a hand to Shad. His handshake was firm and his eyes steady.

"Mrs. Conrad if we are going to be neighbors that Mr. White has to go. It's just plain Albert."

"I'll trade you Ingrid for Albert." Ingrid turned to Shad. "Mr. White... um, Albert brought me some tea. Have a seat and I'll get you a cup. Albert is from England and we have been exchanging stories about the things that happened to us when we first set foot in this country."

Shad sat, silent for the most part, and listened to the conversation, his mind in turmoil. First Ennis, then this soft-spoken Englishman, they were invading his territory and he couldn't think of a thing to do about it.

"What have you been doing Shad?" Ingrid sensed his discomfort and decided to draw him into the conversation.

"The things you wanted are here," Shad said, a little stilted.

"Things I wanted?"

"Yes, the farm implements, a young team of mules, and I found some settlers that were giving up and moving back north. You bought their milk cow. They supposed to deliver her tomorrow. She'll be fresh next month."

"Good!" Ingrid clasped her hands together. "We'll have milk and butter. I'll make cheese."

"I got you a larger turning plow, a go devil, a double shovel, Georgia stock, cultivator, planter, spikes to make an "A" harrow, and a bunch of smaller items, like another grain scythe, cane knives, different kinds of sweeps for the plows, and a few other little things." Shad cast a sidelong glance at Albert. He'd show Albert, who took care of Ingrid.

"My, my," Ingrid nibbled at a fingernail. "I don't know if I can pay for all that."

Shad fished in his pocket, finding a small piece of paper, he passed it to Ingrid. "Here's the bill. Some of it is used but in good condition."

Ingrid took the bill and glancing down the neat row of figures read the bottom line.

"I don't see how you got this much equipment for so little money."

"Mister George had to charter a riverboat to bring in Tendrilhoff's supplies and he said it didn't cost any more to add your equipment to the load. There aren't any shipping charges on the bill. Everything was bought at Tendrilhoff cost. The mules I picked for you are heavier and stronger than Jake and Jack. If there is anything you don't want Mister George said he would buy it for use on Tendrilhoff. He said he owed you a debt anyway."

"Owed me a debt? What for?" Ingrid looked puzzled.

Shad glanced at Albert. "He said something about book-keeping."

"Jake and Jack will sure be glad to get the help. Ennis is about to work them to death. I swear, he's at it from daylight to dark. Then he sits around and splits shingles after supper." Ingrid quickly changed the subject.

"Where is Ennis?" Shad inquired.

"I saw him going south with a load of logs for his cabin just before Mr. White arrived."

"Your purchases are on the dock at Hoffman. If you can send Ennis with the wagon I'll arrange for two of Tendrilhoff's wagons to accompany him and haul it back."

"When should he go after it?"

"You know Tendrilhoff is a six-work day plantation." Shad smiled. "I'm about the only one who works Sunday. A bunch always builds a big fire, sing and dance on Saturday night. He might enjoy that and he could stay over and leave early Monday morning." Shad rose to take his leave.

"How is Junior these days?" Ingrid needed to know something before Shad left.

"Junior and his mom decided he should attend a gentlemen's finishing school in New Orleans. Mister George wasn't too happy about it but they talked him into agreeing. Junior will be leaving soon."

"How long will he be gone?"

"I don't know. It may be a couple of years."

Returning from one of his frequent trips across the plantation, Shad pulled his horse to a stop and watched Ennis urge the laboring mules up to the top of the hill.

"I decided you weren't coming until Monday." Shad said as Ennis pulled to a stop beside him.

"Aw, Miss Ingrid kept telling me I should take a day off and go see the sights. I told her I would if she'd come over with me, but that Albert White fellow is suppose to come over this evening." Ennis propped his foot on the brake lever.

"Lordy, if that woman wants something, you just as well do it. She said, 'Ennis, if you are going to get land, you'll need to be able to manage it. You can't manage it if you can't read and write and figure.' I told her a slave don't do them things. She laughed and said you are no longer a slave. Quit thinking like one. She's got me studying ever night. Just like a little schoolboy. If that woman wants anything, you just as well do it right off, cause she is going to talk you into it anyway."

"She has a way about her. Don't she?" Shad grinned.

"That Albert White man, he said a bunch of people up north are a trying to get all slaves free. You know anything bout that?" Ennis's eyes grew serious.

"I've been hearing something about it. I don't see how the abolitionists are going to have much to say about what happens down here though." Shad toyed with his saddle horn. "Our people need education worse than they need emancipation. If they were educated, they could get emancipated.

"A lot of us came from a totally different culture. Those born and raised here have not been trained to take care of themselves. Most slaves have no concept of getting paid for their labor. They don't understand money or its purchasing power.

"Most planters and plantation owners feel a sense of responsibility toward their slaves. If all slaves were emancipated today, I'm afraid it would relieve the owners of their sense of responsibility and expose the slaves to exploitation by ruthless individuals. The abolitionist tactic of shove and embarrass is turning southern people favorable or at worst neutral on the subject of emancipation into sworn enemies of the proposition. If we get a forced emancipation I fear a frightened and angry public will grind us under their heel. It will take years and years for us to get the education necessary to gain equality. The white man owns the land, money, and has the education. He owns the power. At present, we are a pawn in the north south battle for power and prestige. There isn't anything we can do about it. As soon as we've served their purpose, they'll drop us like a hot potato."

Shad eyed the sun. "Late as it is, supper will be over before we get home. Better follow me. We'll go to the kitchen and see if we can sweet talk the cook.

Upon their arrival, Shad and Ennis took care of their animals and walked to the cookhouse.

With supper over most of the kitchen help had gone on to other chores. They were greeted by the heavyset, matronly old cook with a bandanna tied around her head and another slave.

"Is there any chance of getting some leftovers?" Shad made like he was going to swat the cook with his hat.

"You hit me with that hat and you may end up eating it." The cook laughed. "Honey, if I didn't have your supper ready, Hannibal would have my hide stretched on the barn wall. Who is your friend there?"

"This is Ennis..." Shad turned to Ennis. "Do you have a last name?"

"No, I reckon it be same as Ingrid's, Doppler."

"Well Ennis Doppler, meet the best two cooks in the world, Ruth and Tamar."

"You're gonna choke on words like that." Ruth laughed as she flounced a big hip at him and turned to prepare their supper.

Ennis nodded to the cook and turned to Tamar. When he met her eyes, he stopped. He didn't know what, but there was something different here. She was of medium height, sturdy build with all the curves in the right places. Small tufts of curly black hair stuck out from under the bandana she wore. It was the eyes, he finally decided. Intelligent, active, alive, eyes with little laugh wrinkles around them. He struggled to place them.

"Something wrong?" Tamar was amused.

"No... no, ma'am." Ennis stammered.

"I ain't, no ma'am." Tamar picked up a stack of plates and dropped them. Flustered, she stared accusingly at Ennis then knelt to pick up the pieces.

After supper, Shad took Ennis to a woodpile with a fire already started. Quite a number of people milled around and others from farther parts of the plantation arrived in a steady stream.

A group of hunters were there with their hounds preparing

for a night in the woods. Mister George allowed them to hunt and supplement their food supply as well as for the sport. They weren't allowed to carry guns or any other weapons but they could shinny up a tree and jump old mister coon or possum into the bunch of dogs. They enjoyed the fight more anyway. They were all experts at taking a small stick and twisting old brother rabbit out of his hole.

Shad introduced Ennis to Elias and Moses, then excused himself on the premise that Mister George wanted his services in the office.

Darkness came and the festivities began. Various kinds of food appeared. The hunters donated a brace of coons, which were spitted on the edge of the fire along with several other kinds of meat. A jug of homebrew, which Mister George didn't approve of but failed to see as long as its use was moderate, began quietly circulating.

The singers tuned up and hand clapping began. The dancers began shuffling in the semi-darkness around the fire.

A figure slipped from the darkness and began mingling. It was a woman. Tall and athletically built, she wore an old beat-up hat, man's shirt, and trousers. She moved with ease and grace.

"I'm from the underground railroad." She announced quietly after she managed to gather a group.

There was a stunned silence. All the slaves had heard of the railroad, but none of them paid much mind to it. It was something that operated on bad plantations. They had all heard of these also. The excessive work, starving, and beating, none of this applied to them. It was something that happened over yonder.

"What you doing here?" Someone from the crowd ventured.

"I've come to help you run away. Go north to freedom," the woman announced. "We have an organization that can get you through."

Silence again followed. Running away never occurred to them.

Elias and Moses materialized out of the darkness.

"You're leaving." Moses announced as he and Elias took the woman by each arm. "I don't know why she come or how she got here, but you better think about this. If Mister George finds out something like this is happening at our singing, it will be banned. He won't let us gather and enjoy ourselves if we allow this to go on."

"Take her away."

"Get out of here."

"Don't come back," they warned her. The crowd realized the truth in Moses' words.

After escorting the woman into the darkness, Moses returned to where Ennis sat on a log at the edge of the firelight. "You won't tell Mister George about her visit will you?"

"Ole Ennis ain't ever seen Mister George and most likely never will. Ole Ennis never see nothing anyway." Ennis became more and more restless sitting by the fire. He was born on a small farm and sold to Harcourt. There he was the only slave. While he was trying to go north, he avoided towns and communities altogether. He'd never been in a crowd of this size and this noisy. The milling people bothered him greatly. Besides, he was too busy planning his cabin and worrying about the work he wasn't getting done by being here to enjoy the singing.

Ennis tried to find Tamar in the crowd, but alas, her face was not to be seen. Dancers twirled and the crowd milled until his eyes grew tired searching for her. Restlessly, he rose and walked toward the barn. He could check on the mules anyway.

"What you wandering around in the dark for?" The voice came from a bench in the shadow of a well curb. Ennis immediately recognized it as Tamar's.

"Just going to check on the mules." Ennis could make out Tamar's form as he drew near. She was sitting on a bench, leaning back against the well curb. "Why ain't you down there?"

"At the singing?"

"Yes."

"I don't ever go."

"Why?"

"You sure are full of questions. Did you look for me?" Tamar scooted to the end of the bench.

"Well, I's..." Ennis struggled to remember the proper English Ingrid drilled into him daily. "I thought you were probably off with your boyfriend," Ennis finished bluntly.

"I don't have a boyfriend." Tamar stared intently, trying to see Ennis's reaction to this bit of news. "What part of the plantation are you from?"

"I's... I'm not from this plantation. I'm on my way to pick up supplies for Miss Ingrid." Ennis sat on the other end of the bench.

"Miss Ingrid?" Tamar turned the name over in her mind. "You have a woman for a master?"

"No. I'm a freedman. I work for Miss Ingrid." Tamar felt his weight shift on the bench as he sat upright.

"Are you lying to me?"

"No, and I have a farm too."

"Go on, I know you're pulling my leg now." Tamar's tone was chiding.

"No, it's not much yet, but I'm working to pay for it and I'm building a cabin on it."

Tamar rose, "I ain't got time for fairy tales. I have to get up early and help Ruth with breakfast."

"Wait, can I see you tomorrow? I mean can we talk?" Ennis didn't want her to leave in this mood.

CHAPTER 11

"Mister George might not like it. He don't allow no rutting around on Tendrilhoff."

"Don't allow no rutting around?

"Everyone living together on Tendrilhoff is married."

"Married? Slaves can't marry." Ennis scoffed.

"You don't know Mister George. He makes the law for Tendrilhoff. He says there is man's law and there is God's law and God's Law is more powerful and was there long before man's. Ain't no papers filed, but that traveling preacher marries slaves on Tendrilhoff and he says, "What God has put together let no man tear asunder."

"I have to go." Tamar's steps lingered as she walked toward her quarters in the big house. Twice she stopped and looked back.

Ennis checked on the mules. They stood in their stalls munching hay. Jake flicked his long ears and stuck his head over the half door to rub his forehead on Ennis's chest.

"You're a lucky donkey." Ennis scratched the itchy spot behind Jake's ear. "All you have to do is pull the plow and eat."

When Ennis continued down the hall toward a ladder ascending to the hayloft Jake let out a long mournful bray. He sensed the turmoil in Ennis's mind.

Tossing himself onto a mound of hay Ennis picked a straw from the pile, stuck it between his teeth and stared into the darkness below the rafters. Ennis slept fitfully. His thoughts drifted and swirled around Tamar. Meeting her moved him in strange and mysterious ways. It was miserable in a wonderful kind of way.

What was behind those remarkable eyes and mischievous smile? Why did she glare at him when she dropped the plates? What made her call him a liar and stomp off when he tried to tell her about the farm and Miss Ingrid?

Every time Ennis dozed off, a creak of the barn timbers, a snort or movement of the animals stalled below brought him back awake. When dawn began to push little gray fingers of light into the darkness, he rolled out of the hay and stiffly climbed down the ladder.

After feeding and watering the mules, Ennis found a shovel and a wheelbarrow. Using these, he cleaned the stalls.

Turning the wheelbarrow upside down, he examined the construction. Someone found a perfectly round elm tree, perhaps eighteen inches in diameter, and sawed a four-inch thick piece off and drilled a hole in the center. Placing an axle in the hole formed the wheel. The handles were hewn from a mulberry tree. The deck was formed with split red oak boards. While Ennis was storing this information for future use, Shad entered the hall.

"You're up early." Shad surveyed the work Ennis had performed. "I came to show you the team I picked for Miss Ingrid."

Around a corner, they came to an open corral with a hayrack in the center. Several mules picked at the hay or loafed around the lot. In the far corner, segregating themselves from the strangers stood a pair of cream-colored mules. Head to tail, they were switching flies off each other.

"There they are." Shad pointed to the pair in the corner.

Leaning on the pole fence, Ennis examined each of them. A matched pair, good feet, long legged, deep bodied, and well muscled in all the right places. Must be twelve-fifty or thirteen hundred pounds each, he thought.

"They sure are a pretty team," Ennis ventured.

"They are full sisters. Kate, the one with the bigger star in her face, is a four-year old and Judy is three." Shad whistled and both mules turned their head toward the sound and pointed their long ears forward inquiringly.

"Moses and Elias worked them two days. They said both were fast-traveling, hard-pulling mules. But, they also said they were a little rambunctious for a woman to work, Kate especially. Do you think you could keep Miss Ingrid from working them until they settle down?"

"I sure will try, but you know Miss Ingrid, if she makes up her mind to work them, old Ennis just as well shut up."

Shad checked a rosy glow, the rising sun was beginning to toss across the eastern sky. "Breakfast will be ready and I think we better be on time. We both got in the doghouse last night."

Breakfast was not ready. Ruth stood with both hands on her opulent hips.

"Girl, how much salt do you intend to put in that gravy?" Ruth demanded.

"Oh!" Tamar exclaimed, staring at the salt still running from the bag into the pan. "I... I," she pulled the salt bag away.

"I think you better take the day off." Ruth's hands dropped from her hips and a smile touched her face.

"I don't want the day off." Tamar glanced at the door.

"Don't mess Ruth, child." Ruth moved toward the door. "If you was off you might find somebody to talk to." Sticking her head out the door, Ruth glanced around.

"Dinah!" Ruth yelled at a stocky girl walking across the yard. "Come here."

Turning back to Tamar, Ruth waved both hands. "Shoo, go on, get out of here."

Tamar hesitated, burst into tears, then ripped the apron off and hanging it on a hook, dashed out the back door as Dinah came though the front one.

"What do you want?" Dinah stopped in the doorway.

"Get that apron and help me finish breakfast." Ruth waved

in the general direction of the apron Tamar had hung on the hook.

"I can't. Sampson's coming over this morning." Dinah looked around the kitchen. "Where is Tamar anyway? She always works on Sunday."

"That's right, honey," Ruth's voice grew silky then harsh. "Tamar always works so you lazy girls can talk to the boys. Today, you work." Ruth turned to stare at the door Tamar had slammed on her way out. "All these boys been hanging their chins over her gate and Tamar wouldn't give them the time of day. The best boys we have, and that ugly galoot walks in here and Tamar starts breaking plates, burning the biscuits, and dumping enough salt into the gravy to preserve it until judgment day." Ruth shook her head. "I don't know what to do, except give her time for the kill or cure.

"Now, don't argue, just get that apron and get busy." Ruth ordered sternly when Dinah opened her mouth.

Ennis was disappointed when he and Shad entered the cookhouse. He looked forward to seeing Tamar and maybe talking to her. He wanted to figure out what he had done to upset her the night before and make amends.

She didn't work today because she didn't want to see me, he thought. Well, maybe he could hook up his team after breakfast and go on to Hoffman. He could meet Moses and Elias there tomorrow.

After breakfast Ennis and Shad ambled toward the barn.

"Are you still wandering around like a lost soul?" The voice came from behind the well curb.

Ennis's heart leaped. He'd know that voice anywhere.

"Speaking of lost souls, where was you at breakfast?" Ennis and Shad rounded the well curb.

Hannibal and Bekah were setting the table for Mister George and Miss Anna's breakfast when Hannibal realized Bekah wasn't moving. She stood looking out the window, watching Shad and Ennis talk to Tamar.

Hannibal watched her for a moment, then shook his white

head and smiled. Moving to the sideboard he picked up a small pan.

"Bekah," Hannibal called, then, "Bekah!" Sternly this time.

"Oh," Bekah jumped. "I... I was just...," Bekah blushed.

"I want you to take this pan and go to the henhouse and get some fresh eggs for Mister George's breakfast. I don't want old eggs, I want some laid today. You take this pan, go out there, and tell that sorry Shad and Tamar, I said to help you find those eggs. And if you ain't back here by lunch time, I'll skin you." Hannibal said sternly, waving the finger on his free hand for emphasis.

Bekah stood transfixed for a moment, hugged Hannibal, took the pan and fled.

"I guess Cupid comes in different sizes and colors." Hannibal grumbled to himself as he resumed setting the table.

Shad's heart did a flip-flop when he saw Bekah approaching the group. *Be careful, he cautioned himself; don't turn to thumbs and elbows like you always do when she is around. She must think you're an idiot,* he told himself.

"That old scoundrel!" Shad exclaimed when Bekah explained her mission to them.

"Well, I saw a hen down by the creek yesterday and I'm sure she has a nest hidden around there somewhere." Tamar offered.

"I'll bet we can find it if we look long enough." Shad couldn't take his eyes off Bekah.

Ennis sat on a log beside the creek with a stick in his hand. He was drawing diagrams in a cleared and smoothed patch of ground in front of him. Tamar sat on a rock and leaned forward to get a better view of them.

"I'm building the cabin here and I think I'll put the barn there and the garden here." Ennis drew the outline in the dirt.

"I think you have it backward," Tamar ventured.

"Backward? You mean the garden there and the barn here?" Ennis indicated each spot with the stick.

"Don't the wind blow from this direction most of the time?"

Tamar kept her head down, but watched Ennis through her brows in order to determine how he took the suggestion.

Ennis leaned back and looked at the diagram for a time.

I reckon you're right," he said and changed the diagram. After this, Tamar leaned back and only asked enough questions to keep Ennis talking about the farm. She loved the way he was lost in himself, expressing his plans and forming new ones along the way. Eyes lit, animation showing in every inch of him.

Meanwhile, Shad and Bekah removed their shoes and were wading slow circles around each other in the ankle deep creek, engaged in the idle conversation of two people striving to get to know each other.

All too soon the morning passed and the idyllic interlude ended and each of them returned to the mundane chores of their existence. But, for these four, that existence would never be the same.

Early the next morning, Tamar stood in the cookhouse door and waved until Ennis and the caravan were out of sight.

On the way to Hoffman, Shad's words about mules turned out to be prophetic. They took the wagon and moved in quick, long, easy strides. They quickly outdistanced the wagons driven by Moses and Elias. When Ennis pulled the check lines to slow them, Kate chomped the bit and danced in protest. They were handy with their back feet, Kate in particular. A man had to be careful working behind them or they would rearrange some part of his anatomy.

On arriving at Hoffman, they found the place bustling. All the warehouse docks were full. They would have to wait. Driving their teams into a shady area, Elias and Moses crawled under the wagons to take a nap. Restless at the delay, Ennis went to see if there was a way to expedite the matter.

On the docks, four wagons were being loaded by two men. The drivers were nowhere to be seen. Without a word, Ennis began helping the two men load.

"Go up to the saloon and tell them drivers to get these

wagons off my dock," the dock foreman bellowed at one of the dockhands as soon as the wagons were loaded.

"Who do you belong to?" The dock foreman turned to Ennis.

"Don't belong to anybody. I'm a freeman."

"Oh, you want a job then."

"No. I'm here to pick up Ingrid Doppler's farm implements." Ennis said.

"Do you want a job when you are through with that?"

"No. I already have one."

"Well, back your wagons in as soon as these worthless drivers move out. Here's a dollar for the work you've done and if you change your mind and want to work here, let me know." The dock foreman was persistent.

Ennis looked at the coin in his hand. A whole dollar! Never in his life had he possessed a dollar. When he left home, Ingrid gave him a list for the store and a gold coin. She told him if there was any money left over to buy himself something. But this was a whole dollar and it was his. He earned it. He could spend it any way he wanted. Tamar. He would buy Tamar something.

Wagons loaded and parked in front of Mickey Doon's store, Ennis gave Mickey Ingrid's list and the gold coin. While Mickey was busy gathering Ingrid's order Ennis wandered the store. He had two problems. What would a dollar buy? And an even bigger one, what could a man buy that would please a woman?

Ennis was so occupied with his thoughts, he didn't notice the talk ceased by the stove when he walked in. The spit and whittle crowd silently and resentfully watched his wandering around.

Things had changed since Mister George and Shad were here. The activities of the abolitionist and talk of secession was having its effect on both sides of the Mason Dixon line.

People who had no particular interest in race before, now felt something was being taken from them and something else shoved down their throats. Like all people, when they felt pushed, they shifted stance and pushed back. Why couldn't the damned Yankees stay home and mind their own affairs?

When Mickey finished Ingrid's order, Ennis laid the dollar on the counter.

"What could I buy for a girl with that?" He questioned.

CHAPTER 12

"Hey, Mickey, are you catering to the dark side of trade now?" The voice came from someone in the crowd around the stove.

"I guess it's the black Irish in me." Mickey joked back.

Chairs scraped and feet shuffled as the men crowded around Ennis at the counter.

"Walked right in the front door," a tall man said.

"Wandered around like he owned the place," another volunteered.

"He hasn't done anything but bring in money to buy things." Mickey was getting worried.

"Wonder if a taste of the cat on his back would teach him which door to use." A riverboat man advanced menacingly.

"Whoa!" Mickey held up both hands. "This man has done nothing but obey his master, bring in a list of goods to be picked up, and try to buy a trinket for his sweetheart." Mickey pointed at the door.

"I recognize those two on the wagons. They belong to Tendrilhoff. If I remember right, George Hoff gave us the land this town sits on. Is there any of you that don't remember his night visit? Fire bells and rifle barrels in the middle of the night."

A murmur ran through the crowd. Everyone took a step back. This put a different complexion on the situation.

"He is connected with Tendrilhoff and if you lay a hand on

him, I'm packing my goods and leaving right now, because," Mickey paused for effect. "This town won't be worth a plugged nickel when Mister George gets through with it." Mickey pushed his advantage. "Think it out before you act gentlemen."

"All right for this time I guess, but nigger, next time you park in back and come through the back door, you hear." The tall man turned back toward the stove and the crowd followed.

Mickey pushed a whalebone brush and mirror set into Ennis's hand. "You better go and good luck." Mickey winked and pointed at the comb set.

Ennis's face was burning as he stomped across the porch. Angrily, he loaded the merchandise Mickey carried out of the store. He was a free man! He had done nothing to deserve this treatment.

Ennis brooded all the way back to Tendrilhoff. He paused there long enough to report to Shad and give the comb set to Tamar.

"It's beautiful!" Tamar exclaimed in surprise. She looked at herself in the mirror, stuck her tongue out and turned it over to study the design on the back. Rising up on her toes, she leaned forward and gave Ennis a peck on the cheek.

Ennis blushed. Flustered, suddenly he couldn't find a place for his hands. He started to put them together in front of him, which brought them around Tamar. Reversing directions, he clasped them behind him, shuffled his feet and cleared his throat. He felt ten feet tall. Suddenly, the trouble he had getting the comb set was gone.

"I'll see you next Sunday." Ennis told Tamar as he climbed onto the wagon.

"I don't know, I told you, Mister George..."

"I'll see you next Sunday." Ennis said firmly, not letting her finish. With that, Ennis released the brake and that was all it took to set the impatient Kate and Judy off behind Moses and Elias.

With the help of the bigger, stronger team, Ennis finished

his cabin and started the barn. Ingrid and Ennis stepped up the clearing program, bringing more land into cultivation. Kate and Ennis struck up a truce during this time. The kicks became love taps, of which Ennis would loudly but gently complain. Better yet, Kate consented to let Ennis ride her to Tendrilhoff nearly every Sunday.

Ingrid spent the morning making huckleberry jelly. At noon, she packed a lunch of bacon, beans, hot biscuits, and the freshly made jelly. Taking the food basket in one hand and a jug of cool well water in the other, she set out to join Ennis for lunch.

Upon approaching the area where Ennis was falling logs for the barn, she found Kate and Judy tied to a tree. She could tell they had been tied there all morning.

Memories almost forgotten leaped to her mind. Conrad's death came back and hit her like a physical blow. Fear seized her throat. Dropping the food and water, she gathered her skirt and raced among the fallen treetops.

"Ennis!" She screamed, dodging this way and that way. "Ennis!"

"Over here, ma'am." Ennis waved an arm to attract her attention.

At the sight of Ennis sitting on a stump, Ingrid stopped and stood on trembling legs.

"I... I... thought..." Ingrid stammered, and then took hold of herself. "Are you hurt?"

"No ma'am, I'm not hurt."

Ingrid looked around. No work had been performed here this morning.

"Ennis, are you sick?"

"No, ma'am. Yes, ma'am I am." Ennis waved both hands. "I'm sick over Tamar."

"Tamar? What is wrong with Tamar?"

"Nothing. I'm so in love with her and it's hopeless."

"She's not in love with you?" Ingrid sat on log near the stump. She was still feeling the effects of her scare.

"She loves me, but she belongs to Mister George."

"Have you asked her to marry you?"

"She can't she belongs to Mister George."

"Would she marry you if she were free to?" Ingrid asked patiently.

"She said she would if she could, but she ain't free and never will be."

Ingrid was silent for a time, then arching her brows at Ennis she smiled. "I guess we'll have to find a way to buy her, won't we?" Ennis's jaw dropped and he stared at Ingrid for a moment. Hope was born in his eyes, then died. He wrung his hands in his lap.

"Don't have the money and don't have no way of getting it and if I did how could I support her? Wait a minute! That man on the dock at Hoffman. He told me if I want to work for him I could." Ennis sat up. Hope kindling again.

"What about the farm?" Ingrid asked gently.

"I guess I'd give it back to you. The cabins built and part of it is cleared. I don't think I'd be cheating you."

"What about your dream?"

"Marrying Tamar is a bigger dream."

"Do you know how long you would have to work to earn enough to buy her freedom?"

"I don't care. I'll work long and hard. I'd save every cent too."

"I'm sure you would." Ingrid smiled at him. "But I think there is another way."

"Another way?"

"I have a little money left and I think I could borrow some from Albert. We could pay it back when we sell the crop this fall." Ingrid was putting the plan together as she went along.

"How could I support her?"

"We have enough food for the year. Next spring you'll have your garden spot ready and next fall you'll sell the first crop from your farm."

They sat in communicative silence for a while and Ingrid

said. "Let's see if we can salvage some of the lunch I threw away. When Shad comes we'll ask him how much it would take to buy Tamar."

Ennis rose, holding both hands up, he looked adoringly at Ingrid. "I know you're an angel," He said.

Ingrid and Ennis were on pins and needles until Shad's duties allowed time for a visit. Ingrid approached Albert about the loan and he said he could loan her five hundred dollars. That was all he had. He had no idea what a house servant was worth and he warned Ingrid that it was possible Mister George wouldn't sell Tamar at any price.

"At least a thousand dollars!" Ingrid exclaimed.

Shad nodded. "She's a house servant, young, healthy and specially trained in cooking and custodial services. She can sew, she is congenial, and such a hard worker that she has picked up other skills on her own."

"A thousand dollars." Ingrid repeated deflatedly. "I have two hundred-fifty-six dollars and forty three-cents. Albert said he would loan me five hundred."

"That leaves you broke and mortgages most, if not all your crop this fall." Shad worried. "How much interest does Albert want?"

"None, he said he would loan me his right arm if I needed it." Ingrid smiled at the memory.

"Tamar was born in Mister George's house. Her mother died of typhoid when she was small, so she's been there ever since. Mister George hasn't sold a slave since he purchased Tendrilhoff. The plantation is growing fast enough to keep them all employed.

"When he purchases new land, he moves family units onto it. When two of his slaves marry, he moves the married couple to a different part of the plantation. He thinks it gives them a better start." Shad moved restlessly to lean on a porch post.

"I've been worried about this situation for some time now." Shad moved to another post. "A couple of Sundays ago, Mister George and Miss Anna were sitting on the veranda by the office window. Ennis and Tamar were sitting on the bench by the well, and I heard Miss Anna say 'George, you are going to have to do something about that situation.' I didn't hear his answer but this week, every now and then, he asked a question about Ennis.

"Yesterday, he told me to come and offer you an invitation to visit Tendrilhoff next Sunday." Shad finished, out of breath. That was the longest speech of his life.

"Me? Visit Tendrilhoff?" Ingrid fluttered her hands around. Nervously, she pulled her hair around and looked at it. Shaking her head, she tossed the hair over her shoulder.

"I don't have anything to wear." She hadn't been beyond the mountain since she and Conrad crossed over it six years ago. Butterflies churned in her stomach. Fear crowded into her eyes.

Her only human contact had been Shad, Ennis, and Albert. Not counting Fess and Ferd of course.

"I couldn't possibly go," She concluded.

"I think he wants to talk to you about Ennis and Tamar."

"I just can't... What about Ennis and Tamar?"

"I don't know," Shad hated this. "He may ask you to keep Ennis home."

"Oh no!" Ingrid collapsed into the chair and locked her hands together in her lap. "Do you know what that would do to Ennis. And, I've got his hopes all built up."

"I know what it would do to me if it was Bekah." Shad let it slip out.

"Bekah, who is Bekah?" Ingrid asked.

"A girl," Shad said lamely.

"A girl?" Ingrid smiled. The butterflies and fear was a thing of the past. Her eyes danced as she crooked a finger at Shad. "Come on, tell me about this Bekah."

"She is just a girl. Miss Anna's personal servant. That's all." Shad tried to evade the subject.

Ingrid was amused. They had an easy relationship. They could discuss anything, and here Shad was embarrassed and trying to avoid the subject of his girl.

Ingrid pulled another chair alongside hers and patted it. "Come, sit here and tell me all about this Bekah."

Shad reluctantly flopped into the chair and began. After a few minutes, he wondered why he hadn't shared the greatest thing that ever happened to him with the best friend he had in this world.

They talked and giggled for a long time.

Finally, Ingrid sat upright in her chair. "I'm going to have to go to Tendrilhoff next Sunday," she announced. "We must see what we can do about Ennis and Tamar and I must meet this Bekah." She hesitated, the fears rising again. "Will you come ride over with me?"

"I'll be here before sun up Sunday morning"

After Shad left, Ingrid prowled restlessly. Butterflies churned and fear gnawed at her vitals. She hadn't paid a social visit to anyone since leaving her native Sweden. Keeping enough to live on and improving the farm had taken all her thought, time, and energy. Paying a visit to someone never crossed her mind. And now, not only was she going to make a social call, but there was going to be other women there. Not just any other women either, Miss Anna was a lady.

"Ennis's happiness is riding on your shoulders and the manner in which you handle this, so buck up!" She told herself angrily.

What could she wear? Since moving to the wilderness, she had not even seen another woman or given any thought about what was in or out of fashion.

Dashing to the trunk she kept her dresses in, she threw back the lid and reached for the blue dress and froze. Her hand! Look at her hands! Dropping the dress, she held them out and examined them. Cracked, callused, rough, hard use appeared written all over them.

Closing the trunk lid, she went to the kitchen and poured water in the tea kettle. Tossing a chunk of lye soap into the washbasin Ingrid went to work on her hands. Taking a piece of sandstone she soaked and scrubbed until her hands looked raw. Opening a cabinet door, she took some of the salve, Shad made for Ennis's back, and worked it into her hands. To her delight, the salve soothed and softened.

Ingrid was pleased to find the few dresses she owned were too large for her. The hard work honed and fine-tuned her body. Hanging the blue dress, she removed her sewing kit from the trunk and smiled. All that hard work in the garment factory came in handy. Snipping here, tucking there, adding a frill yonder, she worked on the dress until it pleased her.

The long blond hair gave her trouble. The sun had kissed almost platinum streaks into it. At first she tried to think of a way to get rid of them, then decided she liked the effect. Clipping the ends, she tried putting it up this way and that. After awhile she decided to brush it back and let it hang loose.

Rubbing more salve into her hands, she marveled at the improvement. Taking some on her fingertips, she rubbed her face and neck.

Meanwhile, Ennis washed and curried the mules until they shined. They resented his zealousness, Kate especially, and aimed a couple of kicks at him, which he deftly dodged.

"Not today baby," Ennis laughed at her. Kate brought her back foot forward in a cow kick, knocking the currycomb from his hand. The currycomb landed near her front feet. When Ennis bent over to pick it up, she nipped him in the seat of the pants.

After finishing with the mules, Ennis turned his attention to the harness. He polished it to a fine sheen.

The wagon received his attention next. There wasn't a lot he could do. He had no paint. About all he could do was make sure the iron tires were tight and the hubs well greased.

The days dragged and the days flew. Ingrid fluctuated between anticipation and fear.

When the big day rolled around the mules knew something special was afoot. They came dancing from the lot, heads raised, chins tucked, long ears locked forward, snorting like two steam engines.

"My, they look good. Aren't they a little edgy though?" Ingrid asked when Ennis pulled them up in front of the yard gate.

"Awe, they put on airs sometimes. Kate especially, She likes to play games. She's mostly bluff. Don't walk up too close to her heels though, or the head end either." Ennis placed a hand on the still stinging spot underneath his hip pocket.

Shad came rattling up in a smartly painted, high-wheeled light wagon pulled by a fast stepping team of bay horses.

"Morning." Shad called. Locking the brake lever forward, he wrapped the check lines around it and leaped to the ground.

"What you doing in that fancy getup?" Ingrid nodded at the wagon.

"You like it?"

"It looks great. The horses are beautiful."

"It's yours."

"What?"

"They are yours. I traded for them and I'm giving them to you."

"Traded for them?" Ingrid was shocked.

"A steamboat captain took them for somebody's passage and offered me a deal on them. I explained the trade to Mister George and why I wanted them and he said go ahead."

"I couldn't take them."

"They are broke to ride. Your cow herd is growing and you are going to need them. Besides," Shad looked at his boot toes, "I'm hoping this is not your last visit to Tendrilhoff."

"What will people think?"

CHAPTER 13

Shad stood on tiptoe and took an exaggerated look around. "It's like you told me long ago. I don't see anyone I don't know and don't care. What do you think, Ennis?"

"Are we going to take that get up to Tendrilhoff after all the work I did on them mules and harness?" Ennis was irked.

Shad walked slowly around the mules and wagon, "You sure did a good job Ennis. I never saw better."

"Well," Ennis glowed, "We can take the horses if you want to."

"My lady, your chariot awaits." Shad swept his hat off and bowed elaborately. Ingrid laughed, threw up her hands, and marched toward the smartly painted wagon.

The road to Tendrilhoff, hardly a track, was improving due to use. At least it could be seen. A rider didn't have to stop and try to figure out which way the trail went.

The fast stepping bays pulled the jolting wagon at a spanking trot over all the smoother parts of the trail. It didn't seem long before the wagon topped a hill and there was Tendrilhoff sprawled in the valley below.

Anxiety pulled bile into Ingrid's throat and put a bitter taste in her mouth. Grasping the bouncing seat, she glanced at Shad. He was concentrating on swinging the bays around most of the wicked boulders that lined the trail. Ennis, hanging onto the rail at the end of the seat, was lost in another world.

Ingrid smiled. She could remember her preoccupation

and fascination with Conrad before their marriage.

Shad deftly swung the team around the U shaped drive and pulled them to a dust swirling stop before the veranda steps at the big house. Ennis leaped to the ground and there stood Hannibal. Face shiny scrubbed, silver hair brushed to a gleam, his best suit well adjusted across his ample midsection. He reached up to assist Ingrid from the wagon.

"Lordee, Miss Ingrid I'd a known you anywhere. Shad has told me so much about you I feel like I know you already." Hannibal prattled as Ingrid woodenly stepped from the wagon.

Ingrid allowed Hannibal to lead her up the steps and across the veranda. At the door, she hesitated and looked back desperately. All she could see was Shad and Ennis's back as Shad headed the wagon toward the barn.

"They are waiting for you in the parlor." Hannibal misread Ingrid's hesitation. Down the hall to the third door on the left and Hannibal swung Ingrid into a beautifully appointed sitting room. A man, past his prime and a little unsteady on the first step, rose and advanced toward her. His hair was still a yellow blonde and there was life and iron in the blue eyes.

"Mrs. Doppler," he said, extending a hand, "What a pleasure."

Ingrid returned her hand and to her mortification, he did a courtly bow and kissed the rough fingers. Ingrid fought the urge to yank the offending hand free and hide it in the folds of her skirts. She did manage a small courtesy.

"I'm George Hoff and this is my wife Anna." Swinging around Mister George extended a hand, palm up, to the lady seated behind him. She accepted the hand and rose, nodding in Ingrid's direction.

Anna was a direct contrast to her husband. She was as tall as Ingrid with gray streaked raven black hair and sparkling black eyes. She was thin almost to emaciation. Her white skin seldom saw the sun and had a slight sallow cast to it. There was a lingering value about her that spoke of the great beauty that used to reside there.

"Please be seated. You must be exhausted after your journey.

I will ring for tea." Miss Anna pulled a taffeta covered rope hanging by her chair.

"Shad didn't prepare us for the extent of your beauty." Mister George seated himself after Ingrid and Miss Anna had made themselves comfortable.

"I'm sure he exaggerated." Ingrid blushed.

Bekah entered the room with a heavy silver tray bearing the most beautiful tea set Ingrid ever saw and placed it in front of Miss Anna. Miss Anna began nervously pouring the tea.

She is more nervous about this visit than I am, Ingrid thought. In her anxiety, Ingrid never stopped to realize Miss Anna's position was similar to her own.

While they were in Virginia Miss Anna had been the belle of her social circle. When Mister George uprooted the plantation and moved it to the wilderness there wasn't a white woman within miles around. Miss Anna settled in and took care of her husband and son. There was nothing about the growing settlement at Hoffman that intrigued her, especially after Mister George's raid on the place.

Ingrid was the first white woman to visit Tendrilhoff since Mister George moved it to the wilderness. Anna knew Mister George couldn't fully understand her plight, even if she tried to explain it to him. He was perfectly content to be buried in the wilderness, cut off from family and friends.

"That's a pretty dress you're wearing. Who did you order it from?" Miss Anna passed the tea.

"I made it myself." Ingrid carefully accepted the tea.

"Made it yourself?" The thought startled Miss Anna. Never in her life had the thought of making her own clothes passed through her mind.

"Yes, I used to work in a garment factory.

"I used to visit the dressmakers regularly." Miss Anna sighed. "Now I order them. Would you like to see the latest catalogue?"

"Yes, I would."

Miss Anna rang, stated her request, and in a few moments Bekah entered carrying a sheaf of pages bound together. On the pages were beautifully drawn pencil sketches of dresses.

The women put their heads together, oohing and aahing, as they pointed out this or that feature of each dress. Mister George excused himself and left the room.

As they progressed through the pages, the tension eased and both women began to feel they had found someone who could become a friend.

When Mister George returned the women politely laid the catalogue aside. They talked of the political situation, secession, and emancipation.

"I'm not fond of the institution of slavery." Mister George said. "But, if I freed all my slaves today and started to pay them wages they would starve. They don't know the value of money or how to handle the fruits of their labor. We must have education before emancipation."

"They could learn." Ingrid said tentatively.

"Sure, they could, but with people pushing and shoving, one side yelling freedom and the other yelling secession, the efforts of wiser people are getting trampled. People with no opinion are taking this side and that. The chances of getting the slave education law changed gets less every day."

"I don't know much about what is going on in Washington." Ingrid said.

"Mrs. Doppler, I must say you have impressed me with your farm." Mister George redirected the conversation.

"It has been a struggle. Please call me Ingrid."

"I'm sure it has. It takes someone with energy and nerve to carve a farm out of this wilderness. It was a big help when they moved the Indians west a few years ago." Mister George fell silent for a moment. "We'll call you Ingrid if you will call us George and Anna."

Ingrid nodded acceptance of the names. "It's been somewhat better since Ennis came. Easier I mean. He's a hard worker."

"Ennis is the reason I invited you here today." Mister George took the opening.

Shad leaned forward. This was something new to him.

"Grandfather mostly, old Conrad was a field commander in the lancers. Wilhelm was a young subaltern. Both served in my unit at Waterloo. "Conrad was a great bear of a man, with a huge walrus moustache. Never knew a braver or more honorable man. He insisted on personally leading the charge that broke the French army." Mister George's unseeing eyes were turned toward the window. They didn't see the bright sunshine on the other side of the pane; they saw the flowering of French muskets, the great crash as the lancers charge collided with the French line. Men and horses going down like wheat before the scythe. Cannons roaring, dirt, men, and horses flying in the air.

Mister George shook himself, "I wish those people in Washington had been there. Anyway, Conrad was killed in that charge and after the lancers were disbanded, I lost track of Wilhelm.

"When I saw young Conrad's name on the list requesting land, I asked the agent to settle him in that valley. Coming from stock like that I knew he would make a good neighbor."

Mister George took hold of himself with an iron hand. "Ruth will have lunch ready. After that we have a wedding to attend."

The wedding was a simple one. Ruth was devastated. Things moved so fast she didn't have time to bake a cake. So she took a pan of corn bread, placed it on a gilded platter from the big house and frosted it. Tamar began wedded life with a down to earth wedding cake.

Tamar took to farm life as if born to it. Cooking, washing, working in the fields, it was all the same to her.

For the first time in years, Ingrid found herself with time on her hands. She picked wild flowers and placing them on Conrad's grave. For the first time since those wild days, she sat by the crude stone and wept.

"I came to buy Tamar." Ingrid countered, feeling it was better to strike the first blow.

Mister George was silent for a few moments, considering.

"We don't talk or do business on Tendrilhoff on Sunday, but today I'm going to make an exception. I think there is an ox in the ditch for both of us. Come to my office. Anna, I think you should get some rest before lunch."

After closing the door to his office, Mister George showed Ingrid to a chair and seated himself behind the huge mahogany desk. "So you want to buy Tamar?"

"Yes, what do you think she is worth?"

Mister George put his fingertips together and nibbled on his bottom lip. "Oh, About eighteen hundred dollars."

"Eighteen hundred dollars!" Ingrid gasped flabbergasted and devastated. No way could she come anyway near that amount.

"That is about what she would bring on the open market. I've not sold a slave since coming to Tendrilhoff. She was born and raised in our house. We are fond of her."

Ingrid was silent, defeat a bitter taste in her mouth.

"I was going to tell Ennis to stay away from Tendrilhoff."

"Oh no!" Ingrid said involuntarily, her hand flies to her throat.

"Anna has had several conversations with Tamar. She tells me that Tamar's face lights up and her eyes sparkle when she talks of Ennis."

"Ennis is in love with Tamar and he is a good man." Ingrid was searching for something, anything.

"Tell you what I'm going to do, Mrs. Doppler. I'm going to sell you Tamar for one dollar and consideration." Mister George pulled a drawer open and lay several folded pieces of paper on top of the desk.

"Call me Ingrid..., what did you just say?"

"I'm afraid I can't take credit for the idea. Anna requested it. The one dollar part at least."

"Anna?"

Mister George pointed to the window. Ennis, Tamar, and

Shad, not being able to stand the suspense, moved into the shade of a shaggy barked old oak that shaded the front yard.

Ingrid was too shocked to say or do anything except sit with her mouth open. It was a success where failure seemed so imminent.

"One dollar and consideration, we can't discuss the consideration, but it has been a great help to me." Mister George rambled on, covering Ingrid's shock and confusion. "Of course Anna's request was enough. She gave up everything to follow me to this plantation, and she is not feeling well lately."

"Thank you!" Ingrid found her voice, still too shocked to catch the fact that Miss Anna wasn't feeling well.

"This is a bill of sale conferring ownership of Tamar to you." Mister George picked up two sheets of paper from the top of the desk and held one in each hand. "And this one," he looked at Ingrid and smiled, "I took the liberty of having my solicitor prepare. It's Tamar's freedom papers from you. There is another condition."

"Another condition?" Things were still going too fast for Ingrid.

"Tamar and Ennis will be married here on Tendrilhoff, before she leaves."

"Married?"

"Yes, the traveling preacher is here today, another liberty I've taken."

"Let me be sure I understand this. You sell Tamar to me, I free her. She marries Ennis today and goes home with us?" Ingrid counted each item on her fingers.

"That's about it." Mister George was enjoying himself.

"Why didn't you free Tamar? Ingrid questioned.

"Because I own other slaves. It might make for an awkward situation later."

"Let's call them in and inform them of the proceedings." Ingrid was regaining her composure. "I know they are anxious."

Mister George rang for Hannibal. The nervous couple shuffled into the room holding hands, hoping for the best, but prepared for the worst.

CHAPTER 14

"We have come to an agreement." Mister George informed them. "I've sold Tamar to Miss Ingrid."

Ingrid plucked one of the papers from Mister George's fingers and turning Tamar's hand, palm up, and laid the paper on it. "Tamar, you are a free woman. This paper gives you your freedom. You may do anything you want; you may go anyplace you want."

Tamar's knees wobbled. Instinctively she took hold of Ennis's arm for support. Turning her face to Ennis, Tamar's eyes softened and a lone tear slid down her cheek. "I'll go where Ennis goes," she said.

"I'm not giving you a slave." Ingrid stepped in front of Ennis and pointed at the freedom papers in Tamar's hand. "She's coming to you of her own free will. You remember that."

The couple left the room, hand in hand, stealing sidelong glances at each other.

Mister George took the back of the chair and seated Ingrid again. After she was comfortable, Mister George returned to his seat behind the desk and Shad took a chair against the wall.

"Mrs. Doppler... Ingrid," Mister George corrected himself, "I'm sorry I didn't get to know your husband before his untimely death. I knew his grandfather and father."

"You knew Conrad's father and grandfather?" Ingrid was surprised.

CHAPTER 15

Shad balanced the books and silently pushed them across the desk to Mister George. A sharp intake of breath, a sigh and Mister George hung his head. Since moving to New Orleans, Junior's expenses increased every month.

At first the plantation was able to absorb the added expenses with little effect on the overall operation. With two bad crop years, Junior's steadily increasing expenses not only took all the profits, but seriously eroded the reserve capitol.

"What is the largest item?" Mister George raised his head.

"The five polo ponies," Shad leaned forward to point out the entry.

Mister George walked to the window. His shoulders slumped. Returning to his desk, he took a sheet of paper laid it beside the entries in the book. Item by item, he went down the list. After studying an entry for a while, he would write a much smaller figure on the sheet. Totaling the figures on the sheet, he slammed the pen down.

"He's inflated every figure at least ten times." Mister George rose and paced the floor. "Tendrilhoff is being bled to death on gamblers and whores!"

Shad sat quietly, waiting for the storm to pass.

"I've tried to ignore Junior's spending because of his mother's failing health. If I cut him down, he will appeal to her and cause a messy scene. She is not up to this." Mister George sat down behind his desk, his elbows on the edge, placed his face in his hands.

Shad remained silent, hurting for the man he admired and cared deeply for.

"It has come to the point where I have to rein him in just to keep a roof over Anna's head." Mister George said through his hands.

The plantation is in bad shape, but this year's crop is good. The cotton harvest is almost finished, the price looks good, it should pull us out." Shad ventured.

"Make a draft paying all Junior's expenses, except the ponies." Mister George said, reaching for paper and pen.

Dear son:

Times are getting bad. As you know bugs and drought got most of our last two crops. I'm having trouble balancing accounts. The polo ponies are beyond our means at this point and your expenses must be cut by half. Your mother's health continues to deteriorate and she knows nothing of the present financial difficulties. Please don't worry her by asking for something she doesn't have to give.

Your Father,
George Hoff

Folding the letter, Mister George sealed it with wax and handed it to Shad. "Have a rider deliver this to Junior as soon as possible." Turning, he slowly shuffled out the door.

No one knew the importance of this crop better than Shad. He felt honor bound to oversee every detail of the harvesting and shipping. He rode the far-flung reaches of the plantation day and night; making sure everything was in order. For the first time, he rode the steamboats to the mouth of the big river in order to see the crop loaded onto the big ships. Returning to Hoffman, he saddled his horse for the long ride home. He was exhausted but jubilant, it was the largest crop Tendrilhoff ever produced, harvested at its peak, and was safely on its way to market. It would command top dollar.

Shad dozed in the saddle most of the way home. It was well after dark when he rode into Tendrilhoff. Reining up, he sat puzzled. At this time of night, the big house should be dark but there seemed to be a light in every window. A shadow detached itself from the veranda and met him.

"I' sure am glad to see you." Hannibal took Shad's bridle.

"What's happening?" Shad stepped to the ground.

"I don't know, but Mister George is in a state. He said to tell you to come to his office as soon as you came in. I'll see your horse is taken care of."

Pushing the office door open, Shad stood shocked. Mister George slumped behind his desk. Shad couldn't believe he had aged this much since he last saw him. It was as if the vitality and animation were squeezed out of him. Silently, Mister George motioned him to a chair and handed him two letters. Shad opened the first.

Dear Father:

I am sorry to hear you are having a slight difficulty with accounts but you must dip into the reserves as I cannot cut my expenses and live like a southern gentleman. If I am to maintain my standing here, I must have the polo ponies. The gentlemen are forming a polo club and everyone who is someone is joining it. If I don't join, I will become second rate and I know you don't want that to happen.

You could always sell some of the niggers. You have too many as it is. Stop the loafing on Sunday and put the lazy louts to work and you could run the place with half the number you have. The food the rest consume would go a long way toward my expenses and the price Shad would bring, could pay for two of my ponies. I will be home to discuss it with you.

All we hear is talk of war. Most of the other gentlemen have joined a regiment of some sort. I'm coming home until this war talk cools off. I'm not stupid enough to go live in a filthy tent, eat grubby food, and perhaps get my head shot off for something as silly as states rights. Anticipating your refusal of the ponies I have contacted mother.

Yours, Junior

Shad laid the letter down and picked up the other.

George Hoffman, Tendrilhoff Plantation

Dear Sir;

By this time South Carolina has seceded from the Union. The rest of the South is sure to follow. Abraham Lincoln has vowed he wouldn't let them go without a fight. I have therefore instructed my brokers to withhold payment for your crop. I cannot place this kind of money in the hands of a potential enemy. Should your state not secede, we will have a full and equitable settlement.

Captain Amos Peet, Great Northern Ship Lines

Mister George brought the cane down across the desk with such force that Shad leaped to his feet.

"What can we do?" Shad asked when Mister George subsided.

"What can we do?" Mister George echoed. "If the South secedes from the Union, no court in the North will hear our case. They'll probably give the scoundrel a medal."

Shad stood silent, stunned.

"What can we do Shad? What is the position of Tendrilhoff without the crop? You have all the facts and figures. Mister George's practical side was gaining control.

"Well," Shad scratched his head. "The reserve fund is almost depleted, but we have enough food stored to last us until next crop. There is plenty of feed for the work animals. We have all the seed we need. If we cut the luxuries, we can make it to harvest next fall. This plantation can be almost self-sufficient if need be."

CHAPTER 16

Junior stared sourly out the window. Rain drummed steadily on the backs of the horses and driver, turning the road to a ribbon of mud. The front wheel hit a rock embedded in the mud, slamming his shoulder into a padded wall of the coach. Before he could react, the back wheel hit the same rock. Bouncing off the wall again, Junior grabbed the windowsill to steady himself. Feeling the water soak through his glove, Junior jerked his hand away and cursed vehemently.

Life had been almost perfect. He lived in the top strata of New Orleans society. He joined the best clubs, was accepted into the best homes in New Orleans, and was given the respect he felt he deserved.

After a short time, he had given up the fencing lessons, which was the only effort he put toward the education he was supposed to be getting. He never climbed out of bed until afternoon most days, and he spent the majority of his time gambling, drinking, and wenching. As a handsome, rich young bachelor, he could almost take his pick of the young ladies that inhabited the city.

The possibility that Mister George would reduce the amount of money available to him was always a nagging worry, but he didn't spend much time thinking about it. *He could handle Mother, and Dad always gave Mother anything she asked for. All Dad ever thought about was the plantation anyway.*

What crop to plant, where and which one would make the most money. Work, work, how could Dad live with such monotony?

Junior looked out the window and cursed again. With war fever rising to such a pitch, he was under great pressure to join some kind of military company. He gave the excuse that his mother was ill, needed him immediately and fled.

Oh well, Junior sighed settling back into the cushion, this beastly little war wouldn't last long and he would escape the prison of Tendrilhoff again.

At the top of the hill overlooking Tendrilhoff, Junior turned to the manservant cowering in the opposite corner of the coach. "You better hope you have kept my luggage dry," he growled.

"Yes, massa." The manservant almost bowed, "I wrapped it good."

Junior eyed the servant with a with jaundiced eye. It went against his grain to have a servant inside the coach with him, but he wanted the servant dry so he could serve him immediately upon arrival. The servant, one of Junior's first purchases upon arrival in New Orleans, would have ridden the back step naked in the rain rather than be cooped inside with the irritated Junior.

Mister George was the only person on the veranda to greet him.

When the coach came to a stop on the cobblestones, Junior's head appeared in the window. "Couldn't you get me closer to the steps, you lazy lout," he screamed, then sat still until the footman got the umbrella open and in position to protect him for the three steps to shelter of the veranda.

Black boots, white riding breeches, frilly fronted white shirt, white gloves, topped off with a light gray, small brimmed hat, set at a rakish angle. A light gray cape coat hung on his shoulders. A handsome figure until the eyes settled on his red nose. It contrasted with the translucent, colorless skin and cold, cold blue eyes.

"Hello Father," Junior climbed the steps in an almost effeminate manner and brushed past his father. "Where is mother?"

"Your mother is upstairs, she's not able to leave her bed."

"Oh?" Junior said and sauntered though the doorway.

Mister George stood on the porch for a few moments and walked toward the barn with raindrops bouncing off his hat and shoulders.

Climbing the stairs, Junior turned down a hall that brought back many memories. Pushing Bekah out of the way, he entered his mother's bedroom.

Junior stood transfixed. This shrunken old lady couldn't be his beautiful, vital mother. Miss Anna held her arms up and he crossed the room and hugged her, lightly, briefly.

"What's the matter with you, girl?" Junior snarled at Bekah. "Haven't you been taught enough manners to take a gentleman's coat?"

Bekah slipped the coat from Junior's shoulders. Another girl sat a chair beside Miss Anna's bed.

"How was your trip?" Miss Anna asked after Junior seated himself.

"Beastly, that coach driver hit every rock between here and New Orleans. Junior complained.

"I'm sure he didn't do it on purpose," Miss Anna wanted to start off on a positive note.

"It was fine until everyone caught this war fever and father started gripping about my measly living expenses."

"Tendrilhoff has fallen on evil times I'm afraid. George explained the whole thing to me. That unscrupulous Yankee stole this year's crop." Miss Anna anxiously studied Junior's face. "Poor George was beside himself. Things will be better now that you are home to work with him and carry part of the load. I'm so worried about him."

Junior sat silent. This wasn't the kind of talk he expected or wanted to hear. Spend his days in dusty fields and dirty barns, associating with sweaty, smelly, working slaves? Not likely.

"You must be exhausted." Miss Anna misread his silence. "I'll get us some tea."

"Yes, Mother, I am tired. Don't ring for tea though, I'm going to freshen up and rest."

"I'll ring for Hannibal then."

"No, I brought my own manservant. I'll be back later."

Junior strode down the hall to his old room, slapped the waiting manservant soundly and threw himself on the bed.

What were they talking about? Tendrilhoff had money. It always had money. A big place like this with his miserly father running it? Sure, it had... Wait a minute. Miserly father? That was it! Father had got to mother. He couldn't stand to see me enjoy myself so he came up with this to turn Mother against me. This was undoubtedly the worst day of Junior's life.

Later, Junior sat on the shady side of the veranda and watched Shad lead his horse from the barn and mount. Hatred boiled in the blue eyes.

"Come here, boy." Junior rose and walked to the rail.

Shad rode to the edge of the cobblestone drive and sat silent in the saddle.

"Put the horse up, I have a special job for you." Junior smiled and flopped back in his chair. Maybe this wasn't going to be a wasted day after all. It was time for some amusement in this dreadfully dull place.

"Mister George told me to go work in the Esterbrook fields today." Shad sat in the saddle, unmoving.

"May have, but I'm telling you to put that horse up and clean the toilets behind the slave quarters." Junior sat upright in order to stare at Shad.

"Mister George told me to go to Esterbrook," Shad repeated.

"You insolent lout!" Junior screamed. Slamming his drink on the table, he picked up a riding quirt and dashed down the steps.

Shad stepped from the saddle and stood by the horse's shoulder.

Junior's steps slowed. It dawned on him that Shad was taller and broader than his own stocky frame and he didn't like the look in Shad's eyes. He left the porch, expecting to lash a cowering, whimpering slave until he tired of the sport, but here was an altogether different and shocking situation. Coming to a stop, Junior cast around for help. If he could see any of the slaves, he would order them to help and he would beat this insolent cur into submission. Junior's eyes fell on Mister George, who came to the door to see what all the screaming was about.

"Father, I've given this insolent bastard an order and he is defying me. Even threatening me."

"He threatened you? What did he say?" Mister George walked to the edge of the veranda.

"Nothing, but he hasn't obeyed my order yet."

"Perhaps that is because he is obeying mine."

"What!" Junior couldn't believe his ears.

"Junior, Shad is too busy to be flogged. He is my personal slave. From now on, I'm the only one to issue orders to him. I need him to do my bidding and do it when I tell him. Shad, I told you to go to Esterbrook, now get going!"

Swinging to the saddle without hesitation, Shad turned the horse.

"Are you going to let him..." Junior turned to see his Father's back disappear through the door. Junior swore lustily and threw the crop at the wall beside the door. "I will not be treated lower than a slave!" He roared.

Time wore heavily on Junior. He made a foray into the dives across the river from Hoffman and found that without money, everyone sneered at him.

Fear and hatred of Junior increased among the slaves. They avoided him as much as possible, especially the young women. Shad was constantly fighting the brushfires of hatred, reminding them of Mister George's benevolence and the fact that Junior would not stay at Tendrilhoff long.

Shad was sitting beside the road talking to some of the slaves when a long line of horsemen, dressed in gray and followed by a line of empty wagons, moved by at a smart trot.

Shad watched until they took the fork of the road leading to Tendrilhoff, then swung into the saddle.

When Shad arrived, Mister George stood on the cobble-stones conversing with a tall Captain dressed in a gray uniform.

"What do you mean, requisition grain and supplies?" Mister George questioned.

CHAPTER 17

"The Army needs them, sir. We intend to pay for them."

"I barely have enough to make next year's crop. I don't have any to sell." Mister George stated.

"I'm afraid you don't have any choice sir, my orders are to leave you with enough supplies to see you through to next crop. And, to pay for all the grain and stock, we requisition." The captain was polite but firm.

"Stock? You are going to take my work stock too?

"Work stock, riding stock, cattle, hogs, grain, wagons, food, whatever you have the army can use. We'll pay a fair price for what we take; you can be assured of that."

"What are you going to pay in? I want gold."

"I'm afraid gold is out of the question at present. However, as soon as the Confederate States are able, you may trade the script for gold."

Mister George eyed the line of armed horsemen and seemed to shrink and age at the same time. Without a word, he staggered to the veranda and sat on the edge of it.

At a signal from the captain, the horsemen spread out and the teamsters drove their wagons to the barn. They were like a swarm of locust feeding on an unresisting plant.

The horsemen drove all the work stock, both horse and mule, into the corral. Systematically, they went through them, choosing the good, rejecting the poor, sick or lame. They took all the cattle except the milk cows and young calves. There was much squealing and cursing when they loaded the hogs from the fattening pens onto the wagons. They even raided the chicken coops.

"For our supper tonight," the Captain explained, lamely. At the barns, things were pretty much the same.

The soldiers went through taking harness, bridles, saddles, saddle blankets, grooming equipment, pitchforks, and other tools. They loaded the entire blacksmith shop.

Using the harness from the barn they hooked the work stock to the best of Tendrilhoff's wagons and continued to plunder.

Backing the wagons up to the barn doors, they loaded most of the oats, barley, wheat, corn, and cottonseed. They even took tobacco from the drying barns.

True to his word the Captain had clerks everywhere, vainly trying to record the plunder. Men with no training at all were trying to guess how many pair of harness in this pile or how many bushels of grain in that crib. Scratching their heads, they were trying to guess the weight of this hog or that cow. Some were bewildered or lazy, so they walked away and scribbled some figures on their slates.

A group of horse soldiers came from the barn leading Mister George's hunting horses. They were shouting with glee, appraising the nervous jumping horses.

"Return those horses to their stalls." The captain stood, feet spread, hands on his hips.

"Sir, these are the best horses on the place." A trooper protested.

"We are taking enough from this man. We will not take his personal mounts. A half dozen horses are not going to whip the Yankees."

"But, sir," The trooper began.

"Return the horses, now! That is an order trooper." The captain's jaw tightened.

Leading the horses away, one of the young troopers turned to admire the fine chestnut behind him. "I sure wanted this one," he said wistfully.

A bearded old sergeant, veteran of many years in the US Cavalry before defecting to the southern cause, snorted derisively. "Son, that horse is officer material."

"Officer material?"

"Yep, an officer would've yanked a fine horse like that from under you before you could get a saddle on 'em."

The soldiers bivouacked on the creek in order to give the officers enough time to go over the clerk's report and put a value on the supplies requisitioned.

After ordering the slaves to flee to the far reaches of the plantation or anywhere out of reach of the army, Mister George clumped slowly to his office. Sitting heavily, he placed his elbows on the desk and leaned his face into his hands. There he remained the rest of the night.

The cocks were crowing when the captain and his subordinate officers entered the house, unbidden, and clattered down the hall looking for Mister George.

"Here's a complete list of things we are requisitioning." The captain lied, placing the list in front of Mister George. "Look it over."

Mister George quickly thumbed the pages, raised his red rimmed eyes to meet the captain's embarrassed gaze. "What would be the use? Would you steal any less of my property if I said your list is wrong?"

Reddening, the Captain looked at his boot toes. "These are trying times Mr. Hoff. We are supplying an army to fight the Yankees and we must all make sacrifices. We have left you enough to make a crop with and hope you will supply us with a bumper crop next year."

"A few broken down animals, no harness, no feed, no seed, I doubt we can grow enough to feed the slaves. The Yankees stole our cash crops this year. We were in good shape, ready to grow a fine crop until you came marching in.

"We are paying for what we requisitioned." The captain nodded to one of his subordinates, who placed a large stack of Confederate script on Mister George's desk. "We believe this is fair payment."

Mister George snorted derisively and turned his back.

"Good day, sir." The Captain motioned the other officers out of the room.

Shad watched the last of the wagons disappear behind the mounted horsemen. Clouds of dust drifted through the trees. Shad leaned against the door frame. An intense hatred of the Confederate Army was born in his breast. After the bile settled in his throat, Shad walked thoughtfully down the hall.

"Are they gone?" Junior's pale face appeared around a corner of the hall. It occurred to Shad that he had not seen Junior since the soldiers arrived. "I thought they were coming for me," Junior stepped around the corner, straightened his jacket, and breezed past Shad. "Hannibal!" He yelled, "Hannibal! Where is that old devil every time you need him?"

Shad pushed the office door open and his heart went out to the old man behind the desk. Quietly, he sat for a few minutes.

"It's not as bad as it seems," Shad ventured.

"What do you mean?" Mister George's red rimmed eyes settled on Shad.

"They only hit the main plantation. We still have grain and stock left. I sent a man to check. They came straight from Hoffman to here and returned to the boats to unload what they took from here." Shad leaned forward. "We still have the outlying areas."

"Mister George showed a spark of interest, and then it died. "They'll be back," he declared.

"They will be scouring the countryside. Up in the mountains where I used to hunt there are three large caves. No one is likely to stumble on their location." Shad waited with bated breath for the implications of this to dawn on Mister George.

"Are these caves, dry?" Mister George asked at last.

"Yes, sir."

"How much will they hold?"

"All we got, but I don't think we should move everything."

Mister George leaned back, locked his fingers across his stomach and pondered this new line of thought.

"I don't like the idea." Mister George declared at last. "But, I think it is the only chance Tendrilhoff has of surviving. If the army were to catch us at this, they will strip Tendrilhoff bare."

"Yes, sir. I thought of that. We can scatter the work stock on the open land. The ones we aren't using anyway. Maybe we can give each man a few head to keep an eye on. That way we will know where they are when we need them and they won't scatter too far. We are going to have a lot of idle hands after the raid they pulled on us." Shad was planning as he went along.

"I think a fast demise for Tendrilhoff would be preferable to the slow death we have been experiencing all these last months." Mister George was becoming animated again. He bucked the odds when he joined in the Prussian Army; he bucked the odds when he left Russia for the United States, and again when he moved Tendrilhoff to the wilderness. Maybe, just maybe, his luck would hold one more time and Tendrilhoff could survive.

With his military and political experience, Mister George didn't think this war was going to be over in a short time. He thought it was going to be a dirty war and life, as they knew it, was going to be radically changed, regardless of who won.

"Order the grain moved and scatter the stock."

"We have a problem there, sir." Shad was thinking ahead.

"What kind of problem?" Mister George questioned.

"There are two men on this plantation we can trust completely, Moses and Elias. I believe we can trust Ennis and I'd stake my life on Miss Ingrid." Shad watched Mister George, trying to gauge how well his words were being taken.

"You have evidently given this some thought." Mister George nodded, "Go ahead, I'm listening."

"I've been thinking about it since the Army hit us, like ants robbing a beehive. Taking all our hard work like they were due it," Shad was fast becoming riled.

Mister George smiled for the first time in days. "Get on with it Shad," he said gently.

"Well," Shad scratched his head. "We can only use people

we trust to move the grain and supplies. If we use everyone, the fact a cache exists and its location is bound to get out."

Mister George nodded assent.

"All the moving must be done by Moses, Elias, myself, and Ennis. If you agree with my opinion of him." Shad waited.

"Okay, that will simplify it some. We can't just load up wagons and haul them to the caves. That would create a road the Army would be sure to follow.

"What I think we can do is haul it to Ennis's place and pack it to the caves on mules or horses. We will have to use a different route each time and hope it will rain enough to cover the activity." Shad paused for breath.

"Can the four of you move it fast enough this way?"

"We'll have to leave a working supply and hopefully enough to fool the army." Shad calculated. "We will move about two thirds of it. We should be done in a few days. We will work as fast as possible. You'll need to move people around the plantation so there is no one around where we are working."

Mister George nodded assent. "When are you going to start?"

"Right now, I'll send Moses and Elias hunting wagons and teams and I'll ride over to Miss Ingrid's house and talk to her and Ennis. Providing I can ride one of your hunters. They took my horse."

"Of course you can have any one of them you want."

Sitting on the veranda, Junior watched Shad take the long legged chestnut out of Tendrilhoff at a high lope.

Junior slammed a glass of whiskey on the table. The blow sent the bottle flying. He looked at the flying bottle disdainfully.

That is alright, Junior thought, *I wouldn't have drank that cheap, rotten stuff a few months ago. I always had the good stuff.*

Junior padded drunkenly through the door, meeting his father in the hall.

"I just saw that nigger, Shad, ride off on June Bug," Junior said.

"I sent him on an errand." Mister George answered.

"June Bug is my favorite horse. You know that. What is that nigger riding him for?" Junior demanded.

"Because the army took all of our serviceable horses." Mister George was getting irritated.

"He could have walked." Junior pouted.

"Listen Junior, we must do as much as possible to repair the damage the army did to us. There is going to be a lot of work going on in the next few days. I don't think you want to get involved in work, so you stick close to the house and Mother." Mister George grated sarcastically as he passed through the door.

Shad let the big hunter do his thing. June Bug hadn't been exercised since the day before the army came. He went up the hill in a ground-burning lope, his long legs driving the flinty hooves a drum rolling cadence. He fought the bit when Shad tried to check him.

Over the mountain and down the valley, the great horse's stride never faltered. Bred to the chase, bred to take six-foot fences in a bound. This road was child's play for June Bug. Ears forward, snorting in derision, he leaped a twelve-foot wide creek easily. Massive, well-muscled haunches drove June Bug on and on, stride after stride. Shad settled back, matching his movements to the ground eating strides, maintaining light contact with the horse's mouth. He reveled in the raw power of this magnificent animal.

June Bug was well winded and puffing mightily when Shad pulled him to a stop at the hitching rail beside Ingrid's gate.

"Shad, what's wrong?" Ingrid emerged from the kitchen door, wiping her hands on the tail of her apron. Tamar appeared in the door behind Ingrid.

"The army hit us."

"The army? What army?" Ingrid couldn't picture an army here.

"The Confederate States sent a Cavalry unit and a quarter-master regiment to requisition supplies for the army. They left

Tendrilhoff this morning. They stripped the place, took almost everything." Shad said, bitterly. "Where's Ennis?"

"He's working the north field. Do you need him?" Ingrid motioned vaguely toward the north.

"Yes, Tamar, will you go and get him?" It occurred to Shad that Tamar was a part of the plan he had forgotten. Could they trust her? What else, perhaps more importantly, had he not taken into consideration?

Shad and Ingrid gravitated to the porch while he was filling her in on the happening at Tendrilhoff and his plan for storing supplies.

"They will be here next." Ingrid folded her hands in her lap and looked around the place. She had poured her life's blood into this land. It seemed totally unfair that anyone could come and haul off the gains she made through long days and years of blood, sweat and toil.

"Yes, they will be here. Do you want to store part of your supplies with our stuff? You must be aware, if the army catches us, they will probably take everything. Maybe even take the land itself." Shad waited while Ingrid thought it over.

"It's not my war!" Ingrid blurted, "Why can't they leave me alone? I never owned a slave or fought with anybody."

"I know." Shad waited patiently.

"We are just getting to the point where we can live in peace and not think one bad crop, a drought, flood, bugs, or other catastrophe would bring us to starvation." Ingrid leapt from the chair and paced the porch, slapping a support in frustration, agitation showing in every line of her body.

Shad sat silent, waiting for the anger to pass. He knew Ingrid didn't expect an answer.

Ingrid turned to him. "Sure, we want to join you. I've worked too long and hard to sit by and watch our livelihood taken away without a fight."

"I'll go now. When Ennis gets here, tell him we need him to fashion packsaddles for the horses and mules. Tell him we are making panniers out of wagon sheets, they fit over a regular saddle. I know the animals have never been broken to carry a packsaddle, but we will have to train them on the way. We haven't the time to do otherwise."

Shad swung onto June Bug. "Have everything packed and ready to load onto the animals. I don't know when I'll be back. It will be as soon as possible."

June Bug was in a much more tractable mood, having burned off the excess energy. Letting June Bug pick his way home, Shad went through his vast memory. So much corn here, so many bushels of oats there, five teams of work stock at Esterbrook. What would they need the most? What to move first?

Moses and Elias were waiting for him. They had three teams of mules. Six sturdy, long eared mules per team, hooked to six good wagons. Two wagons per team. They sawed the tongues off three of the wagons, fashioned hitches and hooked them behind the other three.

Mister George was talking to Moses and Elias, when Shad rode up.

"Esterbrook," Shad said without greeting. "We start at Esterbrook. Most of our seed for next year's crop is stored there. Can you send the people to work another part of the plantation until we are done?"

Without a word, Mister George swung to the saddle, on his way to issue the necessary orders.

The men worked like the barn was on fire. They shoveled tons of seed onto the tight-bedded wagons. Sweat popped out on their foreheads, then ran down their bodies until it splashed around in their shoes.

Corn went into one wagon, cottonseed in another. Oats, wheat, beans, and peas completed this trip. Peanuts, tobacco, Irish potatoes, sweet potatoes, cane, garden and various other seed would have to wait their turn.

The wagons were heavy. Moses and Elias were expert teamsters and Shad took his cues from them. At one hill, they unhitched one team and hooked them in front of the team pulling the lead wagons. Twelve sturdy mules, two by two, inched the heavy wagons upward until they reached the crest.

Tying a rope to the brake of the second wagon and running it to the front wagon so the driver could pull on it to operate the brake on the lead wagon with his foot, kept the wagons from running over the teams on the smaller hills but it wouldn't work here.

Moses cut a thick pole and stuck it through the spokes of the rear wheels, tied it in such a manner that the pole rose to catch the bed of the wagon. This locked the rear wheels so they would slide instead of turn.

Moses spoke softly to the mules and descended the hill amid the screech of ironclad wheels and a big cloud dust. By the time the third set of wagons was safely over the hill, it was almost pitch dark. The rest of the trip down the valley was easy going. The soft thud of the mules' feet, jangle of harness, and rumble of wheels gave off a hypnotic effect.

Shad was dozing on the seat when the mules stopped. It took him a minute to rub the sleep out of his eyes and realize they were at Ingrids. Looking at the sky, he judged it to be three o'clock in the morning.

"Let's unharness and feed the teams. We'll sleep for three or four hours while the mules rest and we can load the packs in daylight." Shad said, climbing stiffly from the seat.

The effort to load the mules with their homemade packs turned into quite a chore and would have been amusing if time wasn't of such importance. The mules didn't mind pulling a plow or wagon, but wearing a pack was an indignity they weren't going to endure without a fight.

Kate bucked and bellowed until she was exhausted and out of wind. Running to Ennis, she pushed her face into his chest. Ennis stood, embarrassed, stroking her sweaty neck and talking soothingly.

The tired men received a boost when Ingrid and Tamar announced they were going to help with the packing. This was two more hands than Shad had planned.

Ingrid was better with the mules than the men. Her easy manner and soft voice inspired trust and they didn't fight her as hard as they did the men. With Ingrid and Tamar to help lead the mules, freed Shad to scout the trail and make sure no one saw them.

The three men head and tailed, tied the halter rope of each mule to the tail of the one in front of it. They divided the mules into three groups of six and two groups of three. Tamar's group consisted of the two horses and a gentle mule.

Shad pointed to a gap in a distant mountain. "Work your way up the valley and stay on the left side of the big hollow you see coming down from the gap. It will probably be easier if you use the long ridge to the south. I'll meet you in the gap."

Shad climbed a ridge running parallel to the valley he sent the cavalcade winding into. Moving quickly through the mixture of giant hardwoods and pine, he took station above and slightly in front of the string of mules.

From this vantage point, he could see front, back, and both sides. If anyone appeared, he would dash off the ridge and divert the mule string before they were discovered.

The quiet ride along the ridge was a pleasant chore for Shad. It seemed a lifetime since his carefree days as the plantation hunter. Like most folk, it was easy to remember the good and forget the bad. The whispering breezes and cool shade of the monarchs soothed Shad. The pressures and worries of today seemed to shrink when he looked across the forest, much of which was standing when the founding fathers landed at Plymouth Rock.

He moved steadily upward until he met the others in the gap. Swinging around the mountain, they approached a large hole in the mountain.

Shad rejected the first cave. It faced the valley and had little natural camouflage. It was likely to be found by someone casually passing through. The other two were in a narrow hollow and one in particular had a small naturally concealed entrance. A little help and it would be almost invisible. Shad chose this one to guard the precious seed.

After the seed was stored, Shad took some seed and made a ring around the cache on the floor. Removing a jar of strychnine from the pack, he sprinkled it liberally over the seed in the ring. He hoped this would protect the seed from the rats and mice.

It took three trips to unload the wagons. They used a different approach to the caves each time. A few hours rest and they were off for another load.

Shad picked up more mules to pull the wagons. He left the ones who carried the packs at Ingrid's in order to let them rest as much as possible so they wouldn't need to break another bunch to carry the packs.

Day after grueling day, they continued at a backbreaking pace. Pushing themselves to the brink of utter exhaustion, taking barely enough rest to keep from collapsing.

Finally, the much looked-for day arrived. They had successfully removed all they dared. Unless something unforeseen happened, none of the slaves or animals would starve before the next crop was gathered.

Shad climbed off the wagon at Tendrilhoff, sent Moses and Elias to drop the wagons and disperse the teams. He reported to Mister George and tumbled into bed for the next eighteen hours.

Still feeling the effects of the hard days past, he rose and cleaned up leisurely. After one of Ruth's belt buster breakfasts, he took a stroll around the home plantation.

Shad was in for a great shock. Everywhere he went, the slaves appeared sullen and uncooperative. While Mister George, Moses, Elias, and he were occupied with trying to save the supplies, a bored Junior had only two amusements available to him, drinking and slave baiting.

Shad was taken to the slave quarters where a man lay. His back was an angry mass of welts. In a fit of anger, Junior beat him with a weighted riding quirt. Shad looked at the sullen faces around him. "I will report this to Mister George," he promised.

CHAPTER 18

"Won't do no good, Mister George rides in and out, leaving Junior to do what he wants." One of the stable hands said.

"You saw what the army did to us. Mister George is trying real hard to save the plantation. He hasn't had the time to be here. Think about it, if the plantation fails, we will all be sold. Some of us will be sent down river. It has never been like this in the past and won't be in the future. We have to pull together and see this thing through." Shad felt they were only listening with one ear.

Mister George leaned back dozing in his chair. The stress and weariness of the past months reflected in the deep lines etched into the sun browned skin of his face.

Shad stopped at the door. Was there a way to soften the blow he found necessary to deliver? He cared deeply for Mister George and it seemed the chain of events was shrinking and aging him at a rapid pace. Where would it end? It appeared nothing would go right as of late.

Shad turned, he would talk to Mister George later. Perhaps by then he could find a way to handle the situation or at least have a suggestion.

"Come in, Shad."

Shad turned and stared into the blue eyes. Junior had the same eyes. How could two men have the same eyes and be so different?

"I thought you were asleep."

"I was dozing." Mister George sat up straight and looked at Shad.

Shad hesitated, not knowing where to start.

"What is it Shad?" Mister George knew Shad had something on his mind.

"I've sent for Sara," Shad said reluctantly.

"The medicine woman?" Mister George was wide awake now. "What for? Who's sick?"

"Joshua."

"What's the matter with him?"

Shad squirmed; no way except to say it. "Junior beat him, it's bad."

"Junior beat him? A stable hand? What in tarnation for?" Mister George placed both hands on top of his desk and clasped them together.

"According to Joshua, he didn't hold Junior's stirrup steady enough. It's much deeper than that. All the slaves are in a rebellious mood. Junior has been giving them a rough time while we were storing the supplies." Shad hesitated, hung head, and then added softly, "Especially the young women."

"What?" Mister George roared, his face turning scarlet. "Son or no son, I won't stand for that!" Mister George slapped the top of the desk with such force the stuff on top of it rattled.

"Sir," Hannibal's face appeared in the doorway. "I need to talk to you, sir. It's important."

"What is it Hannibal? Make it quick."

"Them sorry stable hands, Ahab, Jonas, and Dan, they've run away, sir." Hannibal said, highly agitated.

Mister George closed his eyes and settled back in the chair. When he opened his eyes, Shad could see the iron hand around his emotions.

"Shad, take Moses and Elias, and bring them back." Mister George said quietly.

"Get out of my way, Hannibal." Junior gave the old butler a push. "Did I hear right? Three slaves ran away?"

Mister George nodded.

"You're not going to send three more valuable slaves after them, are you? I can get Alf and Jim Bob..." Junior looked into his father's eyes, broke off and paled. He had seen that look before.

"I'd free every slave on this place before I'd allow that scum on Tendrilhoff," Mister George grated. "We are going to have a talk. Until we have that talk, you are not to give one slave an order and if you touch another slave girl, I'll castrate you."

Junior's jaw dropped and his eyes bulged. He could almost feel the knife. Turning, he shoved Hannibal again and dashed for the stairway to his mother's room.

"Get going Shad, I want them back in good shape if possible." It was a military order.

The three sets of barefoot tracks in the road were so plain a child could have followed them. Was it an indication of ill preparation and lack of planning on the part of the runaways? Or, was it part of an elaborate plan? Shad wondered as he followed the tracks at a lope. Moses and Elias followed on either side of the road. They had no problem handling the big horses because they exercised them regularly.

Shad grunted when he saw where the runaways slowed from a trot and began a fast walk. Why were they headed toward Hoffman?

The tracks indicated a slower gait with each mile of travel. A dusty spot indicated where they rested. Several miles down the road was a spot where they milled around. Shad pulled his horse up and studied the sign patiently. He decided they were arguing about which way to go.

It was evident this was an impromptu departure, not a planned thing. This eased Shad's mind. He was afraid they left a plain trail to draw pursuit this direction while another group went off the plantation into the hills.

The trail meandered along the road, giving more evidence every mile. The group of runaways was tiring and still indecisive about which way to go.

Shad pulled his horse to a stop. The runaways milled around this spot and left the road on the right side. The sign crossed a bare spot, and then went up a heavily wooded steep slope.

Shad held a finger to his lips and motioned Moses and Elias off their horses. Follow me, he motioned and led his horse into the brush on the opposite side of the road.

Tying his horse he stood, considering whether to leave Elias guarding the animals. These are stable hands, he finally decided. They wouldn't be crafty enough to lay a false trail, double back, and grab the horses.

He motioned Moses and Elias in close, he whispered, "Bring your axe handles and follow me. Stay as far back as you can see me. Move as quietly as possible."

Shad crossed the road and eased up the hill. Shaking his head, he marveled at the trail the runaways left. Any woodsman could have followed it at a trot. If running away was on their mind, they must learn to do a better job of hiding their trail.

When he approached a large boulder, Shad heard a sound emanating from behind it. It only took him a second to identify the sound as someone snoring. Motioning Moses and Elias to come up behind him, Shad silently circled the rock. Jonas lay on his back, Ahab and Dan lay on their stomach. All three were sound asleep.

Creeping in beside Jonas, Shad motioned Moses to Ahab and Elias to Dan. While he waited for the others to get into position, Shad looked at Jonas's face. An angry red welt ran from below the ear up across the cheekbone. The skin was broken and blood had trickled to the jaw and crusted there. Had they gotten into a fight over which way to go?

With Moses and Elias in position, Shad stepped on Jonas's right wrist and placed the ax handle on his throat.

"Lie still," Shad ordered when Jonas began to struggle. Glancing around, Shad saw Moses and Elias had the situation well in hand. Each grabbed an arm and shoved it up behind his man's back and held their faces in the pine needles.

"Tie their hands in front of them." Shad ordered. "They have a long way to go."

"Please don't take us back." Jonas begged. "Mister Junior will kill us."

"Mister George will decide what happens to you for running away."

"Mister Junior done told us, if we don't shape up, he will beat us to death." Jonas eyes rolled in fear.

"No! Mister Junior will not decide. If Mister Junior decides then I will help you escape." The fear emanating from Jonas was so thick, Shad could smell and even taste it.

Jonas rose to his feet, Shad shoved him to where Moses had finished chaining Ahab. "Chain him, run a rope around their waist, and tie them together. Leave enough slack so they can walk and put the knots behind their backs. Bring them to the road. I'll get the horses." Shad had to get away.

In consideration of the bound prisoners, Shad set a slow pace back to Tendrilhoff. Ahab and Dan marched with their heads up and shoulders back. They looked like men who knew they were going to meet their end, but refused to beg, even if they knew it would save them. Jonas sobbed softly.

The look on Moses and Elias faces told Shad their feelings on the matter. Their loyalty to Mister George was almost as strong as his. It was a dirty job that had to do. No use crying about it, just do it.

Coming in sight of the big house, Shad sat bolt upright in the saddle. People were everywhere. They milled around the cobblestone driveway, the well, cookhouse, everywhere. He had never seen this many people here before. His eyes picked out overseers from the most distant parts of the plantation.

Hannibal parted from the crowd and ambled out to meet him.

"What is going on?" Shad demanded as soon as he was in earshot of Hannibal.

"Mister George called in the whole plantation. He was sure you would bring them back." Hannibal pulled out a handkerchief and mopped his brow. "He even sent for Ennis, Tamar and Miss Ingrid. They are on the veranda."

"What's he going to do?" Shad was becoming very apprehensive.

"I don't know. He's in that mood of his. You know the one where he has a ramrod up his back and don't talk."

"I know the mood." Shad knew Mister George was capable of making harsh decisions and carrying them through. "Is he going to whip these men?" Shad demanded harshly, apprehension changing to anger.

"I don't know what he's going to do. He said to tell you to bring them to the veranda."

Shad stepped his horse forward. His mind was in turmoil. What could he say? What could he do? Nothing! Mister George never beat a slave.

Yes, there was one thing he could do, he'd demand the same punishment dealt out to the three stable hands. Somehow this might atone for bringing them back.

Mister George, Mister Junior, and Ingrid were seated at a table on the porch. Ennis and Tamar stood behind Ingrid. Tamar gripped the back of Ingrid's chair. Ingrid's pale face heightened Shad's anger.

Shad climbed the steps, pulling the sobbing, trembling Jonas and ramrod stiff Ahab and Dan behind him. Crossing the veranda, Shad stopped in front of the table.

"I see you got them." Mister George said, reading Shad far better than Shad would have guessed.

"Yes, sir!" Shad stood, rigid, hands balled into fists.

"I want to say something," Mister Junior rose. "These are three prime slaves. Before we hang them or damage them with the lash, I could sell them across the river for top dollar."

"Sit down and shut up!" Mister George lashed out in a voice that Junior had never heard before.

Blanching, tight lipped, Junior sat.

"Did they fight?" Mister George nodded toward the mark on Jonas's face and neck.

"No, sir, that was already there when we caught up with them."

"Untie them," Mister George's expression had not changed in the least. "Jonas, what happened to your face?"

"Mister Junior hit me." Fear flickered in Jonas's eyes when he looked at Junior.

"Hit you? What did he hit you with?"

"A riding crop."

"What did he hit you for? What were you doing wrong?"

"He said I didn't run fast enough to take his horse when he came home."

"The lazy lout..." Junior leaped from his chair. The cold blue eyes stopped him in midsentence and pushed him back into the chair. A chill ran up his spine.

"Did Junior strike you?" Mister George turned to Ahab and Dan, who stood chafing their freed wrists.

Without a word both men turned and drew up their shirts. Mister George winched at the sight of their backs. It was the first emotion Shad had seen from him since climbing the steps.

Mister George stared at the pulpy, bloody, oozing backs for a long moment, then looked at his shoe toes. Silence reigned. Everyone could hear himself breathe.

Mister George rose, walked stiffly to the rail, relying heavily his cane for the first time. Leaning on the rail, tears streamed from his eyes. All faces in the crowd were turned to him.

"I've not been a good shepherd!" He cried out in a loud anguished voice. "I've allowed my flock to be abused in the vilest manner. No one on Tendrilhoff will obey an order from Junior again." The tears stopped, iron edged into his words. He stood straight and walked down the rail. "Make no mistake; if anyone is disrespectful to him, I will have his head. But, none of you will take orders from him or be abused by him again."

Uttering a frightful oath, Junior leaped from his chair and strode toward his Father. The blue eyes stopped him in mid-stride. Pausing, he turned and ran into the house, slamming the door so hard the whole wall shook.

"I would free everyone of you and let you head north, but I don't think it's the best thing for you. The way north is wrought with frightful dangers. What would you do in a strange land among strangers? How would you live? The abolitionists are using you to set up a frightful clamor.

"They don't want you in their state. They don't want you in their town, home or business. As soon as you are no longer a political tool, they will tell you to go some other place and don't bother them.

I've asked Ennis to come today and tell you his story." Mister George motioned Ennis to the rail. Ennis came trembling to the rail.

"My master freed me." Ennis began.

"Louder!" A voice in the crowd shouted.

"My master freed me." Ennis began again. "He told me to go north. I tried to go north. I starved. Nobody wanted me around. If I hadn't had my papers, they would have taken me back as a runaway. Slave catchers got me. After burning my papers, they did this to me." Ennis stripped his shirt off and turned his badly scarred back to the crowd.

After many oohs, aahs and other exclamations, the crowd settled down.

"They were going to sell me to a plantation down the river, but God was with me. They got drunk and I escaped. Shad found me and took me to Miss Ingrid. The Angel saved my life." Ennis smiled radiantly at Miss Ingrid as he returned to take his place behind her chair.

"These men have received enough punishment." Mister George indicated Jonas, Ahab, and Dan. "They will get no more from me. If they, or any of you, want to run, come to me. I will see that you get a sack of food to travel on. I will not send anyone to bring you back. But, if you choose to run, I don't want to see your face on Tendrilhoff again. Do not try to come back." Mister George spoke the last words very slowly.

To those of you who stay, I don't have to tell you, Tendrilhoff is in trouble. Our cash money is gone, the Yankees stole our last crop, and the Confederate Army is confiscating most of what's left. I don't know what the future is going to bring, but I promise you this, we'll be with you to the end."

"Mister George! Mister George! It's Miss Anna!" Bekah burst through the door hysterically.

Mister George dropped his cane and took the stairs, two at a time, until he burst into Miss Anna's room.

CHAPTER 19

Miss Anna was lying on the bed with unseeing eyes, staring at wallpaper she would never see again. Junior stood at the window, hands in his pockets, back to the room.

Mister George knelt and took the small, shrunken hand in his. "What have you done?" He accused.

"Nothing," Junior's voice was flat. "All I did was tell her I was leaving this God-forsaken-hole forever." Junior shrugged.

Mister George buried his face in the bedcovers. "Please leave this room... now." He added when Junior hesitated.

Junior roughly shouldered Shad aside at the door and rushed down the hall. Shad knelt beside Mister George and placing a black arm around Mister George pulled him into his arms. Both wept unashamedly.

The plantation went into deep mourning. Miss Anna had touched the lives of every slave on the plantation at one time or another. She cared for the sick, consoled the troubled and intervened with Mister George when the situation warranted. Everyone would miss her greatly.

Junior crossed the river the night of Miss Anna's death and wasn't seen until the day of her funeral. After the services, he rode off without a word to anyone.

None of the slaves chose to run away. They all stayed and grieved with Mister George. Jonas, Ahab, and Dan returned to stable duty, although there wasn't much to do since the Confederate Army had taken most of the stock.

Mister George picked a gravesite alongside the road to Ingrid's as a final resting place for Miss Anna. At the top of the hill overlooking Tendrilhoff, backed by a grove of thick trunked, short bodied old oaks; it was a lonely, lovely place.

Miss Anna's funeral was an elaborate, emotional, drawn out affair, as befitted the much-loved, great lady in the pine box.

Albert White drove Ingrid's wagon with the matched bays dancing merrily in the harness. Ingrid perched on the spring seat alongside Albert. Ennis and Tamar stood holding onto the back of the spring seat.

The plain, somber black dress was a striking background for Ingrid's long, sun bleached, blonde hair and clear blue eyes. Albert wore a neatly tailored black suit. As with most of the slaves, Ennis and Tamar wore the same type of clothes they wore every day.

The itinerant preacher was flattered by being asked to officiate at the funeral of someone as important as Miss Anna. He allowed the slaves to sing a couple of mournful tunes before he began his sermon on what a great lady Miss Anna was.

Ingrid, supported by Albert's possessive arm, stood on one side of the casket, which rested on rails over the open grave. Mister George, flanked by Hannibal on the left and Shad on the right, stood on the other side.

The preacher was well into his subject when Albert squeezed Miss Ingrid's arm and pointed across the ridge.

Along the spiny back of the ridge, a long, gray line of horsemen, followed by a string of wagons was approaching the solemn group around the casket.

Ingrid spoke to Ennis, who slowly faded backward through the mourners.

At a hundred yards distance the column halted. The Major spoke to a subordinate officer. The young officer turned his horse and barked an order. The Troopers dismounted in unison and removed their hats.

"Our condolences on your loss." The Major, a Captain, a Lieutenant, and the head clerk approached Mister George. "We shall only be a minute. We've visited the southern part of your plantation. Didn't find much, but we had to take what we found. Sure would hate to find a Union sympathizer holding out on our boys at the front. Anyway, we stopped by to pay for what we requisitioned."

The clerk stepped forward with a thin stack of Confederate script in his hand.

"Major, you are intruding." Mister George ignored the clerk holding the script. "As for sympathies, I have no sympathies for stupid people, at the front or in either capitol! This war was unnecessary. Now, take your men and leave. Let us bury my wife in peace."

"Sorry, the needs of the men at the front..." The Major began.

"Don't try to tell me the needs of soldiers." Mister George grated. "I commanded the Prussian Lancers under Bulcher. I know the needs of soldiers. The ones who have the nerve to be on the front lines anyway." The cold blue eyes bored into the Major.

The Major reddened under the insult. The fact that it was true made it more stinging. The major had pulled every political string possible to stay off the firing line.

Jeb Stuart, whose life and reputation depended on the quality of the men at his back, decided the matter by assigning the Major to the quartermaster corps.

"Mister Hoff, I'll send your pay to you," the Major turned to face Albert and Ingrid. "Is Albert White or Ingrid Doppler here?"

Albert stepped forward, "Major, no officer worth his salt would intrude here. Any further intrusion will be grounds for a gentleman to ask for satisfaction."

"Ask for satisfaction?" The Major was puzzled. "You mean fight a duel?"

"Exactly!" Albert spit it into the Major's face.

The Major started to make a cutting remark. The look in

Albert's eyes stopped him. He's really going to challenge me, the Major thought, quickly stepping back when Albert shifted his gloves.

Under no circumstance am I going to fight a duel, the Major thought, but I don't want my men to see me refuse. Besides, as man with political ambitions the Major could see a valuable ally or a formidable future foe in the stubborn Englishman.

Sweeping his hat off in a mock bow the Major said, "We are on our way to your place. We will wait just beyond the hill."

Albert signaled the preacher to resume the service.

True to his word, the Major was sitting beside a small fire drinking confiscated coffee. Albert didn't check the team as they trotted past the soldiers. With a curse, the Major dumped his coffee and began shouting orders. The soldiers formed a hasty column in pursuit of the retreating wagon.

It was a grim, silent ride for Albert and Ingrid.

The Major watched Ingrid's blond hair swing from side to side and wondered how much of a political asset the young widow would be if she were to become his wife.

Albert wheeled the team around the barn and pulled them to a stop at Ingrid's gate. Ingrid stood in the wagon and surveyed the place.

Jake and Jack stood with their heads hanging over the corral fence. There was no sign of Kate, Judy or Ennis.

"Captain, you take a squad and four wagons to Mr. White's place. Take White with you." The Major extended a hand to assist Ingrid's dismount from the wagon. "I've never had a chance to introduce myself, Major JP Crowe at your service, ma'am."

Ingrid ignored the Major's hand and leaped lightly to the ground.

"Major, I'm not taking orders from the military." Albert came stomping around the wagon.

"It's not orders, we like for the owners to be present so they can see what we requisition. If they are present, we can pay them on the spot." Major Crowe spoke in a conciliatory voice.

"Go with the Captain, Albert, I'm sure Major Crowe can strip this place out with less than half the men he has present." Albert had never seen the smile Ingrid sent his way.

Major Crowe held the yard gate open for Ingrid and held her chair when they sat on the porch.

Troopers swarmed over the place. They took grain from the barn, and drove what cows they could find from the forest. All the while Major Crowe prattled on.

"We will leave your team of mules, they are too old, and enough seed to plant next year's crop. We'll leave your milk cow."

"Why don't you just take everything? Why consign us to slow starvation? Why not take it all and just shoot us?" She raged.

"Miss Ingrid! How can you say such a thing? We are the duly constituted authority here. I plan on being appointed judge for this district when the war is over."

"It's Mrs. Doppler to you and I have been trying very hard to convince myself that you are the present authority." Ingrid leaned back and smiled sweetly at Major Crowe. "Because if I didn't think you had some kind of right to do what you are doing, I would have to shoot you for the thief I think you are." Ingrid's hand slid from her pocket, clutching Conrad's pistol, the sights settled between Major Crowe's eyes.

CHAPTER 20

Major Crowe sat petrified while the pistol was aimed between his eyes. He looked down the enormous, rock steady bore until Ingrid lowered the pistol to her lap. Gathering some of his wits about him, Major Crowe ran shakily for the yard gate.

Several days after the funeral, Mister George wandered aimlessly into his office; Junior sat at Mister George's desk, turning pages in one of the ledger books.

"What are you doing?" Mister George demanded from the doorway.

"I'm leaving Tendrilhoff." Junior flipped the ledger shut.

"I think that is a good idea. What if Ahab or Dan had decided to hang you before they ran or one of the girl's fathers had waylaid you on one of your drunken returns from across the river?"

Junior paled, this thought had never crossed his mind. As far as a slave was concerned, he had always considered himself an untouchable god. He could see his father's point clearly.

Man to man, he would be no match for Ahab or Dan. Either one, much less both backed by what little Jonas could contribute.

"They wouldn't have the nerve, besides, it doesn't matter much anyway. I've stopped by to pick up my inheritance and I'll be off for New Orleans or someplace." Junior squared his shoulders. He had prepared for this battle.

"Inheritance? What are you talking about?"

"I've put years into this place. Since you've publicly relegated me to a position lower than the lowest slave, I want my money. I'm leaving."

Mister George was stunned to silence, and then he laughed. "You've put..." Mister George laughed again. "Junior, your inheritance is in New Orleans, along with the rest of Tendrilhoff's cash. You gave it to the gamblers and whores while your mother was so ill. I didn't feel she could stand the fight it would've taken to stop it."

"Don't tell me you didn't convert your extra cash to gold and bury it or deposit it in England like the rest of the planters did when this beastly war began. I'll take that and be out of your hair. Now that Mother is gone, there is nothing here for me."

"I told you Junior, you spent your inheritance and mine too. No, wait a minute; I do have money for you." Mister George walked around his desk and stooped to open the bottom drawer.

Junior had to scurry out of the way, but he didn't mind. Mister George was beginning to cave in. *When I get this I'll keep on until I get it all,* Junior decided.

Straightening, Mister George handed Junior the stack of Confederate script the officer left on the day of the raid.

Junior stared at it, horrified. Then, he flung it in Mister George's face. The silver-headed cane began an upward arc, but stopped halfway. Mister George stood, his mouth working, but only unintelligible sounds came out. Slowly, like a mighty oak, he toppled to his side on the floor.

Junior stared at his father, mildly puzzled for a moment. "Hannibal! Hannibal!" He yelled.

Hannibal called Moses from the barn. Together they rolled Mister George onto some planking and moved him to his bed. They made him as comfortable as possible.

"Go bring Shad in as quickly as possible." Hannibal whispered to Moses while they were moving Mister George.

The closeness between the men had let Shad sense Mister George's need to be alone with his memories. Shad saddled June Bug that morning and set off on a circuit of the outlying reaches of the plantation. It was several hours before Moses caught up with Shad.

Spotting Moses on his back trail, Shad pulled June Bug to a stop, stepped off and leaned against him while he waited for Moses to catch up.

"It's Mister George. He had some kind of spell." Moses said without greeting.

"Spell?"

"Yes, he fell to the floor. He can't move his left leg or arm and he can't talk. He just makes noise. He's still alive, but it don't look good. Mister Junior is there." Moses called the warning as Shad was swinging into the saddle.

Shad gave the big hunter his head and took the short cut home. Early darkness was enclosing the world by the time June Bug's shoes rattled on the cobblestone drive in front of the house.

Shad left the sweaty, winded horse for the stable hands to care for and took the veranda steps in a single bound.

Hannibal met him at the door."He's a little better. He can talk now. Not very good, but you can understand him now. One whole side of his body doesn't work. Mister Junior is up there. He hasn't left all day." Hannibal shook his head.

Junior sat in a chair facing the window. When Shad entered the room, he rose, turned the chair facing the bed and sat back down. A single light cast shadows on the walls.

Mister George lie on his bed, a mere caricature of himself. The whole left side of his face sagged. The left eye partially covered by the drooping lid. Spittle oozed from the corner of the slack mouth.

Shad bent over Mister George and saw recognition in the good eye. Shad glanced at Mister Junior. Junior leaned back in his chair and placed his hands in a steeple in front of him. He was determined to stay in the room.

"Shad," Mister George struggled. Reaching up with his good hand, he took Shad by the arm that he had propped on the bed. "Too late," Mister George's good eye moved in Junior's direction. "Tendrilhoff."

"It's not too late." Shad said. "Hannibal said you have improved a lot since this morning."

"I want... I want some venison. That... that... that," Mister George checked himself. "That little buck in the swamp. I want him."

"Okay, I'll get him for you." Shad promised.

"I want him now." The hand holding Shad's arm tightened to a surprising degree, and Mister George's good eye bore into Shad's. "I want my cotton. Find my cotton."

"I'll get him for you." Shad promised again.

"Find my... my... cotton. Where the scoundrel is. Get cotton." Mister George raised his head slightly.

"He's wandering. You better leave." Junior's flat voice cut in.

"I'll get the venison for you." Mister George's hand relaxed and Shad straightened.

Junior followed Shad out of the room with the express purpose of countermanding Mister George's request for the venison. Before he got to the door, he remembered the look in Shad's eye the day he started to whip him with the riding crop. By the time he went through the door, he realized he was alone. Not one soul on this plantation would raise a hand to help him. It could wait, he decided. He had been sitting in that chair making plans for Tendrilhoff. He wouldn't be alone very long.

"Don't be long with that venison," Junior growled at Shad's back. Shad never looked back.

"How is he?" A worried Hannibal met Shad in the hall.

"Wandering," Shad didn't want to be short with the old butler, but he felt he must, simply must get out to the privacy of the open air.

The screen door slam behind him, Shad crossed to the far

end of the veranda. Leaning across the rail, gulping the soft evening air, Shad gave vent to the passion building inside him. The money, the stolen crop, the army, Junior, the runaways, and the death of Miss Anna. Now, the incapacitation and impending death of Mister George, and the end of Tendrilhoff. It was more than he could hold up under at the moment.

Junior followed Shad to the door. Standing inside the door, he listened for a moment.

"Hannibal," Junior yelled, turning back down the hallway. "I want you to prepare Mother's room for two gentlemen." Walking past Hannibal, Junior ordered, "Have it ready by tomorrow evening. Alf and Jim Bob should be here by then."

After his tear ducts ran dry and the sobs died, Shad sat in a daze. *What could he do?* There was nothing he could do sitting here, he decided.

Shad walked past the big barn, up the ridge, and continued toward Ingrid's house. *How much did Junior know of his involvement with Ingrid?* He decided to take precautions.

It was a highly unusual trip for Shad. He didn't hear the chirp of the crickets or the song of the cicada. He never changed stride or direction at the frying buzz of an angry rattlesnake.

Poor Mister George, Shad told himself. His mind was gone. He was rambling around somewhere, perhaps in the past. "Too late... Tendrilhoff... little buck, swamp... find my cotton... where the scoundrel is..."

Shad stopped abruptly. *Wait a minute! Maybe? Could it be that Mister George was telling him something?*

"Too late... Tendrilhoff." A look at Junior. "Too late to save Tendrilhoff? Little buck in the swamp."

Once several years ago, Shad found a small buck bedded in tall swamp grass. While he was drawing a bead on the deer, a runaway slave stood up on the other side of the buck with both hands above his head. The runaway thought the rifle was being aimed at him.

Mister George turned his horse and rode away. When Shad

followed Mister George, the runaway lowered his hands and dashed for the timber. "Little buck..." A runaway slave.

"Find my cotton..." The Yankee skipper took the cotton north, so you would have to go north to find it.

"Where the scoundrel is..." Stay in the north.

"Too late for Tendrilhoff. Runaway. Go north and stay there." Shad said to himself. It hit like a board to the side of the head. If Mister George was capable of passing this message in a form Junior couldn't understand, there was nothing wrong with his mind.

Shad was still wondering what he could do for Mister George when he arrived at Ingrid's yard gate.

The coffeepot made a rattling sound when Ingrid slid it across the lids on top of the wood cookstove. She measured a small amount of coffee into the pot, she poured several dippers of water on top of the coffee. Lifting a lid Ingrid stirred the coals, dropping a piece of kindling followed by a stick of wood. All this puttering around was done for the purpose of giving her time to think.

Shad sat in front of the dead fireplace. He had not moved since explaining the happenings of the past few hours. What could be done? Junior was apparently in charge of Tendrilhoff now. This made him Shad's owner. Ingrid shuddered at the thought.

She watched Shad rise and pace the floor. My God, she thought, what a man he has grown to be. Six-foot-two, at least two hundred pounds and he came out of the chair and paced the floor like a big cat, all his motions smooth and fluid. To Ingrid, he would always be a child.

"Shad, you are going to have to run. I can see no other way."

"What about Mister George? I can't just take off and leave him there." Shad stopped pacing.

"He told you to run. He told you it was too late for him and Tendrilhoff."

"I can't abandon him. I'm all he has left." Shad's jaw was set.

"There is nothing you can do Shad. Junior won't let you do anything. He will kill you if you go back. I'm worried."

"Junior won't kill me. He might beat me, but he won't kill me. I'm worth too much money. He needs money desperately. He will sell me down river, the first chance he gets." Shad continued to pace the floor.

"If I could get Mister George out of the house, take him to Hoffman. They have a doctor there now." Shad desperately searched for a way.

"Junior won't let you or Mister George go to Hoffman. He sees a way to get Tendrilhoff. He will do anything to keep you from spoiling this chance." Ingrid cast around for a more persuasive argument.

If Shad ran, Ingrid knew it was highly possible she would never see him again, even if his escape was successful. It wasn't what she wanted, but she was desperate to keep him alive and well.

I can't run and go north. Besides not abandoning Mister George, I have you and Bekah to think of. The rest of the slaves need me," agitated, Shad paced faster.

Ingrid intercepted him. Taking him by the hands, she pulled him to a chair and pushed him into it.

"Shad, I have something to tell you. Albert asked me to marry him. I'm going to say yes. I'll have Ennis and Tamar. I won't be alone." Ingrid waited for this to soak in. "Could you take Bekah with you when you go?"

Shad contemplated this for a while. "No," he said reluctantly. He thought it was an enticing idea. "If I go, Junior will send Alf and Jim Bob after me. Their big brag is that no nigger has ever gotten away from them."

"Can you get away from them?" Ingrid thought no one could catch Shad.

"I think so. About all the people they have run down were field hands." Shad scratched his head. "I've heard they stay clear of anything that looks like the work of Harriet Tubman or the Underground Railroad."

"Could you get in touch with Tubman or the railroad?" Ingrid asked.

"I don't know there wouldn't be enough time. They are probably swamped. Elias and Moses escorted Tubman off Tendrilhoff one time. She might not be well disposed toward us."

"I have something for you. I made it some time ago." Ingrid went to the trunk where she kept her dresses. Rummaging around, she dug out a ragged old coat. It had patches on patches. It looked more disreputable than anything Shad ever saw the slaves on Tendrilhoff wear.

"Ennis was going to throw this away. I had an idea and asked him for it." Ingrid held a sleeve out. "Feel here," she ordered.

"Feels like a coin sewn into the lining," Shad said.

CHAPTER 21

"It is your half of the gold, from the long hunters, sewn into the lining. It's scattered all over the coat."

"All over the coat?" Shad began probing, finding a coin here and there.

"Yes, I thought the day might come when you would have to run. You'll need money and it's not likely anyone will take or steal this old coat from you."

"I can't go!" Shad rose and started pacing again.

"For the ones of us that love you, you are going to have to go. How good at slave catching is the rest of the bunch, if Alf and Jim Bob were taken out of it?" Ingrid watched him walking to and fro.

"Not very good if Alf and Jim Bob were taken out of it. Shad was beginning to see which way Ingrid's mind was drifting.

"Get Bekah out and send her to me. I'll dress her as a man and hide her, or perhaps we could put her in the caves for a while. We could keep her there until you could come get her." Ingrid tossed the blonde hair.

Shad had to grin at the thought of disguising the shapely Bekah as a man. "If I couldn't get away from Alf and Jim Bob, I could probably keep them busy while the slaves who chose to run leave Tendrilhoff. Some of them might make it."

"I don't think you have any choice. Tendrilhoff is a dead carcass. Junior will pick on it for a while, then leave for other parts." Ingrid hated to say this. She knew how much pain Tendrilhoff's demise was causing Shad. She had to get it across to him.

"Junior has several problems. He has expensive tastes and he is broke. Tendrilhoff is broke. Everyone in the south is broke or hanging on tight until they see which way this war is going. He may sell the slaves, but they won't sell for much right now. I don't think he can sell the land at any price. The army has taken most near everything else of value.

"Junior left New Orleans because of money problems and he was under severe pressure to join one of the military outfits. The little coward doesn't have the stomach to face a Yankee with a rifle in his hand.

"Tendrilhoff is not dead as long as Mister George lives. I'll go to the swamps and stay there until I can get Mister George out of there." Shad decided.

Ingrid knew there was no use arguing the point any further. All she could do was pray Junior never got Shad under his control.

Leaving Ingrid's gate, Shad looked at the stars. If he wanted to get to Tendrilhoff before dawn, he was going to have to hustle. He settled into a long striding trot. He could hold this gait for miles. He didn't need much light, for his feet seemed to have eyes of their own. In the open places, there was the starlight. When he passed under the canopy of the huge oaks, it was almost pitch black.

What to do about Bekah? He had no doubts about Ingrid, she was intelligent, tough, and would do her best to protect Bekah. Should he put Ingrid in this kind of jeopardy on his behalf? Did he have the right to let her take the risk?

About Albert White, he didn't know. He wished he had spent less time resenting the man and more time getting to know him. Albert had shown he had iron in his backbone when he called Major Crowe at Miss Anna's Funeral, but would he be willing to risk hiding a runaway slave?

What about Bekah? What were her feelings about him? He

thought he knew. Now, he wasn't so sure. Would she be willing to risk running away and taking the hardships and danger running away would involve?

He cursed himself. Most of these questions should have been answered. He thought there was lots of time, but in reality there was none.

Did he have enough skill to lead Alf and Jim Bob away? He was sure Junior would give them the job of catching him but he had to make sure it happened. He could wait and ambush them. The thought of cold blooded murder was repugnant to him.

He needed to talk to Bekah and Hannibal. He had no doubts about the old butler. The timing of Bekah leaving Tendrilhoff would have to be right.

He would gather his few belongings together and watch Tendrilhoff until he got a chance to talk to Hannibal and Bekah.

What if... what if... His mind kept asking while his feet beat a steady pit pat tattoo on the ground.

The eastern sky was softening a little when Shad slipped into his quarters. He threw a quick bedroll together. His hunting pack and shot pouch were already well supplied with flint and steel, lead, powder, primers, bullet molds, and a few odds and ends.

Food, he didn't have, but that didn't matter much. He could live off the land.

Glancing around the room, Shad realized it might be the last time he saw it. Tendrilhoff had been his life since he could remember. The last few years it had been his whole life. Almost all his waking hours had been devoted to working or planning for the betterment of Tendrilhoff.

Leaving was almost more than he could bear.

Rolling the coat Ingrid gave him in the bedroll, he lashed it across the top of the pack. Slinging the shot pouch over one shoulder, he pulled the straps of the pack over both shoulders and picked up a rifle in one hand and a double-barreled, twelve gauge fowling piece in the other. Stepping into the fast softening darkness he turned toward the Hoffman road. When he passed the shadows at the end of the veranda, a hand shot out and took him by the arm.

He dropped the shotgun, broke the hold on his arm and brought the rifle into striking position.

"Don't hit me! It's just old Hannibal," a voice whispered from the dark shadows.

"Hannibal? What are you doing here?" Shad lowered the rifle.

"I've been waiting for you. I thought you would be coming by."

"How is Mister George?"

"Much worse, I'm afraid. Bekah is sitting with him, nursing him day and night."

"Is there any chance we could slip him out of there?"

Hannibal shook his head. "He couldn't stand the move. It would kill him for sure."

Shad was silent, wondering what else could go wrong.

"What I've been waiting on you for is to tell you, Mister Junior sent for Alf and Jim Bob."

"Alf and Jim Bob? What for?" Shad was finding out what else could go wrong.

"They're going to live here. Leastwise, Mister Junior told me to prepare Miss Anna's room for them."

Shad shook his head, "I hope Mister George don't know this."

"I don't think Mister George knows much of anything. It's like he was hanging on real hard, until he talked to you, and then he let go. He's been slowly sinking since then.

"I think Mister Junior sent for some men. They will be coming with Alf and Jim Bob this evening or tonight." Hannibal finished with a sigh and a shake of his white hair.

"Hannibal, I think Mister Junior needs something else to think about. Do you think you could let it slip that Mister George had gold here?" Shad was planning as he went. "You don't know what happened to it, but I might."

"That would be easy. Mister Junior done been tearing the

place up, looking for it." Fear showed in Hannibal's eyes. "Shad, that would put them on you like a duck after a June bug."

"I know they will have to come after me. But they would need me alive wouldn't they? Do you know where Devil Dog Bayou runs into the swamp?"

"Is that the one with the quicksand?" A shiver escaped Hannibal.

"Yes," Shad nodded.

"I know where it is."

"I'll be camped there. If Mister George improves to where we can move him, we'll take him out of there regardless of the cost. I have to be going. It's breaking daylight."

"I don't think we have to worry. Mister Junior is sleeping behind locked doors with a jar of whiskey and his daddy's guns," Hannibal chuckled at Junior's fear.

"If you can get Bekah out of the house without waking Junior, have her meet me at the creek behind the barn, the first place we went with Ennis and Tamar."

Shad paced the creek bank restlessly until Bekah appeared.

"Bekah, I must have some answers and we don't have time for the niceties," Shad said. "Will you marry me?"

Bekah stood, shocked, for a moment, then squealed and threw her arms around his neck.

"Wait a minute." Shad took her by the shoulders and gently pushed her back to arm's length. "Are you willing to run away, take all the hardship, and danger this will entail?

Bekah looked him in the eye. "Let's go."

"I wish it were that simple. I don't think we could get away from Alf and Jim Bob together. We must wait and see how Mister George does. If he gets better, I'm going to move him to safety. If he dies, I want you to go to Ingrid and do what she says while I lead Alf and Jim Bob away.

"Mister George is getting worse. He has lost the will to live." Tears appear in Bekah's eyes.

"Get word to the rest of the slaves. Don't run right now.

Don't tell them what I'm planning. After Alf and Jim Bob are gone, they stand a chance of getting away."

"Moses, Elias, Ahab, and Dan are planning to go. Bekah counted them off on her fingers.

"Tell Moses I want them to wait. He'll understand. I don't know how or exactly when we are going to get you out. Stay ready to go on a moments notice. I think you can trust Hannibal completely."

"I know I can trust Hannibal. He's been like a father to me. Are you coming back for me?" Bekah voiced her fear.

"Don't be silly. How can we get married if I don't come back for you?" Shad pulled her into his arms and kissed her passionately. They clung to each other until Shad pushed her back to arm's length again.

"I promise, I'll come for you." Shad picked up his pack. "You better get back now. We don't want to make Junior suspicious. I'll be camped at the mouth of Devil Dog Bayou. Hannibal knows where and Junior has a good idea where it is."

Shad picked up a coil of small rope when he passed the barn.

The sun was warm on his back. The colors were beautiful. Breezes rustled the new fallen leaves back and forth. Squirrels suspended their nut and acorn gathering long enough to bark at the intruder.

Head down, fore foot up, a doe froze in the act of picking an acorn from the ground. The doe raised her head and then turned the big fan of ears in the suspicious direction. At the grinding sound of a foot on a rock, she flipped the long flag of a tail up and down to alerting the yearling feeding a few feet away. A swirling breeze brought Shad's scent to her. An explosive snort, a stamp of the front foot and she was off toward the heavy brush with the yearling on her heels.

Shad flipped the rifle over and smiled down the barrel. "If I was hunting, you were too late young lady," he said.

He left the road at Devil Dog Bayou. Crossing the bayou, he climbed the ridge at a slant. Staying on the rocks as much as possible, he was very careful to leave no sign of his passing. He watched the timber as he moved along. About four miles above the crossing, he found what he was looking for. Someone had cut the big trees, some years before and a strong young second growth replaced them.

Shad selected a tall, slender tree, he tied the rope to the base of a nearby tree and began climbing the taller slender tree. Working the rope up through the limbs, he climbed until his weight began bending the tree. Wrapping the rope around the tree, he pulled until his weight and the force of the rope brought the treetop to a few feet above the ground.

After working in the area for perhaps forty-five minutes, he laid the makings of a small fire. Peeling the inner bark from a dead tree nearby, he rolled it between his hands. After rubbing the bark for a while he examined it. Satisfied it would make good tinder, he struck it under the makings of a fire.

Carefully, foot by foot, inch by inch, he went over the ground where he had been working. He obliterated or covered any signs of his presence. Surveying the area, he grunted his satisfaction picked up his pack, and carefully retraced his footsteps to Devil Dog Bayou.

When he came to the crossing, he turned down the bayou. After crossing the road, he was no longer careful of the sign he left. He let his feet blunder along. Turning rocks over, kicking partially buried sticks out of the ground, letting brush hang on his clothes, and flip twigs and leaves on the ground. He left a trail anyone could follow.

A small hummock appeared on the left side of the trail. Shad carefully sidestepped off the trail and climbed to the top of the hummock. From here he could see the swamp. At the edge of the swamp, a knotty old cypress tree grew out of the damp earth. Underneath the cypress was a clear area. Marking the clear spot in his mind, he eased back to the trail and walked to it.

Dropping his pack on the ground, Shad picked four saplings. He pulled the tops of the saplings together and tied them there. Filling the openings on three sides with brush formed a nice little lean to.

He went back up the ridge and cut enough pine limbs to make a bed in the lean-to. Taking his bedroll from the top of his pack, Shad spread the first quilt over the pine boughs.

He cast about until he found a dead chunk about as long as he was. Placing the chunk on the bed, he stood two smaller chunks at the end of it. The two smaller chunks looked like feet when he spread the second quilt over the bed. He balled up some pine limbs to resemble a head and stuck them at the other end of the large chunk.

Shad looked the job over. Up close, it obviously wouldn't fool anyone. From a distance in the semi-dark lean-to, it looked like a sleeping man.

Work done, he eased along the edge of the swamp until he killed a swamp rabbit, which roasted nicely on a fire in front of the lean-to. Before dark, he dragged a load of wood in and threw it on the fire.

Taking his guns and pack, he moved back to the hummock. Satisfied that anyone going past him into the camp would wake him, he slept.

The swish of brush against fabric woke him. He came wide-awake. No fumbling around. No befuddlement. He was clearheaded and wide awake. Most woodsmen developed this trait.

He looked at the sky and realized he had not been asleep long. It was still a couple of hours to midnight.

He lied still until a figure passed his hiding place. Rolling to his stomach, he watched the camp. The figure stopped just outside the light of the dying fire.

"Shad," a woman's voice called softly.

Bekah! What was she doing here? "Bekah?" Shad called softly.

Bekah jumped and peered into the lean-to, then realized the voice came from behind her.

"What are you doing here?" Shad asked gruffly.

"Hannibal sent me."

"Sent you? Why didn't he send one of the men?"

"He couldn't. Alf and Jim Bob came earlier than expected. They brought a bunch of men with them. They've rounded up all the men and locked them in the barn."

"Locked them in the barn?" Shad had not expected this.

"Junior told the slaves, Alf had arranged a sale for a lot of them and the rest were going to do the same amount of work the whole bunch did." Bekah fidgeted. "I heard Alf tell Junior he had a special cotton planter in mind for you. He said this man didn't mind working slaves to death because by the time they died, he got enough work out of them to pay for another." Bekah hesitated.

"Hannibal let it slip that you knew where Mister George buried some gold and Alf put the sale off. Him and Jim Bob are coming out first thing in the morning and bring you in before you get itchy feet." Bekah's eyes grew round with worry. "I don't think Hannibal intended to let it slip."

"There is no gold. I asked Hannibal to plant the idea so Alf and Jim Bob would come after me and maybe it would make them hesitate to kill me." Shad smacked a fist into an open hand. "Don't Junior know Tendrilhoff is done for?"

"Junior doesn't know anything about the plantation except it furnished him a good living, without him having to work for a long time. He can't understand why it can't go on doing so."

Shad took her by the hands. "How did you get out?"

"I sat with Mister George. I guess they got used to seeing me walk in and out."

"Hannibal didn't send you here to tell me this." Shad stated.

"No, there ain't no easy way to say this, Mister George died not long after you left this morning."

He dropped her hands and walked to the edge of the firelight. Sobs wracked his frame. Bekah came up behind him and wrapped her arms around him. Turning, he pulled her to him and leaned on the comfort she offered.

Think, Shad told himself when the first flash of grief passed.

I must get a hold of myself and think. I can grieve later. Bekah comes first.

"You can't go back now." Shad continued to hold her tight. "You have to go to Ingrid. I can't see another way."

Bekah snuggled closer to him, looking up at him with soft, adoring eyes. "This might be the last time I see you." She laid her head on his chest.

"You can't leave now. You can't go back the way you came. The risk of meeting Alf and Jim Bob would be too great. You will have to go around the swamp and you can't do that until daylight."

Bekah wiggled against him again. He had to quit pretending he didn't have a soft and beautiful woman in his arms.

He kissed her willing lips tenderly. Then again, more passionately this time. Releasing her, he took her hand, and led her toward the lean-to.

Dawn was creeping up to peek over the Eastern ridges. The last star winked at the world and went to sleep. Day birds were shifting and chirping on their roost.

Shad picked a blade of grass and tickled Bekah's nose.

Bekah rolled over and buried her face in the quilt. He tickled her ear. Slapping at the offending grass woke her. She rolled to her back and rose to a sitting position, rubbing the sleep out of her eyes.

"Traveling time," Shad announced.

"With you?" Bekah pulled her knees up under her chin and hooked her arms around them.

"That's my dream." Shad rose. "Unfortunately, it's not possible."

"Why not? We could leave right now." Bekah pouted.

"Alf and Jim Bob should be leaving Tendrilhoff about now. Much as I dislike them, I don't underestimate them. I don't want them to get their hands on you." This thought sobered Bekah. She held a hand up and Shad pulled her to her feet.

"Follow the edge of the swamp. It will turn south. The third stream is the one that runs behind the barn at Tendrilhoff, wait until you are close to Tendrilhoff. Don't go within sight of the place. Circle around and go over the hill to Ingrid's." Shad was still holding her hand.

"All my things are at Tendrilhoff."

Ingrid and Tamar will have something you can wear. You couldn't take them when I came after you anyway." Shad pointed out. "Now listen carefully, don't walk on soft ground, and don't walk in the road. If you need to follow a road keep to one side as far away from it as possible."

"I don't want to go." Bekah came into his arms. They clung to each other for a long kiss.

Taking her by the shoulders Shad pushed her away, turned her toward the swamp and swatted her fanny. "Off with you girl, there's work to be done," Shad said, a lot lighter than he felt.

Shad watched Bekah until he could no longer see movement among the trees. Returning to camp, he set it up as it was the evening before.

He went back to his hiding place on the hummock and worked himself into the grass so he could peer through the blades into the camp and sideways onto the trail. He dozed.

Footsteps on the trail woke him. Peering through the grass, he saw Alf followed by Jim Bob. They were coming steadily down the trail.

Alf came in sight of the camp and immediately eased to his stomach in the trail. Jim Bob dropped to the ground and crawled alongside Alf.

"Damned nigger is still in bed," Alf whispered.

"He's probably got that wench in there with him." Jim Bob peered into the semi-dark lean-to. "I don't know how we let her walk out of the house last night."

"Don't worry about it, we'll collect them both and be back to the house by dark." Alf was looking the situation over. "Open ground to the left. If he tries to run, it will be to the right or back toward the swamp. You go around and come up on that side. I'll cover you from that log beside the trail." As usual Alf gave Jim Bob the job with the most work attached.

Rifle across his arms, Alf slowly inched toward the indicated log. Stopping, he carefully moved some twigs out of his way. Jim Bob turned at right angles to the trail and crawled toward Devil Dog Bayou.

Shad realized he was holding his breath. Exhaling silently, he waited until Alf was almost to the log. Backing off the hummock Shad came onto the trail. Staying out of sight and hearing of the pair working the ambush, he ran up the trail to the crossing on Devil Dog Bayou.

Shad crossed the road and took the same slant up ridge he had taken the day before. This time he ran through the leaves to stir them up and was careful to leave a trail that would be easy to follow.

Meanwhile, Jim Bob had completed his circuit of the camp and lay at the edge of the clearing. Something was wrong. He could feel it in his gut. He expected Shad and Bekah to burst from the lean-to before this.

Jim Bob checked Alf. He could see the barrel of Alf's rifle over the log, but not much else. Rising to his feet, Jim Bob snuck up to the side of the lean-to. Gripping the rifle in both hands, he leaped around to the front.

"Come out!" He yelled. Slack jawed and with an oath, he dropped the rifle to his side, reached in and tossed the quilt in Alf's direction.

"He set us up!" Jim Bob yelled at Alf. Silently Alf rose from behind the log and began walking a slow circle round the camp. Jim Bob did the same on the opposite side.

They met on the Hummock.

"Wench went out around the swamp. Buck lay on his back trail and let us pass him. It looks like he didn't leave until we were past. Alf surmised.

Jim Bob grunt assent.

"You go get the wench. I'll catch him," Alf said.

"You would like that, wouldn't you? She don't know where the gold is. He does. I'm not as stupid as Junior. He thinks we're going to split the gold with him."

"Let's go get the buck, then the sooner we catch him the sooner we get the gold." Alf started down the trail.

"Do you think he will talk when we catch him?" Jim Bob worried.

Alf smiled evilly. "They all do, sooner or later. We'll persuade him."

After crossing the road, Shad went straight to the site he had prepared the day before. Taking flint and steel from his pack, he struck sparks into the tinder. A tiny curl of smoke appeared. He didn't have time to blow it to full life. He was sure it would catch and be burning merrily by the time Alf and Jim Bob got there. Leaving the ridge, he struck a ground-eating trot. He didn't particularly try to hide his trail. He didn't make it easy for them either. His plan was to travel faster than they could for a while.

"I smell smoke." Alf halted.

"Me too." Jim Bob stepped up beside Alf.

They moved a few yards apart and approached the fire. Standing still, they silently searched the woods for signs of an ambush.

"What do you make of that?" Alf nodded at the fire.

Jim Bob shrugged, "Stopped to eat and we ran him out?" Jim Bob questioned.

"I doubt that, he knows we're after him."

"I don't know, we've seen them do some dumb things." Jim Bob scratched his head. The smell of the smoke was so strong in his nostrils he could taste the tannin.

Alf strode into the fire and started to make a circle around it. There was a sizzling sound as a rope flew from the leaves, circled Alf's leg and yanked him upside down off the ground.

At the first whisper of sound, the wary Alf's thumb rocked the hammer back on his rifle. With the shock of his feet being jerked out from under him, he pulled the trigger. The heavy bullet slammed into the fire, throwing hot coals and burning embers all over Jim Bob.

"Get me down, get me down!" Alf screamed.

Jim Bob was too busy trying to brush hot coals and embers from his burning hair and shake the same from inside his hunting shirt to pay any attention to Alf's predicament.

Jim Bob went around the hillside doing a bucking, stomping, slapping twist. The coals and hot rock splinters stung like a nest of hornets. Thoroughly panicked, Alf swung to and fro, screaming for help.

Jim Bob, minus much of his hair, finally controlled the fires about his person and looked at Alf.

"Hanging like a Christmas turkey," he cried derisively, despite the many stinging spots burned into his body.

"Cut me down! Cut me down!" Alf cried, still panicked.

"Well, I don't know." Jim Bob began. "I've got a lot of burns that need treating."

Alf stopped struggling and stared coldly at Jim Bob. "Get me down now, he said in a deadly voice."

Jim Bob hesitated; he knew laughing time was over. Pulling his knife from its sheath, he approached Alf.

There was the sizzling sound again and a sapling came swinging around like a baseball bat and struck Jim Bob across the shoulder and the back of the head. He rolled under Alf, unconscious.

"What...?" Jim Bob groaned.

"Big help you were. I had to cut myself down."

Rolling to his stomach, Jim Bob painfully pushed himself erect, rediscovering each of the burned spots. Struggling out of his hunting shirt, Jim Bob surveyed the damage. His shoulder and back were already blue. Most of the hair on top of his head was missing. The back of his head was matted with blood. His upper torso was speckled with burned spots.

"He done a job on you." Alf wasn't going to own up to his part in the affair.

"That boy tried to kill us."

"No, he didn't try to kill us or you would be dead. Here would have been spikes on that sapling he whooped you with." Alf surveyed Jim Bob. "One thing for sure though, you've been thoroughly nigger whipped."

Jim Bob gingerly felt the back of his head, then blushed brightly when the import of Alf's words sank home.

"I'll kill him! Ain't no nigger going to get away with touching me. I'll..." Jim Bob broke off, staring at Alf. "You ain't going to say anything. You looked too funny hanging like a Christmas turkey."

"He sure had this figured out. He spent some time thinking about it. He knew right where you would walk to cut me down. I think he's going to be the smartest runaway we ever chased." Alf balanced the coffee cup on his knee and said coldly, "We'll get him though. If we have to chase him into Abe Lincoln's office, we'll get him."

"He didn't do this to stop us or throw us off his trail. He did this to insult us. To shame us, show us a nigger was smarter than us." Alf leaped to his feet, spilling the remaining coffee, "I'll kill you!" He screamed, waving both fists at the forest. "I will kill you and drink your blood!"

"Your blood, your blood, your blood," the echoes mocked Alf.

CHAPTER 22

Shad labored to the top of the mountain and collapsed against a tree. He was hungry, wet, cold, and miserable. A steady rain and drizzle had been falling for the past three days.

He dared not stop for fire or shelter. He had traveled westward in a zigzagging line barely keeping out of Alf and Jim Bob's clutching hands.

Alf and Jim Bob traveled slowly for the first few days owing to Jim Bob's injuries, but were pushing him hard now.

Shad leaned against the tree and watched the approaching clouds. Huge black boiling clouds, streaked with lightning, and issuing a steady hissing sound.

Hail. Shad groaned. This was all he needed. His joints ached, his head ached, he felt feverish since yesterday afternoon.

Shad studied the country ahead of him. He had long since left the terrain he was familiar with. Ahead of him was range after range of small mountains carpeted with hardwood and pine trees. He looked carefully for habitations or other signs of man. He could use food and shelter, but he dared not stop.

With anxious eyes, Shad studied the approaching clouds. It was time to lose Alf and Jim Bob if he could. The slaves that were going to leave Tendrilhoff ought to be gone by now and their trails would be very cold by the time Alf and Jim Bob could get on them.

With the onslaught of hail, Shad rose wearily and started down his back trail. He traveled carefully, leaving as little sign as possible. He was sure Alf and Jim Bob would hole up during the hailstorm and he wanted to use the storm to put as big a break in his trail as possible.

The hail beat Shad mercilessly. It increased in fury and size until his gait became a stagger. He knew he must find shelter or perish.

He found a small red cedar tree sheltered by a larger cedar. Crawling under the trees, he found little comfort. The cedars slowed the icy missiles from heaven, but did nothing for the chills that seized and shook his frame. Throughout the afternoon and night, his fever raged. His teeth rattled. His frame shook and demons chased one another through his brain.

The dawn came, fair and clear. The sun cast its brilliant light across a blue sky.

Shad crawled from his nest beneath the cedars. Climbing to his feet, he staggered away. His vision was a mist. The world tilted this way and that. He had no direction. He wasn't quite sure why, but he knew he must keep moving.

"Stop! Hold where you are!" The voice was close yet so far away. Demanding yet indefinite, was it real?

Shad was barely aware of a powerful hand gripping his arm.

"Why, he's burning up with fever. Give me a hand."

Shad tried to locate the voice again and failed. He was aware of a door opening and closing then total darkness claimed him. He felt like he was falling into a black hole with no bottom.

Squeak, squeak, the sound echoed through his skull. Shad opened his eyes. A woman sat in a rocking chair that squeaked with each forward and backward motion.

She was in her early thirties with a pretty face, firm jaw line and strong white teeth. Red tinted dark hair and freckles across the bridge of her nose. These and the green eyes gave proof of her Irish ancestry.

Full bosom, small waist, rounded hips; a slight smile tipped the corners of her mouth upward. A beautiful woman, Shad decided. Letting his gaze stray from the woman, he saw he was in a barn. His bed was a pile of hay, covered with beautiful handmade quilts.

It was a cozy barn. With the exception of him and the woman, everything was neatly stored or hung in its place.

"So you're back with us." The woman laid her needlework aside and rose. She was taller than Shad had supposed.

She opened the door. "Dane! He's awake." She stood by the door and waited for Dane to make his appearance.

The light in the door was momentarily blocked as a big man ducked into the room. Red gold hair and beard, six-feet three-inches from the ground. Twinkling blue eyes, crooked nose, broad shoulders, large arms with strong hands. He would have been at home standing on the deck of a Viking ship.

Dane squatted on his heels about three feet from Shad, "Feeling better?" He questioned.

"I think so. I don't remember coming here."

"Sven and Johnny found you wandering in the field. We brought you here. Allie made you some willow bark tea. It seems to work on fevers."

"Thank you." Shad looked at Allie.

"We be the Svensons. I'm Dane and this is my wife Allie." Dane frowned. "Who might you be and are you one of them runaway slaves?"

Shad sat up abruptly and saw Dane tense. "I'm Shad Hoff and I'm a runaway slave. I have two very bad men after me. I have to go."

"You're not able to go yet." Allie leaned on the door.

"I have to. You don't understand. These men might hurt you or your family." Shad tossed the cover back.

"Not so fast," Dane held out a hand. "Sven, our oldest, killed a deer. Allie is making deer stew. You stay and have some. Allie, send Sven to Pap and finish the stew."

"You don't understand. These are hard men. When they trail me here and find you have not held me for them, they will

be very mad. They might hurt you, your wife or children."
Shad located his rifle and pack beside the back door.

"Nobody leaves Svenson's hungry." Dane maintained
stubbornly. "You lay back."

Shad lay back. Even though the fever was gone and his
clothes were soaked in sweat, he was still very weak. It had
been several days since he ate a decent meal. Staying a step in
front of Alf and Jim Bob left no time to hunt or cook.

Allie walked slowly from the house to the barn carrying a
steaming bowl of venison stew and a large chunk of cornbread.

A lad of twelve or so raced up the rutted track that served
the farm as a road. "Pap, Pap!" He shouted. "Two men just
crossed the creek."

Dane looked at Shad. "You lay still," he ordered. Joining
Allie in the yard, Dane shaded his eyes with his hand. The
twinkle died in his eyes as he watched the pair. He had seen
their kind before.

"They look kind of rough," Allie ventured.

"They are. Don't look back; the slave went out the back door."

"He's not able to travel and he looks starved to me. Stop
him, Dane." Allie still held the stew.

"He's a man, Allie. A man does what a man thinks he has
to. By golly! Look at that!" Dane exclaimed.

"What are you talking about?" Allie stared at Dane.

"He's trying to lure them off. See him in the cornfield. He
could have stayed in the brush, but he walked out where they
can see him and he's staggering like a drunk." Dane smiled at
this show of nerve and appreciation. "I told you he was a man."

"They're not going after him." Allie was apprehensive.

"Looks like they want to come on in." Dane crossed his
arms in disapproval. Both Alf and Jim Bob saw Shad enter the
field. Long training kept them from turning their heads or
altering their strides.

"There goes our man." Jim Bob stated after a few steps.

"I see him. From the looks of his tracks and other sign, he is
about all in. We can scoop him up later." Alf pointed ahead,

"I'm liking the looks of that woman. Let's ease in and at least look the place over."

Dane still stood with his arms crossed when Alf led Jim Bob into the yard.

"We're chasing a runaway slave." Alf announced without any introduction. Keeping his eyes off Allie, Alf watched the house, barn, and surrounding area closely.

"He's not here," Dane stated quietly.

"Are you saying he ain't been here?" Alf questioned sharply. Where was the kid he saw run from the creek? His eyes darted here and there. No kid and nobody else he could see or hear.

"I said he wasn't here now." Dane stood like a statue.

"I don't suppose you crackers know the law says you're supposed to turn runaways over to us?" Alf was looking at Allie and smiling. She was prettier than he thought.

"We know what the law says. We don't hold with it, or abide by it."

"We don't hold with it." Alf mocked. "Mister you've bought yourself trouble. I'm going to search this place for the nigger. I'm going to take the little lady with me to open the doors. Jim Bob hold him here."

"Oh, no you don't," Jim Bob said, "we go together."

"Dane?" Allie questioned.

"Ain't nobody going anywhere." Dane said quietly.

Alf looked at Dane. The quiet assurance of the man gave him pause. "What do you mean, ain't going anywhere? We're the men with the rifles."

"You are two men with rifles. There are other men with rifles." Dane flicked the fingers on his left hand and the ominous clicking sound of a rifle hammer being slowly drawn to full cock filled the air.

Alf froze, but was unconvinced. "You better tell that kid to put the rifle down before I kill him."

"If you think you can kill him, go ahead and try." Dane was as unmoved as ever.

A long moment passed.

"The runaway said you were bad men. I sent Sven to bring the kinfolk in. Times they get a bit edgy."

"Put the rifles down," Dane ordered. "Hold them by the barrel and lay them out in from of you. Alf and Jim Bob hesitated, unsure.

Now!" Dane barked.

Alf literally tossed his rifle when Dane barked. Jim Bob reluctantly followed suit. The boy they saw run from the creek dashed in and removed the rifles.

"You boys sit down." Dane took the stew from Allie. "Have some deer stew. Nobody leaves Svensons hungry. No matter what condition they leave in."

"What's going on?" Alf demanded.

"Why, we'll be deciding what to do with you." Dane seemed offended they didn't know.

"We ain't going to no court!" Jim Bob avowed.

"You're right about that. No outsiders allowed in our gathering." Dane said.

"You can't try us without us being there. It's against the law." Alf was beginning to worry.

"We don't hold with the law." Dane explained. "We moved way back in these here hills to get away from the law. Shucks, they tried to tell us it was against the law to wipe out the Jenkins clan, but everybody knows that was a feud."

"They come in here trying to tell us we got to feud with Yankees we ain't ever seen or heard of, they want our young 'uns to go off and feud with them someplace else." Dane frowned at the stupidity of it. "We decided since everybody was withdrawing from everybody, we'd withdraw from everything and set up our own country here in Svenson county."

"Sit down and enjoy your stew. If you try to run you won't make three steps."

Alf could see at least four rifle barrels. He could not see anyone behind the rifles. These guys are good he decided.

Alf and Jim Bob ate the stew. Eating was a serious business. When food was available, you ate.

"That pretty little gal sure can cook." Alf stated as he took the last of the stew.

"I wouldn't say too much about her. Here comes her husband." Jim Bob spoke nervously.

"Pap and Uncle Zed said this was a war deal, you chasing runaways and all. We ain't takin' part in the war. So they said let you go. Uncle Clem wanted to turn you loose in the field and put the boys that haven't been blooded after you, but Pap and Uncle Zed outvoted him."

"We'll give your rifles back." At Dane's signal, the boy laid the rifles at Dane's feet. "Don't load them until you cross the river. You are to go back down the pike you came in on. Don't come into Svenson County again. If you do, I'll butcher you like fattening hogs. I saw you look at my wife."

Alf picked up his rifle and trudged off down the hill. Jim Bob hesitated, looked around the clearing and followed Alf.

They watched shifting shadows and heard birdcalls all the way to the river.

Now what?" Alf rammed a ball home in his rifle. "Our man is on the north side of this county, we're on the south side, and them crazy people are in the middle."

"I ain't going back in there." Jim Bob shuddered. "They'd take it personal this time. I think we should go see Cousin Bobby Ray."

"Cousin Bobby Ray?" Alf turned on Jim Bob. "Does every member of your family have a Bob or Bobby in his name?"

"Well, there was old Grandpa James Robert. He had five boys and he put Bob or Bobby in every one of their names." Jim Bob snapped his fingers. "There was Fess and Ferd. Neither one of them had Bob in their names."

"You still call them cousins? After they got us drunk and ran with the money we stole?" Alf was getting agitated. "What in tarnation would we want to go see Cousin Bobby Ray for?"

"Because he's got the best pack of nigger dogs in the country," Jim Bob was unperturbed by Alf's outburst.

Alf chewed on this for a while. "How much will he want?"

"All he can get."

"Here is the way I see it." From habit, Alf dropped to his heels and doodled in the dirt. "Every day we are gone gives Junior a bigger chance to find the gold."

"We'll take it from him when we get back. Junior is a fool."

"Junior is a fool. What if he finds that gold and somebody else takes it from him before we get back?" Alf could see this thought had never occurred to Jim Bob.

Anger rising at the dilemma, Jim Bob fingered his still tender shoulder. "Let's get the dogs so we can get back quicker. I've got a score to settle with that boy."

A plan formed in Shad's mind while he staggered across the field in sight of Alf and Jim Bob. He was about to turn back to the barn when they ignored him. A lone man with a rifle appeared at the edge of the brush and waved him onward.

Shad labored to the top of the ridge, glanced at the sun hanging on the western horizon and dropped against the trunk of a massive oak.

In the hours since departing from Dane's, he burned the last of his reserve energy. The well was dry.

It had been several days since he'd eaten any real food and the little bit of soup Allie gave him only reminded his stomach how deprived it really was.

Eyes closed, he leaned against the rough bark and endeavored to work up enough energy to begin hunting.

Turning his head on the bark, he smelled it... meat. A couple of sniffs... pork. Sugar cured, hickory smoked pork.

Opening his eyes Shad spotted a tall skinny old black man leading a decrepit old black mule. On each side of the old mule dangled three great big beautiful hams.

Shad let the man approach within a few feet of him and rose. The old man's eyes grew large and he ran backward into the mule.

"I won't harm you." Shad said gently.

"Are you a haint?" The old man asked fearfully.

Shad glanced down at the ragged old money coat Ingrid made him. "No, I'm not a ghost, I am hungry though. Could I have some of that ham?"

"It's almost dark and you come out of the ground like that..." the old man exaggerated.

"The sun is still up and I'm real. How about some of that ham?" Shad persisted. The smell was driving his stomach crazy. It was rumbling and growling.

A crafty look replaced the fright. "This ham is for Mister Joe's table. It ain't for some ragged runaway. You got any real coffee?"

"No, but I have a gold piece."

"What use does a slave have for a gold piece?" The skinny old man snorted. "How 'bout that rifle? Old Jack could shoot some food with it."

Sitting his pack down, Shad removed the double-barreled, fowling piece and handed it to Jack.

Jack took it reverently. He had been on many shooting expeditions, retrieved many birds, and spent days beating the brush in an effort to drive game to the gun. This was the first time he ever actually held a firearm in his hands.

Awkwardly, he mounted it to his shoulder and squinted down the wobbling barrel.

"Can you load and shoot it?" Shad asked.

"I've watched it done many times. Load it and let me shoot it." Jack was eager.

"No, they may be close behind me. I'll have to have a whole ham for that." Actually, Shad had been considering dumping the shotgun because of its weight.

"A whole ham? What'd I tell Mash Joe?"

Shad silently reached out for the shotgun.

"No," Jack wasn't about to let a prize like this escape. "I'll tell Mash Joe old Jack got careless and let a ham fall off and couldn't find it."

Shad threw a small fire together, cut a thick slice of ham and hung it over the fire. Large drops of fat formed along the bottom edge the slice. More and more frequently, the drops of fat fell sizzling and smoking into the fire. The sight and sound got to Shad. The aroma drove him into cutting another slice and eating the first one before it was done.

"What's this nigger worth?" Bobby Ray asked.

"He ain't worth hardly anything," Alf answered a trifle too quick.

"Yeah, we're chasing him for a friend," Jim Bob added.

Bobby Ray raised himself to his full five-feet-six. He pulled the long thinning hair out of his face with a dirty hand. "Now cousin Jim Bob," he began, "you wouldn't pull old Bobby Ray's leg, now, would you?"

Neither Alf nor Jim Bob answered, Bobby Ray continued. "This has to be a big one. He must be a smart nigger for you two to come in here and ask for old Bobby Ray's help. I just want a fair share, that's all."

"The price of slaves is shot all to hell and you know it," Alf flared. "Seven-fifty was all we could get for this one and we don't get it until we catch him. We'll give half for you and the dogs."

"Now, that's a little better," Bobby Ray said as he stepped back. "How do I know you'll get the money if you get him?"

"We won't turn him over until we get the money. He's a prime slave. He is worth way more than seven-fifty."

Bobby Ray raked at the graying hair again. "Why don't you just bring him in?"

"We can do that, excepting we are in kind of a hurry. We have another job after this and we thought..." Alf didn't get a chance to finish.

"You thought you'd get old Bobby Ray to do it for nothing," Bobby Ray spoofed. "My rumatiz has been bothering me. Right here in this leg. I guess I'll have to pass this time."

"Rider coming." Jim Bob warned.

Bobby Ray shaded his eyes. "Looks like Joe Martin. He owns a plantation. I reckon you boys are out of luck because he wouldn't be coming here unless he had a nigger that needed running."

"Step down and rest your saddle." Bobby Ray offered.

"Bobby Ray," Martin nodded curtly, staring at Alf and Jim Bob.

"This here is my cousin Jim Bob and his friend Alf," Bobby Ray said by way of introduction.

Again Martin nodded. Pulling a double-barreled, twelve gauge from a scabbard, he handed it to Bobby Ray. "A runaway traded this to one of my slaves day before yesterday."

Bobby examined the shotgun. "Good gun."

"Stolen, no doubt, I want you to run this slave down and bring him to me."

"I have something of a problem, Mister Martin. Cousin Jim Bob here asked for my help."

"Five hundred dollars," Martin said. He understood Bobby Ray.

"Well, now," Bobby Ray began. Alf stepped up and took the shotgun from Bobby Ray's hand. After examining it, he silently passed it to Jim Bob.

"Is that boy the one you 'ns is after?" Bobby Ray asked.

"Circle T branded into the stock." Alf took the shotgun and passed it back to Bobby Ray.

"I want that runaway," Martin demanded. "We can't have him arming slaves."

"Sorry Martin, Jim Bob and I have a prior claim on him."

"I want him!" Martin seemed to swell in the saddle.

CHAPTER 23

"Hold on, stop just a minute." Bobby held both hands up. "There is a way for everybody to get what they want. Alf and Jim Bob are the best slave catchers around. When they catch this boy, he ain't going anyplace. Right, Jim Bob?"

"He's going to die."

"Mister Martin, what if we use my dogs to run this boy to the ground and I bring you word of his demise?"

"Well." Martin stared at Alf. "I'd rather do it myself."

Alf showed no sign of relenting.

"However, if Bobby Ray will keep me posted." Martin turned his horse.

"Uh, Mister Martin? There is that little matter of the five hundred dollars." Bobby Ray held out a hand. Martin reluctantly dropped the bills into Bobby Ray's hand.

"I'm liking this better. Bobby Ray, don't put that money in your pocket." Jim Bob said as soon as Joe Martin was out of earshot.

"Why shore, I'm going to put my money in my pocket. You and Alf get the use of the best nigger dogs in the country and I get this cash plus three-hundred-seventy-five when you catch him."

"You're not going with us?" Alf sneered.

"I told you, I had rumatiz in this leg." Bobby Ray pointed to the opposite leg this time. "Give me the shotgun."

Alf took the gun from Jim Bob and glared at Bobby ray.

"Oh no, I've got to have this shotgun to give Mandy and Traveler a sniff of this runaway and you are going to need to travel fast. I better keep this shotgun safe here."

"Here's the handkerchief he dropped." Alf decided it was futile to argue with Bobby Ray.

While Alf and Jim Bob visited Bobby Ray, Shad drifted north and east. The effects of the fever wore off and his health and vigor returned.

He was traveling slowly now. Careful not to be seen, he worked hard at leaving no trail for Alf and Jim Bob to follow. Topping a mountain, he found a rock under a tree and leaned back to look at the terrain ahead. Below him, he could see a large valley. Surrounded by mountains except for a small slit at the lower end, the valley was apparently inhabited by quite a number of people.

A large mansion pushed its red roof above the oaks in the top end of the valley and a collection of barns, houses, sheds, and smaller structures were scattered from there to the foot of the valley.

He was in no real hurry. Besides, he told himself, you need to know the location of everything at the point you are going to cross this valley.

Shad began thinking of Bekah. *Do I dare circle back for her now? Should I go all the way north and get a place to take her to? Could I go back now?* It had been days since he had seen any sign of Alf or Jim Bob and he thought he had lost them.

The pastoral scene was so peaceful. He could faintly hear human voices carried up on the rising breeze. Doors and feed pans rattled as the people went about their chores. Cows bawled and dogs barked. A hound dog bayed.

Again the hound gave tongue.

Shad's eyes popped open. That hound was behind him! Rising, he walked a few paces and his heart sank. That dog was coming down his trail.

Higher pitched barks mingled with the heavier, deep bell

tones that drew Shad's attention. Dogs, one thing he hadn't taken into consideration.

What to do? Shad was confused, almost in a panic. He searched for a place to hide his trail, nothing close. His eyes fell on the mansion in the top end of the valley.

Shad picked up his pack, eyed it a moment, and tossed it aside. He was wearing his money coat. Picking up his rifle, he ran. He calculated the distance to the plantation and set the fastest pace he thought he could hold between the two places.

Shad took stock as he loped along. Stopping to fight the dogs was out of the question. Before he could kill all of them, Alf and Jim Bob would be on him. What could he do?

Alf and Jim Bob were sweating profusely. Since Mandy, a large black and tan female bloodhound, known for her superior cold tracking ability, found traces of Shad's scent by the pile of ashes where he cooked the ham.

Traveler was the enforcer. His job was to catch and hold or tree a runaway. His long ears told of some hound blood, his hairy, rough coat came from some wolfhound ancestor. The stiff whiskers went straight back to his Airedale grandmother.

Taboo and Pinkie were young dogs of bloodhound and foxhound mixtures that could already hold their own in tracking or fighting.

At first Mandy could only catch a little whiff of Shad's scent here and there. Traveler was perfectly content to let her carry the load.

The track became warmer and warmer as they worked their way down it. By the time they reached Shad's resting spot from the night before, all the dogs were working Shad's scent.

Shad ran hard. His breath came in ragged gasps. Pain crawled up his ribs like little streams of fire. His legs grew rubbery and his knees wobbled. His ears kept track of his pursuers. Approaching the plantation cookhouse, Shad estimated his lead about a quarter mile.

The cook squealed and leaped behind the stove when Shad exploded through the door.

"Pepper!" Shad gasped. The cook stared.

"Where is the black pepper?" Shad demanded.

The cook glanced out the window at the fast approaching pack of hounds and took a cloth bag off a shelf and handed it to Shad. Taking the bag, Shad burst out a door on the other side of the cookhouse. If he could get enough room to use it the pepper would slow the dogs down.

The cook selected a large broom and took station beside the door. Traveler came through the door at high speed with Shad's scent burning hot in his nostrils.

Wham! The broom caught Traveler alongside the head, knocking him off balance. Toenails pulled shavings out of the pine floor as Traveler tried to gain enough control to hit the open door on the opposite side of the room.

He failed to make the correction enough to hit the door, his one hundred pounds plus frame skidded into the stand that held the flour barrel. The partially filled flour barrel went airborne landing upside down on Traveler with an explosion of white dust.

Tabo was next to receive the broom treatment followed immediately by Pinkie. Pandemonium ruled. The cook was laying about mightily with the broom, screaming at the top of her lungs. Pots and pans were banging and flying wall-to-wall. Dogs were yelping and dashing to and fro. Everyone was blinded. Clouds of flour, sifted out every crack of the cookhouse. Mandy pulled up short of the door to bay at the whole mess.

Slaves appeared from all directions to investigate the ruckus. They caught each dog as it managed to escape the cookhouse.

Alf and Jim Bob appeared at a run. Jim Bob leaped into the cookhouse and received a whack with the broom.

"Not here!" Jim Bob leaped clear of the cookhouse. The broom whacked the door facing behind him. The flour gave Jim Bob an almost ghostly quality.

"Turn the dogs loose," Alf ordered. The men looked at each other and held the dogs. "Turn the dogs loose!" Alf demanded, taking hold of the forearm of his rifle in a threatening manner.

The cook burst through the cloud of flour issuing from the door. She was totally white from the top of her head to the ends of her bare toes. Still screaming, she charged Alf and let loose with a mighty swing. The broom left a trail of flour in the air Alf occupied a fraction of a second before. Alf didn't know any woman could run as fast as this cook. She chased him all the way to the woods screaming and swinging the broom.

Jim Bob and the dogs caught Alf in the woods.

"Come on; let's get the dogs back on the track. I'm going to kill this nigger if it's the last thing I ever do, Alf swore.

"Could have been the last thing you ever did if that cook had caught you." Jim Bob was laughing. He enjoyed the race thoroughly.

At top of the ridgeline, Shad stopped and listened to the commotion at the cookhouse. He didn't know what was going on but he knew something had stopped the dogs and he was grateful for this.

Traveling quickly, Shad knew the break would be temporary and the dogs would be on him again.

Shad fled down a small creek until he found what he was looking for, a small pool of water surrounded by ledges of smooth, flat rocks.

He knew he was leaving two trails of scent when he moved. One was like a cloud of smoke that hung in the air and the other was where his feet touched the ground.

Placing the black pepper on a rock, Shad lay down in the cool water and rolled. The water felt so good, he wished he could stay and enjoy it.

Regretfully leaving the water Shad picked up the pepper and walked across the ledge rock scattering it left and right. The water on his body would mask the scent trail in the air and the water running out of his clothes would wash out and diffuse the scent his feet left.

When the dogs got to this spot they had to put their heads down and snuffle the ground in order to figure which way he went. While snuffling the ground the dogs inhaled the black pepper causing them to sneeze and temporarily lose their sense of smell.

Alf stomped the ground and swore. "He must have got pepper at that plantation."

"Well," Jim Bob said, uncoiling leashes from his shoulders. "We just as well catch and lead them dogs until they get over it. Perhaps tomorrow."

Leading the dogs and trailing Shad was posing quite a problem for Alf. He had Mandy and Traveler. Even though they temporarily lost their sense of smell both dogs were still in the blush of the chase and eager to go.

Curses and vicious kicks failed to keep the dogs behind him. Alf cut himself a green club and beat the dogs into submission. Traveler resented this and growled so threateningly that Alf drew the hammer back on his rifle.

"Don't shoot that dog," Jim Bob warned.

"I will if he jumps me."

"You shoot that dog and you'll have Bobby Ray on you like white on rice."

"I ain't worried about Bobby Ray."

"You may not worry about Bobby Ray but you better worry about the clan."

"Does that include you?"

"Most likely." Jim Bob warned.

Shad plunged on westward. He continued after it got dark. He had to put as much distance between himself and the dogs as possible.

At the top of another small mountain, Shad looked down a vertical bluff into a large pool of water. Closer examination revealed no possible way off the bluff in either direction.

Shad backtracked to a large oak tree and climbed it. Walking down a huge limb, he leaped into another tree which reached the edge of the bluff. Praying for deep water, Shad leaped into the air over the pool. He hit the water, lost his rifle, and went down, down. When his feet reached bottom, he shoved mightily, lungs burning for fresh air.

Back at the surface, Shad looked frantically for the rifle and swam for the far shore. He knew he must be out of sight before the dogs arrive.

The dogs reached the top of the bluff and found where Shad's scent went up the tree. Casting about, they couldn't find where he left. Mandy stood with her front feet on the tree and began to bark treed. Tabo and Pinkie immediately honored Mandy's tree. Traveler made another large circle and reluctantly joined the group.

"Treed! They got him treed" Jim Bob chortled.

"All four dogs are there." Alf listened thoughtfully.

"Sure, did you expect some to quit? Bobby Ray told you this was the best pack of nigger dogs in the state."

"I didn't expect this boy to tree that easy. I thought he would kill some of the dogs or make a try for us. You run on in there if you want." Alf checked the load and prime in his rifle. "I'm taking my time to look for a trap."

"Yeah." Jim Bob gave his shoulders a shake. He could still feel a little stiffness." He didn't have time to do much of anything this time."

Alf and Jim Bob approached the tree from opposite sides. Silently, and very cautiously they approached the empty tree.

Alf worked himself up alongside Mandy. She stood with her front feet on the tree sending out one rolling tree bark after another.

"Stupid bitch! He fooled you." Alf sent a bone rattling kick into Mandy's exposed chest. Mandy collapsed into a wiggling, wailing heap at the foot of the tree.

Traveler launched himself from where he sat. Striking Alf at shoulder height, Traveler's hundred plus pounds knocked Alf down. Alf shoved his forearm between the great teeth coming for his throat and screamed in pain. Traveler pulled the arm out of the way and went for Alf's throat again.

Jim Bob wrapped his fingers around Traveler's collar and threw his full weight backward. Traveler's teeth left red marks on Alf's throat, then met with a mighty pop in thin air.

"Shoot him! Shoot him!" Alf screamed, rolling to his feet.

"Nobody's going to shoot him," Jim Bob was calm.

"I'll shoot him." Alf turned to look for his rifle.

"Go for that rifle and I'll turn him loose."

"I'm going to kill him. Nobody attacks me that way and lives."

"This dog is Bobby Ray's. He trusted me with him. Nobody shoots this dog."

"Bobby Ray rented that dog for five hundred dollars and whatever else he can get out of us," Alf said, sarcastically.

"Makes no, never mind, we're blood. No other way he would have let the dogs go. Check on Mandy and see if she is badly hurt." Traveler began to struggle when Alf moved in Mandy's direction.

"You better set up camp and I'll calm the dogs down."

"It's too early to camp. We're close to him. We can't stop now." Alf argued.

"Mandy's hurt. Do you want me to turn this one loose right now?" Jim Bob was tempted to do just that.

"No, I'll set up camp as soon as I tend this arm. Alf knew Jim Bob and his moods.

Shad kept a steady pace. He was tired, gut-wrenching bone-tired. The dogs would be after him again soon. The trick would slow them for a while, but it wouldn't stop them for long. Shad didn't know Alf's indiscretion was holding them up even longer. He did know he had to find a way to get away from the dogs, but how?

On the second day after the loss of his rifle, Shad was moving through a country ribbed with small ridges, carpeted by a liberal mixture of hardwoods and pines. Huge trees, virgin forest, a perfect place to work dogs. He knew he had been very lucky up to now, and if things didn't change, his luck was going to run out.

How could he lose them permanently? This question keeps circulating through his mind as he trudged on and on.

Shad descended a ridge that seemed a little longer than the rest and was about halfway across a broad valley when the dogs came over the top behind him. Stopping, he searched the country as far as he could see. *Where can I go? What can I do?* He beat his tired brain into action and came up with nothing. One thing for sure, he couldn't stay here. *Why not? Why not take his knife and make a stand. Wouldn't that be better than torturing himself to the inevitable end?*

Get going, his tired brain ordered, and his feet obeyed. Forcing his feet into a shuffle, he listened to the bawl and squall of the hounds grow louder and louder.

The constant singing of the hounds beats in his ears and grates on his nerves.

On and on his rubbery legs carried him. Shaking, the legs betrayed him and he fell often.

Something, anything, to slow the hounds. Nothing! Gotta be something.

Shad's nerve snapped and he ran over a hummock in a panic. About halfway down, he jumped a dead log. A blur passed his foot but he was too tired and too panicked to give it any thought.

Mandy increased her pace. Coming to the place where Shad panicked, she recognized the panic tint to his scent. Experience taught her that when the quarry panicked it wasn't going to be long before she caught it.

The big rattler tried to pull his coil tighter and shuddered. His fight with a large buck deer had left him in a dangerous position. Wounds punctured the length his body from head to tail. The bucks slashing feet had torn large pieces of skin loose and cut all fifteen of the rattles from his tail. Crawling to a log, the snake coiled to recuperate. Shad caught him asleep and he missed the strike at Shad.

Mandy came roaring over the top of the hummock, the rattler drew his head back behind his coils. He missed last time, but he wasn't about to miss again. He was furious and vibrated the bare stub of his tail vigorously.

Mandy came down the hummock in a rush. The hot smell of panic convinced her the race was about over.

The big rattler launched himself. At the extreme end of the strike, his huge head was traveling in a downward arc with inch long fangs leading the way. Both fangs entered the small of Mandy's back. One of the fangs penetrated an artery.

Mandy's momentum jerked the snake out of his coil. The pain of the wounds caused an involuntary contraction of the muscles around the poison sacs, pumping all the poison in them through the fangs.

Mandy stopped, turned back as if trying to figure out what happened. Her back legs gave way, rolling her to her side. One big sigh and it was over.

Traveler came to Mandy's side. He nudged her plaintively, begging her to rise. The rattler's scent and the scent of death filled the air.

The huge head hit Traveler in the shoulder, driving the fangs deep. They were dry fangs, though; there was no more poison. Traveler sank his teeth into the rattler and shook him until all life departed. Tabo and Pinkie ran in and took hold of the rattler. Traveler lowered his head, bared his teeth, raised his hair, and gave the younger dogs such a stern warning they tucked their tails between their legs and ran to Alf and Jim Bob.

Traveler returned to Mandy, circled several times and lay beside her. Resting his head on her shoulder, he whimpered softly. He didn't understand, but he knew his life had changed.

Traveler stayed with Mandy until he heard Alf and Jim Bob approach. Rising, he stood irresolutely for a moment. Making up his mind, he took Shad's trail and left at a long lope. He didn't give tongue this time. The thud of padded feet and occasional swish of brush was all that marked his passage.

Alf and Jim Bob approached the scene slowly and cautiously. To their woods trained eye everything was as clear as the written word to most people. There were some items of doubt.

"Traveler left on the track. Wonder why he didn't bark on track?" Alf pointed the direction Traveler went.

"Yeah, and why did these two come back to us instead of going with Traveler? Let's get 'em going, Traveler may need help." Jim Bob followed Shad's tracks. "Sic 'em, hurry man," he encouraged the dogs.

Tabo smelled Shad's tracks, looked around uncertainly, and bawled. Pinkie raced in to add his high-pitched squall. Encouraging each other, the dogs took to the trail again.

Shad splashed across a small creek and climbed the opposite bank. Standing on the bank, Shad bent over with the dry heaves. He could hear the roaring trip hammer of his heart beat. Swinging an arm, he tried to ease the pain in his side. He couldn't hear the dogs. Why? He tried to hold the whistling gasp of his breath. No dogs. It won't be for long, he told himself.

Fatigue caused Shad to turn slowly. What was that shining through the trees? Rocking back and forth to get a better look, Shad realized it was water. A river. A big river.

New hope brought new energy. Shad began a joyful shuffle toward the river.

The vines slowly parted and first one eye then two peered up and down the river. It was mud red and rolling bank full. Sticks, chunks, and other debris rode the muddy crest.

Shad looked for boats first, and then carefully checked both banks. His eyes move along the banks with the practiced ease of a woodsman. Shad swiftly checked each large tree, clump of brush, rock and anything else large enough to hide a man. Nothing was out of order and no people in sight. Now check the banks for alligator or alligator sign.

A drum deep, rolling bawl floated down from the mountain crest and died in the tangled vegetation of the river. Before the bawl died, it was joined by another a few octaves higher in pitch. Despite himself, he admired good dog work. How many days and nights had he spent running from these bloodhounds? He slowed them down a couple of times, but he could not stop them.

Shoving a log off the bank Shad pushed it far enough out for the current to take hold of it. Shad moved behind the log in order to watch the bank.

What was that swimming toward him? A dog. The realization struck fear into his heart. Franticly he looked for more dogs or humans. Nothing.

Shad listened to Tabo and Pinkie coming across the flat land bordering the water. Why was this dog so far ahead of them?

Shad worked his way down to a wrist sized limb sticking from the log. Taking a firm grip on the limb with his left hand, Shad pulled a knife from his belt. Baring his teeth, Shad waited. He didn't want this fight, but if it had to be, so be it.

Strong swimming strokes pulled Traveler to Shad's log. Hooking both front paws over the log Traveler used his strong toenails to hang on.

The pair drifted down stream staring into one another's eyes. Neither Shad nor Traveler bothered to look upstream when Tabo and Pinkie reached the water.

CHAPTER 24

"Is this nigger that smart or just plain lucky?" Jim Bob asked, watching Tabo and Pinkie cast around in a fruitless effort to find Shad's trail.

"We've had a string of bad luck. Wonder what happened to Traveler?" Alf eased himself to the ground and stretched out. I haven't seen anymore tracks around. If he lost the trail, it looks like he would have left more tracks hunting it. Yeah, the boy drowned him." Jim Bob convinced himself.

"What now? We can't follow him on the water."

"Think about it. This river runs south. He had to drift down. I don't think he could swim against that current. That nigger has to go north. He will have to come out of the river and he will be farther away than ever. My guess is, he won't go far down stream." Alf watched Jim Bob out of the corner of his eye. "Are you ready to quit? Are you ready to take your nigger whipping, tuck your tail, and run for home?"

Jim Bob's face grew red. "I told you I'd kill him even if I had to chase him into Abe Lincoln's office, and I have more reason to want him now than I had then. He's killed two of Bobby Ray's dogs."

"I think we've been going about this wrong. We should rest here for awhile. Give him time to head back north. We can keep these dogs on a leash and make a big circle. They will find his trail and we can move in kind of quiet like." Alf began rummaging in a pack, looking for more of the stolen coffee.

Alf's figuring was right about how far south Shad would go. Still holding the knife in his hand, Shad backed from the water.

Traveler swam to the bank, shook himself, and disappeared into the underbrush. Shad watched the big dog go with relief. Finding a grassy spot Shad collapsed. Two minutes later, he was in a deep exhausted sleep.

Shad's eyes opened. Dawn was chasing the stars away. He couldn't believe he had slept all afternoon and night. Lifting his head showed him how sore he was. Rolling to his side, Shad stopped. Not two feet away, Traveler lay rolled into a circle. Between the two, lay a rabbit Traveler brought to Shad several hours earlier.

Traveling north and a little east, Shad had no particular destination in mind except the vague North.

The pair moved through the winter-stripped woods like waifs. After several uneventful days, Shad decided Alf and Jim Bob had lost his trail. He was still afraid to make any human contact. Shad left as little sign of his passage as possible and he worried about the sign the big dog romping at his side was leaving.

On the third day of drizzle, Shad sat against a tree. The loss of his rifle was a real problem. Hunting for food with a sling-shot fashioned from the tongue of his boot and most of its lacing was for the most part unproductive.

A patter of feet and a shower of gravel announced Traveler's arrival. Following Shad's scent, he failed to see Shad's still form until he was close. A fox squirrel dangling from his mouth, Traveler stared at Shad. Whimpering softly, Traveler dropped to his stomach, crawled to Shad and lay his head in Shad's lap.

Gingerly, Shad slid a caressing hand down the dog's head and back. It was the first time he touched the big dog. The caressing hand revealed Traveler was suffering from a shortage food also.

"Why did you bring this to share with me?" Shad asked, dangling the squirrel and ruffling Traveler's ear.

Alf and Jim Bob spent days traveling in great loops. Mile after mile they traveled, each leading a dog. After his experience with Traveler, Alf was much more patient with Tabo.

Discouragement was riding Alf and Jim Bob's shoulders. Each privately wondered if they had made the right decision. They were trudging up a steep hill when Tabo caught a whiff of Shad's scent through the trees.

Meanwhile, Shad and Traveler were moving parallel to a road. Finding a dump, he searched until he found the barest stub of a pencil and a small piece of paper. He sat on a rock and wrote a short list of supplies on the paper. He considered putting a rifle and ammunition on it and decided this wouldn't do.

Shad stretched his stride. It was good to travel on a road with unobstructed footing. He reminded himself to stay alert. He must see anyone before they saw him. Man, the road felt good after all those days and miles in rough country.

Traveler gamboled around like a puppy. Every so often, he came to Shad for a reassuring pat on the head. Shad had not realized how lonely he was until the big dog decided to join him. Now he had someone he could talk to for hours and get no back talk.

It was a rundown, ramshackle old cabin but the sign on front said COUNTRY STORE. Shad took the point of his knife and removed a gold coin from the lining of his coat before he entered the store.

"What do you want?" A voice growled from the semi-dark counter. Shad's heart sank. It was Boughton from Hoffman.

"My massa sent me after supplies," Shad slurred.

"I bet he did. Are you a runaway? Is there a reward for you?" The thought of a reward brought Boughton to a sitting position.

"Massa camped down de road." Shad laid the brogue on as thick as possible. "He sent me with this note and this money." Shad placed the paper and coin on the counter.

Boughton laid greedy eyes on the gold. Gold was a scarce commodity in the south and the very sight of it moved his avaricious soul and clouded his judgment.

"I guess it's alright. It's writ in a clear hand." Boughton turned the note upside down and right side up. "Do you by any chance remember what he put down here?"

Shad struggled to suppress a smile. Pretending to strain to remember, he hesitatingly began naming items.

"Your master has more of these?" Boughton bit the coin.

"I don't know."

"Has he sent you for supplies before?"

"Yas suh."

"How many men are with your master?"

"Two white men."

"Where they camped at?"

"Bout five mile down the road."

"Tell your master that bacon is expensive, what with the war and all. This coin won't pay for the supplies you got but I'm going to let you have them anyway."

Shad knew this was robbery, but decided not to argue. Taking the groceries he silently departed. He could feel Boughton's eyes on him until he went around the bend. Thank God, Boughton was one of those people to whom all colored folks looked the same.

He climbed a hill alongside the road and built a small fire. Shad and Traveler feasted on half of one slab of bacon and hoe cakes baked on a flat rock. The sun was warm and the world was beginning to turn green. Shad lazed against a tree. Traveler's head lay on his lap. Through droopy eyelids Shad watched his back trail. He saw two figures come around a bend of the road. They were leading something.

Alf and Jim Bob! Shad leaped to his feet with an oath. *How did they find my trail after all this time?* Standing still until they dropped behind a ridge, he gathered his meager supplies and fled.

After talking to Boughton, Alf and Jim Bob decided to turn

the dogs loose and once more try to run Shad to earth.

Shad ran for all he was worth, but the dogs gained steadily. After a couple of hours Shad could go no further. His legs turned to rubber. The stitch in his side was almost unbearable. Gasping for breath, he pulled his knife and leaned his back on a tree.

Tabo came into sight, with Pinkie a few yards behind. Spotting Shad, Tabo let out a triumphant bawl and increased his speed. A tawny blur passed Shad and slammed into Tabo.

Knocking Tabo from his feet Traveler took him by the throat. Pinkie slammed into Traveler knocking him loose. They became a snarling, snapping ball of dust. The younger dogs, being unable to take this, tucked their tails and ran back in search of Alf and Jim Bob.

Shad turned north, traveling steadily always conscious Alf and Jim Bob were one step behind. The first thing Shad saw was a dead horse. Approaching the horse, he saw an officer's body at the edge of the clearing.

It was the first union blue uniform he had seen. Circling the scene, he decided the officer and horse had been wounded somewhere else and the horse made it this far before succumbing to its wounds.

The officer was young, painfully young to have the stamp of death on his face, Shad decided. The uniform was neat and tailored to fit. Even in death Shad could see this young man came from good breeding. Shad couldn't bring himself to go through the dead man's pockets.

He had no such qualms about the horse. He could see the butt plate of a rifle sticking out from under the horse's neck. Shad raised the horse's head and pulled a rifle from a scabbard attached to the saddle. He looked at it curiously.

There was no ramrod and no place for one. Turning the rifle over he read the word, "Spencer," engraved on barrel. There was a funny looking lever behind the trigger. A pull on the lever dropped a shiny brass object at his feet. Picking it up, Shad looked at the first self-loading bullet he ever saw.

Pulling the lever closed, Shad noticed the hammer was back and pulled the trigger. The morning air was assaulted by the blast of the rifle. Working the lever, Shad noticed the hammer was back again and lowered it.

A look in the saddlebags revealed they were full of the shiny brass cartridges. Rifle in hand, tossing the saddlebags onto his shoulder, Shad turned east. He moved quickly but quietly because he was sure Alf and Jim Bob heard the report of the rifle.

Several days later, he sat on the edge of a flat waiting or daylight. He came down a creek all night and worked his way through blue clad pickets. Now he sat at the edge of a large camp of Union Soldiers. He was north. He had made it.

Now that he was here, he didn't know what to do. One thing for sure, he was going to wait for daylight. Most of these sentries looked young and jumpy.

Lying down in a leaf bed, he slept. A distant popping sound awoke him. A few more pops, then a tearing sound like fabric being torn. About the time he figured out the sound came from musket fire the camp turned into bedlam.

Officers shouted orders. Soldiers dashed to and fro. More soldiers came into camp from the other side. These soldiers had fear stamped on their faces. Most had thrown their rifles away or run off without them. Through the camp they ran causing more confusion.

Shad held his ground. He checked his back trail. He didn't see Alf or Jim Bob but he knew they were there. He didn't think they would quit.

Shad listened as the firing progressed in his direction. Traveler pressed against his leg. He had not been ten feet from Shad's heels since they found the first picket.

The tide of refugees grew to a torrent. Officers shouted and flailed with their swords to no avail. The men were panicked and no order from the officers was going to stop the rout.

Shad could see the smoke of the approaching barrage over the trees now. Tossing the saddlebags over his shoulders, he watched his back trail. Anger began to rise in him. The strain of the loss of all he held near and dear, being pushed beyond human endurance came to roost on him.

The first Rebel soldier came in sight. He was wearing the same uniform as the ones who raped Tendrilhoff. Shad shot him. Dropping to one knee, he worked the lever as fast as he could. This barrage of deadly accurate fire checked the leading Confederates.

Swinging the saddlebags around in front of him Shad reloaded. An officer stopped beside him.

The officer grabbed two fleeing soldiers by the collar and pointed at Shad. "Are you going to let him outfight you?" He shouted. "Load!" He ordered. Automatically they obeyed.

The battle lust grew in Shad until there was no sound but a roar in his ear. Time lost all meaning. The only thing he existed for was to load and fire. There was no room for fear. No room to take notice of the injured and dying around him. Every Confederate soldier wore Alf's face.

Kill the oppressors. Baring his teeth, he gave a scream that drowned out the Rebel yell and pumped lead into the advancing gray wall.

More soldiers collected around him. More officers. Shoot, shoot. The smoke choked him.

The gray line was upon them. Dropping the hot rifle, Shad snatched a bayonet tipped rifle from the ground and ran the first soldier through. A soldier in gray lunged at Shad's back. Traveler took him by the throat. Another gray clad soldier shifted his aim from Shad to Traveler. At the boom of the rifle an officer decapitated the soldier with a single swipe of his sword.

Shad danced. Cut and shoot. He lost all reason. He was a magnificent killing machine. When the Confederates realized the color of his skin, they concentrated on that part of the line. Blade and shell both bit into Shad's skin, but it seemed he had a charmed life. Nothing could stop him.

It seemed the thin blue line must disappear. It wasn't

moving, but it was being annihilated. Over the bank on the Confederate flank came a howling mob of blue coated soldiers. Recruited and regrouped in the shelter of Shad and the thin blue line.

Sullenly the gray line gave way and retreated. Back they came, shouting and singing, more banners, more muskets. It seemed there never was, or ever would be anything else.

Suddenly it was over. Shad didn't recognize where he was. Dazed, he wandered. An officer approached him. The officer was saying something when an orderly yelled, "General Sherman, they need you at headquarters immediately."

Shad looked for Traveler. Not seeing him, pulled Shad back to reality. He now realized he had advanced with the other soldiers in pursuit of the retreating Confederate Army.

His woodsman sense told him which direction to go. He could not believe the number of dead and wounded, he stumbled past. Coming to the point where the fight started for him, he saw Traveler's body.

"No, oh no!" He moaned. Gathering the dog's body to his chest, he let the dog's blood mix with his. Stumbling up the hill, he headed for a stand of tall timber on the hill. He had to get Traveler away from all this destruction.

He stopped, put the dog's body down and vomited. He had never been this tired and sick before. Retrieving the dog's body, he stumbled into the darkest part of the woods.

A whistling sound and a rope settled around his neck, jerking him to the ground. He held onto Traveler on his way down. A rope was placed on his feet and he was being stretched, choked. The last thing he saw before he passed out was Alf's leering face.

"Got you, nigger! Got you, nigger!" Jim Bob sang over and over, as he tied Shad's hands.

"Shut up. We ain't the only ones around here," Alf cautioned.

"Them blue bellies are too busy licking their wounds and burying their dead to pay us any mind. After us chasing him so far, how come he walked right into our arms?"

"I'd like to know why he killed that dog we had after him and was carrying it around with him." Alf turned on Jim Bob. "What in tarnation are you building a fire for?"

Jim Bob rubbed his head. "This nigger is going to know what it is to burn. Shame he can't live to enjoy it." Jim Bob stuck the blades of Shad's knives into the fire. First, a little light, then a terrific burning in his throat and lungs, Shad moaned.

"Where is the gold, old man Hoffman hid?" Alf demanded.

Shad fought to clear his head. He couldn't think.

"You may as well tell us and save yourself some grief." Alf slapped Shad.

"There is no gold," Shad croaked at a whisper.

"We know better," Jim Bob chimed in.

"How does it feel to be outsmarted and whipped by a nigger?" Shad asked in a whisper, still fighting to get his voice back.

Jim Bob let out an oath, snatched a piece of rope, and cursing with each blow flailed at Shad.

"That will be enough of that!" The voice carried authority.

Alf turned to face the unexpected visitor. A lone figure in a blue uniform stood at the edge of the clearing. He had no visible weapon except the sword hanging on his side. Alf's grip on his rifle tightened. He checked the bushes on either side, then changed his mind.

"Bushes are full of them." Alf warned Jim Bob.

"What's going on here?" The young officer advanced, holding his hand out to receive Alf's rifle.

"We've arrested a runaway, sir." Alf tried to put the best face on.

"Runaway?" The officer took in Shad's condition, from head to toe. The young eyes had seen far too much war. He knew where the wounds and crust of powder smoke came from.

"We'll just take him and go," Alf tried.

"We better put this before my C.O." The young officer motioned his men to advance and secure the situation.

Heads turned and the soldiers stared as the group marched into camp. A burly soldier marched on either side of Shad, Alf, and Jim Bob. The ones marching with Shad put out a steadying hand each time he stumbled.

General Sherman rose from consultation with his officers to take in the sight.

"Bring them here," Sherman ordered.

The small column wheeled and the lieutenant snapped to attention.

Sherman pulled the stub of a cigar from his mouth. "What do we have here?" He growled.

"I'm not sure, sir. These men claim this darkie is a dangerous runaway. Claim he has hurt white people."

"If you count Reb soldiers as white people, I can vouch for that. Cut this one loose and take him to the infirmary. Take these two to the guardhouse. As soon as the doctors have treated his wounds and he is able, I want the whole bunch back here." Sherman stuck the cigar back in his mouth and turned in dismissal.

"Will you have my dog buried?" Shad croaked. Sherman looked at the lieutenant who nodded. The doctors treated Shad's wounds as well as battlefield conditions permitted, fed him a bowl of soup, and put him on a makeshift bed under the spreading limbs of an old oak tree.

A rosy dawn found the lieutenant shaking Shad's shoulder. "General Sherman wants to see you."

"What for?" Shad was apprehensive.

"I don't know. Come along."

CHAPTER 25

Alf and Jim Bob were standing in front of Sherman's tent when Shad arrived. The lieutenant pushed Shad alongside Jim Bob and stood at attention.

"At ease," Sherman barked, tossing the flap of his tent back. His breath smelled of whiskey.

"We'll take the contraband off your hands, General," Alf offered.

Without a glance at Alf, Sherman turned to Shad. "I was at the drop off yesterday. That was the greatest piece of soldering I've seen. You furnished a rally point. Damned Rebels nearly drove us into the water. If you were a soldier, I would recommend you for a metal. Who and what are you?"

"I'm Shad Hoff, and I am a runaway slave."

"Not anymore, you are Shad Hoff, member of the First Massachusetts Scouts."

"But, sir!" An aide gasped. "He's a darkie."

"He's a man!" Sherman lashed out. "He proved it in battle yesterday. If I had a few more men like him here I wouldn't get surprised and stomped by the Rebs like I did yesterday."

"Take these two to the guardhouse and keep them there." Sherman motioned toward Alf and Jim Bob. "Send me Major Goforth, of the First Massachusetts Scouts."

"Can you count? Can you determine how many soldiers in a group?" Sherman questioned Shad, grinning at the way Jim Bob stomped off.

"Yes, sir. I can read, write, and do sums."

"Tell me how you learned."

Shad found himself telling the General about Tendrilhoff, Mister George, Ingrid and Bekah. "I must go back for Bekah," Shad entreated.

"Stay with me and we'll have the whole Union Army to bring her back." Sherman offered.

"I must go now. I promised."

Sherman considered a moment. "I'll give you a few days, but I want you back soon. I don't want any more surprises like I got yesterday. At ease, Major."

The major eased his brace and eyed Shad dubiously.

"Major meet Shad Hoffman, your newest recruit."

"He's a darkie, sir."

"I'm not blind, Major."

"The other regiments, sir, they don't have any darkies in them. We'll become the laughingstock of the army, sir."

"I thought you were a member of the Abolitionist Society before you joined the army."

"I am a member. We want to free them in the south, not have them in our regiment." Major Goforth argued.

Sherman turned to his table, wrote a set of orders, and passed them to the major.

"Lieutenant Hoff? But sir, this means he will be able to command white troops!" Reading further, the major turned red then white. "Report directly to you, sir? That could mean he outranks me in some respects!"

"He may outrank you in all respects after an investigation into how the Rebel Army completely surprised us yesterday. Take the lieutenant and fix him up with uniforms, gear, and find him a horse. Dismissed, Major. I know you will do your duty," Sherman added pointedly.

An almost unrecognizable Shad rode back to Sherman's tent. Kid leather boots, clean uniform, white gauntlets, and saber. The major went whole hog.

"You look like a soldier," Sherman commented with a

this war now. Would Sherman keep his word and use the resources of the Union Army to find Bekah after the war was over? Shad refused to think a Southern victory possible.

Returning to the Union Army, Shad threw himself into his work. With his drive and intelligence, he managed to get himself into the work gangs inside the Confederate Army.

For a time, he was assigned the duty of cleaning General Beauregard's office. He could read whatever they left laying around.

Shad's service was of such magnitude that Sherman transferred him to whatever unit Sherman was given command of. Shad carried papers ordering any officer in the Union Army to forward immediately his dispatches to Sherman from any point.

In November eighteen-sixty-three, Shad discovered the Confederates pulled most of their troops off the impregnable western slopes of Missionary Ridge. Shad passed the information to Sherman, who in turn made it available to General Thomas. At the Battle of Chattanooga, Thomas led his troops in a charge on the western slopes of Missionary Ridge, breaking the Confederate Army in half and defeating it soundly.

Sherman's march to Atlanta was especially hard on Shad. Joe Johnston, the Confederate commander, was a wily officer. His long suit was to wait for the opposing commander to make a mistake and pounce. Ambush was Johnston's favorite tactic.

The Union Army was forced to move south through the mountains in segments. Johnston was perched as an eagle, sure he could catch at least one segment off guard and destroy it.

It was a chess game on a large scale with thousands of lives at stake. Move and countermove. Shad was on the prowl day and night reporting Confederate troop movements. At times, making sure where the Reb troop wasn't was as important as being certain where they were.

The Union troops were safely through the mountains and slowly strangling Atlanta. Everyone knew it was a matter of time.

Shad rode in to report the taking of another section of the

railroad. He was tired and worn. He lost twenty pounds and the skin was taut across his face.

"You look like hell," Sherman growled, handing Shad a bottle of whiskey.

Shad took the bottle, noticed it was almost empty, and sat it beside him. "I want to get this war over with."

"Still pining over that girl?" Sherman's question was more of a statement.

"I have to find her. She wanted me to bring her with me. I don't think we could have gotten away from Alf and Jim Bob."

"Speaking of Alf and Jim Bob, I had the whole stockade transferred down here. I think we can make them work for their living." Sherman lit a cigar. "You better get some rest; this war is fixing to take another turn. I've received permission to cut loose and take Savannah."

"Savannah? But sir, what about supply lines?"

"We'll take our supplies from the Rebs. It's about time they realize what they did when they started this war. We'll burn their homes and barns, kill or take their livestock, confiscate their grain, and lay waste to the land. Starvation will show the bastards. When I'm through with them a crow flying over their country will have to carry a knapsack." Sherman's eyes glittered with an unnatural light.

Shad shuddered. This was a side of the General he had never seen and his thoughts flew to the persistent rumors that Sherman was crazy.

Until the beginning of the war, Shad spent most of his waking time working or planning for the betterment of Tendrilhoff. The thought of wanton vandalism sickened him. To take someone's lifework and destroy it because you had the upper hand was a perverted, sick act.

Sherman was watching him and read a large part of his thoughts. "You'll get used to it." He grinned. "I'm transferring you to General Rudat. You will report to him from now on. I think he plans to send you back into your part of the country. Who knows, you might run into that girl again."

CHAPTER 26

Clutching a new set of orders, Shad left Sherman's tent with a heavy heart.

Next morning Shad reported to General Rudat. He would have been a small man if he wasn't fat.

General Rudat read Shad's orders slowly. Standing up surprisingly easy for a fat man, he extended a hand. "Trying to put a new outfit together is always a chore. Even with hand-picked personnel, like yourself. There will be a staff meeting at the old Dither mansion tomorrow at noon."

"Is that the one converted to a prison?" Shad was perplexed. Why was a staff meeting being held in a prison?

"That is the one."

"We're not going to become prison guards are we?" This thought bothered Shad.

General Rudat smiled. "No, but save your questions until tomorrow and I can answer everyone at once."

At loose ends, Shad climbed a mountain and looked down on Atlanta. He didn't realize this beautiful city would be a pile of smoking ashes before the next weekend. He had not plumbed the bottom of Sherman's sadistic lust for destruction.

Shad considered going to look for Bekah. He wondered if Sherman was going to honor his promise. There had been several times when Shad would have thrown up his hands and walked if he knew where Bekah was.

Shad prowled around the mountaintop. Being alone had been his lot since leaving Tendrilhoff. The nature of his scouting kept him alone. Even though he was part of this six-hundred-thousand man army, no one in his immediate vicinity wanted to associate with him.

When they organized the colored divisions, Shad put in for a transfer. Sherman canceled the idea and told him if he wanted help finding Bekah he better stick close.

Tonight he was lonely. His soul cried out for the warmth of a friendly smile. Death and destruction had been a constant companion for these long months and years. Tonight, he needed someone to lean on. Someone to share the burden.

Shad's services were invaluable as the Union Army drove through the mountains. The Confederate commander shifting and desperately trying to catch him in a mistake, Sherman expressed his gratitude to Shad. Now, the Army was on the verge of victory at Atlanta and was preparing for a perilous march across Georgia. Preparing for a journey, many of the highest ranking officers thought impossible and Shad was being transferred?

Shad longed for the war to be over with so he could find Bekah and pick up the pieces of his shattered life. *Where would he go? What would he do?* He could not answer these questions. He didn't feel the north was a place he wanted to stay. It would be fine if he could get Bekah there in safety until the war was over.

What would he do when the war was over? He would take Bekah back to Ingrid and see what he could do about picking up their shattered lives.

Moroseness sat on Shad's shoulders. He alternated between fitful sleep and anxious prowl until the roosters announced the new day.

Old James Dithers built his mansion on the edge of a swamp. Long strands of moss hung from the surrounding trees. The mansion itself was built of stone. A cold, gray stone that seemed to huddle onto itself.

The sun was at high noon when Shad tied his horse to the brass ring in the stone jockey's hand at the edge of the yard.

Dithers was one of the first men to go down when the cannons roared at the first battle of Bull Run. No one had taken care of the mansion or grounds since. The fact it was built of strong stone, was isolated and had impenetrable swamps on three sides, persuaded Sherman it would make a good prison.

The guard at the door told Shad which room he was expected in and unlocked the outer door.

Pushing the door open, Shad came eye to eye with Jim Bob. Before either could react, General Rudat pushed between them.

"So nice to see you fellows know each other." The General boomed. "Make one move toward one another and you are mine," he said just above a whisper.

Shad glanced around the room. He saw Alf and several other men of the same general stamp glaring at him.

General Rudat motioned for a guard to take station by the door and turned to the room.

"Gentlemen!" General Rudat glanced around the room and grinned at the use of the term. "You have been brought here to discuss a commodity near and dear to your heart, gold Gentlemen, lots of gold."

"Now that I have your attention, shut up, sit down, and listen." The General paused while everyone found a place to sit except Shad, who leaned against the door facing.

"Most of the more affluent planters did one of two things with their ready cash when the war began." General Rudat slowly strolled across the room. "They either put it in gold and hid it on the plantation or deposited it in England. A lot more of them put it in gold than send it to England. They didn't trust banks here and they trusted foreign banks even less.

We are going to let you go out in front of the army heading for Savannah and collect this gold. Think about it gentlemen, all that gold and no law. The only law will be the Union Army and it will be backing you.

"We will furnish you a Lieutenant's rank, men to help you,

whom you will have to pay, arms, horses, and protection. For all the things we are going to furnish, we will get fifty percent of the take.

"We know our system will work. We tested it on the Meridian Mississippi campaign.

"You gentlemen have been chosen because you have proven yourself capable of performing this type of work.

"Each of you have been chosen from a specific area. You will be operating on familiar ground. We hope you know who is most likely to have gold.

"There are two things you must not do. First, do not leave a witness to any robbery alive. Black or white, male or female, old or young, makes no difference. We want no witnesses filing wild claims after the war is over.

"Second, and perhaps more importantly from your point of view, *do not take one cent of our fifty percent*. We will go deeper into this downstairs in a few minutes.

"Are there any questions?"

The men all sat in shocked silence for a moment. A hand rose in the corner of the room. "Who is getting the other fifty percent of our take?" A sharp faced man wanted to know.

"All you need to know is fifty percent of the gold will be turned in to me."

Shad was sick to his stomach. The General was talking about robbery, murder, in fact he was not only legalizing any kind of crime, he was demanding murder of innocent people, including women and children.

Shad knew it would be instant death to openly oppose the General but he wondered what he was doing here? The others were riffraff from prison, but why did they include him?

The General rubbed his hands together. All you gentlemen except Alf, Jim Bob, and Shad wait at the back entrance to the wine cellar.

"What's that nigger doing here?" Alf growled.

"He's here because I ordered him here, same as you."

"He didn't come in chains like we did."

"You better make friends with him. You three are going to serve together." The General's good old boy smile slipped a little.

We ain't serving with this nigger or any other. We're going to kill this nigger. That's what we're going to do." Alf stated emphatically.

All General Rudat's good old boy fell away. His eyes seemed to shrink back into his head and become pig like. His jowls quivered. "After the war I might like to be invited to this occasion. For now, you will serve with this nigger or go back to the brig. Up to now, we thought there might be a use for you so you've had an easy time of it. If I send you back, there is no reason for us to worry about you."

Alf gave Jim Bob a "we'll settle this later look."

"We feel this man will be able to increase your take by obtaining information you can't get from slaves." General Rudat stood ramrod straight. His fat flesh no longer looked soft. His eyes glittered with an internal fire fueled by a personal demon. "If anything happens to this man you better be able to prove quickly and conclusively it was due to enemy action."

Both men quaked before this onslaught. They had seen iron resolve in the form of Mister George, but before them stood the devil himself. The unholy light in the General's eyes penetrated to the very depths of their souls.

After a moment of silence, the General eased and shrank. A portion of his good old boy smile returned. "You boys run along and join the others. We'll take this up later if need be."

Alf and Jim Bob hoped there would be no need to take this or anything else up with this man.

The General led the way down the stairs into the wine cellar. Empty wine racks lined the walls. Upon closer examination, Alf decided these racks were full not long ago. The soldiers had a ball with that much wine he thought.

"I shipped it north and sold it." Alf looked up to find General Rudat staring at him.

Alf shuddered. Can he read minds, he asked himself and

quickly looked at the General. The General laughed uproariously and led the group deeper into the cellar.

At the end of the cellar, a collection of benches was lined in rows on one side and four burly guards held two prisoners in front of them.

General Rudat motioned the men onto the benches. "The biggest problem we ran into on our Meridian experiment of the gold collection system was the men we used. Most were greedy. They didn't want to share properly with us, after all the hard work we went through. This was hard on us, fortunate for you and very tragic for them."

"General, I gave that money to..." One of the prisoners struggled with the guards.

"Silence that man!" General Rudat pointed an accusing finger at the guards.

"We lost a large part of our collectors on the Meridian expedition." The General's voice grew silky and he drifted toward the man the guards held. "The trouble was, their hearts were not in the right place. Was your heart in the right place Sergeant?" The general drifted closer.

The guards held the prisoner by the arms. One guard dropped to one knee, the other guard took the prisoner by the hair and pulled him backward over the guard's out thrust knee.

A knife glittered in the general's hand. Leaping forward he ripped the lower part of the prisoner's chest open. Thrusting his hand into the prisoner's chest, a couple of deft cuts, and turned triumphantly to the crowd.

In his left hand, held aloft for all to see, was the man's still beating heart.

Oaths were uttered, a scrape of benches and clatter of shoes as the men leapt to their feet. Silence.

The General morbidly watched the heart until it became still. Raising his eyes, he looked at the other man, "Well, Lieutenant, this leaves you on the hook for the rest of it."

At this cue a soldier entered carrying a rope attached to a large steel hook used to hang beef.

The General took the hook, placed it just below the prisoners ribs and jerked. The hook entered on one side and came out on the other. The prisoner convulsed and screamed, still held by the guards. The rope was thrown over the rafters and the prisoner was jerked to hang facing the ceiling.

Primordial, gut-wrenching screams shook the cellar. The man's arms and legs flailed about, then went limp. The screams died off.

"Sissy," The General spit in the Lieutenant's direction. "Sorry gentlemen, he didn't put on much of a show. I assure you he will in the next three days or so, but alas, we don't have the time to wait.

"I hope you are getting the message, though we will not tolerate anyone who tries to keep our cut." The General looked pointedly at Alf and Jim Bob. "We will not tolerate insubordination."

The General came alongside Shad on the steps and said quietly, "If you want to find that girl you will keep your nose clean."

The next few days were hectic. Since Alf and Jim Bob were going to be operating further east of the army than any other group, their outfit was to be the largest of all.

Men and material poured in. The troops were split equally between Alf and Jim Bob. Jim Bob was especially pleased with the turn of events. He felt he was gaining equal status with Alf at last.

Both Alf and Jim Bob were a little put out when they realized Shad technically outranked them, due to seniority. They were somewhat mollified when he wasn't assigned any troops or other real responsibilities.

Shad was worn and tired from the previous months and years of service. He had pushed himself relentlessly during the advance on Atlanta. Operating on the theory the sooner the war was over, the sooner he would be reunited with Bekah. Shad had driven himself extremely hard since the Battle of Shiloh.

Sick at heart, disillusioned, and worried, Shad prowled the camp. He transferred some of the loyalty he felt for Mister George to Sherman. *Why did Sherman cut him off and drop him in an outlaw band? His first thought was to flee. But, what about Bekah?* He staked everything on the army's help to locate her.

Shad began trying to remember everything he told anyone about Bekah. *Was she in danger? Was the General's words on the cellar steps, a veiled threat to Bekah?* Alf and Jim Bob certainly knew Bekah.

Shad knew General Rudat would put Alf and Jim Bob on his trail if he fled, and this time they would have the full resources of the Union Army behind them. Where could he go? He was already in the Northern Army. Leaving would make him a deserter and a wanted man.

Deciding to go to the mountains and see if his thoughts would clear up away from the hustle and bustle of the camp, Shad saddled his horse and rode out of camp.

He failed to appreciate or even notice the cooling air and touches of fall color creeping into the foliage on the mountains. He was riding with troubled thoughts.

"Sir, hold up, sir." The words finally penetrated the gloom surrounding him. Surprised, Shad looked at a Sergeant trotting along at his stirrup. Looking back, he realized he was only about a hundred yards beyond the camp perimeter.

The sergeant saluted smartly. "The General's compliments, sir. He feels you would be more rested and ready if you stayed within the confines of the camp, sir."

Shad returned to watch Alf and Jim Bob put their outfits together. They were each allowed to pick nine men from the prison. General Rudat figured twenty fast moving fighting men should be able to handle any plantation and most bush-whacking units.

Four of the men, two from each group, were detailed to learn how to operate the small cannon issued to them.

The group wore regulation uniforms, ate regulation food, and slept in regulation tents. That was as close as they came to resemble regular troops. They were an unruly, undisciplined, loud group. Alf lashed one and sent him back to prison the first day, which subdued the rest.

General Rudat held another meeting of the group commanders. Each group was assigned a territory to operate in.

Shad, Alf, and Jim Bob were to swing far to the east of the Union Army's proposed line of march. Since they were traveling over such a long route, they were to be the first to leave.

They marched eight days to the west, then they turned south and hit their first plantation. During the march it was clear to Shad, he was being watched closely. Two men rode on his elbows by day and four bedded down on all sides of him at night.

The first plantation fell into their hands with ease. Coming out of the gray dawn they caught everyone with sleep still in their eyes. Rounding up the white people on the veranda, they drove the slave women into a stall in one barn and the slave men into a stall in the other barn. The slaves went willingly, singing to their liberators.

On the veranda, Alf separated an elderly aunt from the plantation owner and his two teenage daughters. One daughter, he estimated to be about eighteen, the other sixteen.

"Put her in with the slave women and detail a party to search this place." He ordered, shoving the aunt toward Odie, the man he picked for his sergeant.

You can't do this." The owner stated.

"You are going to find, we can do anything we want. Where is your money hid?"

"There is some in my desk. It's in the bottom drawer." Alf nodded to a man who entered the house.

Jim Bob drew his sergeant aside, "Vernon, go and take the men slaves out of the stall one at a time and strangle them quietly. The idiots think we are going to free them, so if you work it right, there should be no trouble."

The soldier returned from the desk carrying a stack of Confederate script.

Alf took the script and tickled the man's nose with it. "What kind of fool do you take me for? I want gold."

"I don't have any gold."

A soldier took the man by each hand.

"That's too bad," Alf turned to cup a hand under the chin of the youngest girl. "I thought I might be able to do some business with you."

"What are you talking about?" The man's eyes cast about wildly.

"If you had enough gold, you could buy me off and I wouldn't give this pretty little thing to that nigger there."

"If I had gold, would you let us go?"

"If you have enough."

"Do I have your word on this? If I give you the gold, will you ride on and leave us alone?"

"We are going to burn this place down. You can count on that. If you can come up with enough gold, we will set you and your daughters loose in the woods."

The man believed Alf. "I'll have to show you where it is buried."

Shad tried to walk away. A soldier blocked his path.

"Odie take him and dig up the gold. Put a rope around his neck and tie his hands. If you let him get away you will take his place." Alf settled into a rocker to leer at the girls.

Odie returned excited. He held a small chest with the lid open. A pile of gold coins glittered in the sunlight.

"What kind of fool do you take me for?" Alf roared at the plantation owner. Leaping from the chair, he grabbed the girl by the breast.

"Father!" She screamed, recoiling. Alf took her by the hair and shoved her toward Shad.

"Wait! Wait," the man stood with his hands pushed up behind his back. The rope around his throat was taut. "Behind the barn."

"Keep him here until I yell at you." Jim Bob headed for the barn.

"This is more like it," Alf fingered the golden pile of coins.

"That is all I have. Let us go." The plantation owner said.

"I believe it's all you have." Alf leaped to the girl, wrapped his hand in the top of her dress and ripped the front out of it. She squirmed this way and that trying to cover her nakedness, but the soldiers held her upright.

"You gave your word!" The man lunged forward but was jerked back by the rope around his neck.

"Stop it! Turn her loose," Shad snapped.

Jim Bob pushed a rifle barrel into Shad's face. Shad felt two more muzzles between his shoulder blades. Hammers clicked ominously.

"I've waited a long time to kill you, nigger." Jim Bob's face was twisted, ugly.

CHAPTER 27

"Jim Bob!" Alf's voice lashed out. "Remember General Rudat, the cellar, I'm not in this with you."

Jim Bob hesitated.

"You have to know some of these men are the General's stool pigeons."

Jim Bob growled in frustration and struck Shad in the temple with the rifle barrel. Shad crumpled. "Vernon, tie this man, put him in the barn. I want two men guarding him at all times."

"The men don't want to guard him, they want to join in the fun." Vernon didn't move.

Jim Bob shot the plantation owner, pulled another rifle from a soldier and pushed it against Vernon's chest. "Want to join him?" He grated.

Vernon hastened to carry out the orders. Jim Bob, his face growing uglier motioned to the men holding the screaming girl. "Bring her to the edge of the porch."

Shad regained consciousness lying on his back. He rolled to his side and curled into a ball, trying to block out the screams and groans of the women, black and white.

Vernon and Odie untied Shad's feet and led him from the barn. The house and the other barn blazed fiercely, covering the rising sun with a black pall of smoke.

The rest of the group was prepared to leave. Alf loped from

the front of the line. "Were all the bodies taken to the top floor?"

"We put the men on top of the corn in the crib. It'll burn hot enough to do the work."

"Tie him on a horse and bring him up front. I want to keep an eye on him." Alf pulled his horse around.

The column moved slowly, planning to pull another dawn raid on the next plantation in their path. Alf and Jim Bob deployed pickets to insure no one reported the presence of the column.

The road wound down a long point and crossed a running stream in the floor of a flat valley. A cool breeze rustled the turning leaves and carried away the dust raised by the horse's feet. A flurry of activity up front, then a soldier on picket duty scurried back to report. "Bushwhackers, I saw a line of them on the ridge."

"Where?" Alf eased his seat in the saddle.

"They are along the ridge top across the road, behind that big water oak beside the road."

"We need to know how many." Alf's eyes fell on Shad. "What we need here is a scout, an experienced scout."

"Are you crazy?" Jim Bob interfered. "We can't turn him loose and send him up there."

"Who said we'd turn him loose? We'll send him out to draw their fire. Remember General Rudat said if he died, it better be by enemy fire. Well, maybe them Rebs can be of service to us." Alf motioned Shad forward.

"Cut my hands loose and I'll go." Shad was looking the ridge over.

"Turn one hand loose," Alf ordered. "Bring three sharp-shooters up. Shad you ride up the road to that big water oak. If you ride out of the road or pass that oak, our riflemen will shoot you."

A soldier freed Shad's left hand, then retied the right one to the saddle horn. Shad's feet were still lashed together under the horse's belly.

The track that served as a road ran straight to the water oak, then made a slight bend and sharply ascended the hill. Deep dust to the water oak, then harder, faster ground beyond.

Picking up the bridle reins in his left hand Shad stepped the horse forward. *If they miss the first shot, I'll duck behind the big oak,* he thought.

Step by step, he kept waiting for the shot. The horse's feet made soft plop and suck sounds. Fear rose in Shad's throat and mixed with the smell of dust, leaving a copper taste in his mouth.

Maybe the bushwhackers can see I'm tied in this saddle and won't shoot at me, Shad reasoned with himself. Looking back, he saw Alf spread the sharpshooters out and have them kneel. Shad could feel his back prickle, anticipating a bullet from the sharpshooters. It was getting to the point where he was beginning to wish someone would shoot.

When he came to the Water oak, Shad put his heels into the horse's ribs and jumped him past the tree, then swerved to bring the tree between himself and the sharpshooters. The air was instantly ripped by blasting rifles and passing bullets.

The horse laid his ears back and charged the ridge with mighty bounds. The way Alf spread the riflemen, it was impossible to keep the oak between his back and all of them. Weaving the fleeing horse back and forth gave the riflemen an uncertain now you see it, now you don't, target. Shad could see figures dashing to and fro, but no bullets came from the ridge.

When he was far enough over the hill to be out of the hail of lead, Shad pulled the running horse to a sliding stop. Around him stood a group of runaway slaves.

"Run!" Shad bellowed. "Scatter and don't stop."

Without waiting to see if the runaways took his advice, Shad pulled the horse's head to the left. He raced along the ridge until he heard the shooting, shouting group behind him come over the top. Pulling his horse left again, he went back over the top and pulled his horse to a trot. He was sure they would keep going pell-mell down the other side or perhaps they would chase the runaways, but he kept to the brush and slowed even more so they wouldn't hear him. He knew Alf and Jim Bob would find where he turned without much delay. The question was how badly did they want him?

Shad rode until nearly dark before he stopped to work the ropes off his feet. He managed to untie his right hand while underway. Dropping to the ground, Shad leaned wearily against the horse.

The horse cropped grass while Shad chafed his wrists. *What to do now? What would Alf and Jim Bob do now? Would they come after him? Would they continue the raid?*

Shad knew the sadistic General had made an impression on the pair, especially Alf. Their greed and fear would keep them raiding, Shad decided. *What am I going to do now?*

He could forget any military help in finding Bekah. He realized this was never a real offer. It was just something to keep him sticking his neck out. He kicked a rock and spit in the general direction of Sherman's camp.

Not only was he not going to get help finding Bekah, he was a wanted man. A deserter. How bad would General Rudat want him back? The thought made Shad shudder. Be better to die out here than to be invited to the General's games.

Alf and Jim Bob can find and follow my trail rapidly, he warned himself. *Get going in some direction.*

Shad decided to go north again. This time he would go far north and east. Who would think of a black man as a deserter? He would go past the war.

He had his fill of war. His fill of destruction. Since Mister George's death the world had gone crazy. Death and destruction surrounded him everywhere he turned. He longed to go somewhere quiet. He longed to build something.

One thing he realized suddenly, he wasn't going North without Bekah. He would hunt for her until he found her and he would take her from anyone who claimed her.

He would find Bekah, claim her for his own, and kill Alf and Jim Bob should they make it necessary.

Where to start? Ingrid. He would go to see Ingrid and take the cold trail from Tendrilhoff. He was a different man from the one who left Tendrilhoff, when? Two years? It seemed a lifetime ago.

While he had been gathering information for Sherman, his quick wit, observant eye, and huge memory were working overtime. Cities no longer awed him. In fact, he had learned it was easier to hide there than in the woods. All in all, he had picked up many skills that would help him find Bekah.

Climbing to the saddle, Shad headed the horse toward home.

"Damned!" Jim Bob looked down Shad's trail. "I'll bet that nigger is headed for Tendrilhoff."

Shad had been correct when he thought it wouldn't take them long to arrive at this spot.

"We'll go get him." Alf walked a few steps down Shad's trail.

"What about collecting the gold?"

"We'll do both. You know Junior has found the old man's gold by now. We need to get it before somebody takes it from him." Alf found he was actually a little homesick.

Hunger rode Shad's shoulder. He possessed neither knife nor gun. The early fall woods furnished him a lot of berries, muscadines, black and red haws, hickory nuts, and the like but no meat.

Being in a hurry, Shad picked berries while the horse grazed and pulled his belt in for the rest of it.

Arriving at Ingrid's, Shad had the largest meal he had eaten since the last one Ruth cooked for him. Ham, corn bread, fried tatters, beans, black-eyed peas, and fresh milk.

Albert was in Hoffman. Ennis and Tamar finished their cabin a long time ago, and were working on their second child. Shad and Ingrid thoroughly enjoyed each other's company and filled each other in on the happenings since they parted.

"Good food." Shad mopped his plate with the corn bread.

"They haven't found the cache," Ingrid explained.

"Have you heard anything about Bekah?"

"I'm sorry Shad, we've not learned any more than we already knew about Bekah." Ingrid was thicker through the waist.

"It was a traveling slave trader and he's not been through this part of the country since he picked up Bekah. Hannibal will send a message if he hears anything."

"There has to be something. They didn't disappear into thin air." Shad paced. "I'm going to Tendrilhoff."

"Junior has white trash working for him. They run the place with an iron hand. They have the slaves so browbeaten, they might turn on you."

Shad caught his horse, saddled him, and rode out of the corral gate. He saw a rider come through the gap at the end of the valley. Pulling the horse to a stop, he sat watching. The distance was too great for detail. Another rider, followed by a third, Alf! Shad recognized Alf, even at this distance.

Shad's heart sank. They followed him after all. He hoped they would go ahead collecting the gold and let him alone.

"Ingrid!" He shouted. Leaping from the horse, he ran for the door.

"What's the matter?" Ingrid came to the door with a rifle in her hands.

"It's Alf and Jim Bob. They're coming down the valley. We have to go right now."

"Go? I'll not leave my place for them to pillage." Ingrid snorted.

"You don't understand, they are robbing, raping, killing, under the cover of the war and with the army's blessing." Shad took her arm and guided her toward his horse. "You being a woman would only make it worse. They would rape you, kill you, and burn your body in the house."

Shad raced into the house and came out carrying another rifle and a double-barreled shotgun. Two pouches of ammunition hung from his arm.

"Will Ennis and Tamar be home or in the field?" In his haste Shad picked Ingrid off the ground and placed her in the saddle.

"Be careful; don't get too rough, I'm with child." Ingrid informed Shad.

Shad stopped in his tracks. It was OK for every woman in the world to be pregnant, except Ingrid. It didn't fit into his way of thinking.

"Are we going to go or are you going to just stand there with your mouth open?" Ingrid smiled at his dumbfounded face.

CHAPTER 28

Shad studied the group weaving down the valley. There were too many men to stay and fight. Alf and Jim Bob would follow if they left. Ingrid was in no shape to run from them. Perhaps he could get to Ennis's house. Any help was better than none.

Topping the first ridge, he heard the yells of Alf's men charging the house. Topping the second ridge, they saw the smoke.

Ingrid climbed stiffly from the saddle, wrapped her head in her apron. Sobbing, she sank to the roots of a tree. All the years of sacrifice, blood, sweat, and toil. All gone.

All gone because of one perverted, warped, and crazy man entrusted with the might of his nation. A man so perverted that he not only ordered rape, murder, and destruction, he reveled in it. The progress of his army, like that of Attila the Hun, could be traced by the death and destruction it rained on a helpless civilian population.

Shad needed help and more firepower. He had the weapons he snatched at Ingrid's but there was no way he could stand against that many men.

They found Ennis and Tamar at home. It was obvious Ingrid was tiring. Shad decided to make a stand in Ennis's cabin.

It was a well-built cabin, copied from one built while the Indians were still a problem. Ennis had been so true to detail that he put loopholes and firing steps in the cabin. A well was situated so water could be obtained without exposing oneself.

Ingrid and Tamar could handle a rifle almost as good as Shad and Ennis. With the women loading, Shad and Ennis could keep up a good rate of fire.

Shad was glad Alf ordered the field gun abandoned on the third day out. It slowed them down.

There were several things he didn't like about the position of the cabin, but there was no time to correct them. Prepared to repel an attack, they settled in to wait. The day dragged on. The only thing that came out of the woods was the scream of a jay and the bark of a squirrel.

Dusk rose from the low places and devoured the earth. Shad decided Alf and Jim Bob wouldn't attack until dawn. If he could find their camp, he might get close enough to shoot Alf and Jim Bob. Deprived of leadership, the others would bicker among themselves over who would be leader and break up into small factions.

Shad dug his uniform out of the saddlebags. There was a chance the camp would be poorly lighted. If this were the case, he might get the opportunity to walk into the camp without challenge.

Shad explained his plans to the group.

"Too risky, even if you got to Alf and Jim Bob you would never get out alive." Ingrid complained.

"It might work." Ennis was thoughtful.

Shad donned all the uniform except the boots. He preferred the soft soles of his shoes.

Riding down his back trail Shad was surprised when he failed to find the camp within two miles of the cabin. He didn't find it there, or between there and Ingrid's place.

The smoke was strong in his nostrils as he circled the still glowing pile of ashes. He eased out onto the road and back into the bushes. Someone had passed up or down the road recently. He could smell the dust raised by their passing.

On the road to Tendrilhoff Shad could smell the fresh horse droppings regularly. Moving swiftly, Shad's ears heard the swish of bat's wings, the rustle of the crickets, and questioned every hoot of an owl. Was it real or was it a man imitating an owl?

At the foot of the last hill before Tendrilhoff, he found the camp.

Continuing over the hill, he descended on Tendrilhoff. The deterioration shocked him. Doors sagged, fences were down, and weeds overran the open spots. The buildings were in the right location. That was about the only thing that matched his memory of the spic-and-span prosperous Tendrilhoff.

Carefully, Shad slid from shadow to shadow. Movement at the end of the veranda gave Shad the location of a guard on the front door. A dog barked in the distance.

On his way to the back door, he made out the form of a sentry sitting on the doorstep. Shad swore, Junior didn't have enough cash to keep the place up but he sure could pay guards to watch the doors. With times being what they were, these men were probably working for what they ate.

Shad decided not to chance it and backed away.

Would Hannibal sleep in the same room he used to? Shad decided not to chance it and backed away from the house.

The slave quarters were deserted. They hadn't been occupied for some time. Shad leaned against a doorframe contemplating his next move. A dog began barking furiously near the log barn. Shad froze. The dog spotted him when he leaned in the doorway. A spat of cursing and a whistling rock hit the dog in the ribs, sending him yelping and limping for the brush.

Shad stood immobile until he felt the sentry settled down and slipped behind the weed grown corrals. Slipping around the end of the tall weeds, he decided it was impossible to warn Hannibal and the rest of the slaves. They were in no position to help themselves if they were warned.

"Rise and shine. It's time to go say hello to Junior." Shad heard Alf shout as he was backing away from the camp. He must try something else. They would spend time drinking coffee and preparing to ride.

Shad climbed the hill toward Tendrilhoff. Many times he had climbed this hill, but never with murder his heart. Even the death and destruction he witnessed in the recent past did not prepare him for murder.

The very thought of ambushing Alf and Jim Bob made him queasy in his stomach. The thought of what this pair would do to Ingrid if they got the chance stiffened his resolve.

A huge tree flanked by a boulder and a small draw flanked by thick brush. It was close to the road, close enough the picket would pass outside it and the brush would prevent the picket from seeing back into the small opening between the tree and the rock.

Working the shotgun into the grass so it concealed the barrel while it was pointed at the road, Shad napped while he waited.

The click of a steel horseshoe on stone woke Shad. The column of raiders were coming, two abreast. Alf and Jim Bob were riding in front.

Shad nestled the shotgun to his cheek and listened to the sounds the picket made passing behind him. Holding the triggers to kill the sound, He eared both the big hammers back on the shotgun. Three more steps. Two, one, his fingers took up the slack in the triggers.

Shad couldn't pull the triggers. He cursed himself and tried again. At one point he might have hit both Alf and Jim Bob in the blast from a single barrel. He could not manage the squeeze that would send the big buckshot on its mission.

He had killed before, but it was in the heat of battle, not cold-blooded murder from ambush. For Ingrid he could kill, but they weren't after her now. Perhaps they wouldn't bother her again.

Lowering his head, Shad held his breath and prayed no one looked directly at him. Lying still for sometime after the last rider passed his position Shad tried to figure what to do. After half an hour passed, he withdrew and began a circuitous trip to Tendrilhoff.

Approaching Tendrilhoff from the opposite side, Shad could hear a man screaming up near the big house. Cautiously working his way around the stables, Shad looked at the only horse in the long line of stalls.

June Bug! Shad found a gentleman's saddle and bridle on the door across the aisle. Saddling the big horse, Shad rode toward the big house. Placing the rifle in a boot on the saddle, Shad held the shotgun at arm's length beside his leg.

After clearing the stables, an overgrown lot of tall weeds gave Shad cover. Near the well Shad could see blue uniforms surrounding the bunched slaves. Beyond this, Hannibal stood alone. On the edge of the clearing near the first tobacco barn was Alf and Jim Bob. They stood before Junior, who was spread-eagle between two trees.

No one paid any attention to Shad as he let June Bug amble across to Alf and Jim Bob.

"You cut too deep!" Alf screamed at Jim Bob. "He ain't never going to tell us where that gold is now."

"Aw, suppose there isn't any gold like he says?"

"That's right, there is no gold." Shad pulled June Bug to a halt. Bringing the shotgun into line, Shad watched as they looked at the blue uniform and realized who wore it.

"Tell the men behind me, I will kill both of you if they shoot." Shad demanded.

Alf eyed Jim Bob, "I don't think he could get both of us."

"I'll take the one he leaves." Ennis's voice came from the barn loft. A rifle barrel stared between the slats in the barn wall.

Hannibal stepped to the well curb, reached into a recess and pulled a fine English twelve gauge into his arms. "Stand easy," he said to the men guarding the slaves.

Albert White and Ingrid rode around the barn.

"What now?" Albert looked to Shad.

"Put your guns down." With Albert, Ennis, and Ingrid watching the pair, Shad turned to the men guarding the slaves.

"No, don't put your guns down." Vernon ordered.

"They've got the drop on us, but we're not becoming their prisoners. There are enough of us to make a fight of it."

"Will you stand and let the slaves go?" Shad was willing to do almost anything to keep the shooting from starting until he got Ingrid away from there.

"Yes."

Shad rode to Hannibal. "Take the slaves and scatter them in the swamp. After Alf's bunch is gone, gather at Ingrids. She has food and will take care of you."

After the slaves disappeared from sight for a few minutes, Albert turned to Ingrid. "Ride around behind the barn and leave. We will follow you."

"I'm going after Bekah." Shad looked at Ingrid, who waved and turned the corner.

Albert caught Shad's attention and wiggled a finger. Shad nodded and both men drove the spurs into their horses and headed in opposite directions. June Bug's first reaction to the spur was a twenty-foot leap. Rifles crackled like fireworks.

"Kill the nigger, kill the nigger," rang in Shad's ear as he guided June Bug's mighty strides toward the tall weeds.

CHAPTER 29

For three days, Shad dogged Alf and Jim Bob's footsteps and they traveled steadily back to the point where they quit raiding. The specter of General Rudat rode one shoulder and greed the other, driving Alf and Jim Bob off Shad's trail.

Both vowed to take up the search again as soon as possible. Each told himself the fortune they would amass in the next few days would make the search for Shad easier.

The blame for letting witnesses escape was laid squarely on Sergeant Vernon's shoulders. The controversy following the escape led the group to leave Tendrilhoff without burning a single building.

Shad followed the ridge where he escaped. He sat on top until the last soldier disappeared over the hill beyond the valley. Turning June Bug, he devoted his entire being to finding Bekah.

Being south and west of the bitterest fighting and most of the men being away at the front, allowed Shad to move more freely than he expected. Control over slaves was much slacker than before the war.

Shad traveled constantly. He followed this lead and that lead. All were false and led nowhere.

Everyone knew the traveling slave trader and no one knew where he came from or where he went. All knew he bought and sold slaves everywhere he went. It was possible for him to sell Bekah anywhere.

Discouraged and dispirited, he trudged on, searching everywhere possible. Entering the cities, he took great risks checking the slave sales places as thoroughly as possible.

Circling back, he started the trail again. The third day of this new beginning found him sitting on a hill looking into a valley. A woman with a small child was woman grubbing for roots in the far end of the valley. This was a common sight in the South. Millions of acres of prime farmland lay fallow. The few that were planted had armies vying for its production.

The woman straightened, then placed both hands on her hips and stretched over backward. Shad watched this with a sort of blind eye as he tried to think of someway to find Bekah.

Bekah! Leaping to his feet, he bent forward to concentrate. It's Bekah. That woman digging roots is Bekah. He would recognize her profile from any distance.

Shad leaped to the saddle and put the willing June Bug into a hard gallop. June Bug threw showers of gravel into the air, making the turn onto the track that leads up the valley.

Shad pulled June Bug to a stop in a cloud of dust and leaped from the saddle. There was no woman here. There's where she was digging, but she was gone. A movement by the creek caught Shad's eye. A woman carrying a small child snuck through the brush. Shad broke into a stumbling run, then realized what his hell-for-leather approach was doing.

"Bekah!" Shad yelled, forcing himself to stop. The woman hesitated, then moved on. Leaping up on a boulder, he yelled "Bekah," more softly this time.

Glancing over her shoulder Bekah halted. Shad! That was Shad's voice. She had given him up for dead, but it was Shad. Shifting the child to her other arm, as she started to run back and suddenly stopped. What was she going to tell Shad?

Shad came off the small rise leaping brush, boulders, and any other obstacles in his path. He forgot everything. All he dreamed of, the fruit of all the nerve-wracking danger and hard fighting was in front of him.

A cloud of dust followed him off the hill. He threw his arms around Bekah and the child in an all-encompassing bear hug. The child tried to twist around and climb Bekah's shoulder. When that failed and he felt the pressure of Shad's bear hug, he began to wail with a healthy set of lungs.

"Whose boy is that?" Shad released Bekah.

"Mine." Bekah comforted the baby, gathered her resolve, looked Shad in the eye, "Shad," she said in measured tones, "meet George, your son."

"Not my..." Shad began and realized it was possible. He turned and walked a couple of steps trying to understand.

Bekah's heart fell. Her knees trembled and she wished she could disappear into the dust.

"Are you... Is he... We were..." Shad stumbled forward with his hands out, waist high palm up. Shad let loose with a yell and scooped Bekah and the baby up in his arms and swung them around. George began to wail in earnest and for once Bekah didn't mind.

"And he sold me to a Scotsman named Alex McKay." Bekah was winding down her narration of what happened to her since she and Shad parted.

"Are you ready to start north?" Shad figured he would have many years to fill her in on the things he lived through.

"We're starving, including Mister Alex. There is no food available at any price. Mister Alex is a close man with a penny, but he has been good to me."

"Perhaps I could find a deer or some other kind of meat." Shad couldn't take his eyes off her.

"I think if we had a couple of decent meals George and I would be strong enough to go." Bekah laughed because George twisted his little fingers into the cheap fabric of her dress in case Shad reached for him again.

"How many slaves in the big house?"

"Six and counting Mister Alex, seven."

"How many in Mister Alex's family?"

"None, he don't have a family. No wife. No kids. Nobody I know of."

"You go back and prepare to run. I'll find some food and follow you." Shad boarded June Bug and rode away.

Bekah walked around the barn deep in thought. Mister Alex was a nice man and took good care of her during her pregnancy, but he was very close with money. She didn't think he would let her go. He would be losing two, Bekah and George.

She would have to run away. What to take with her? What would George need the most?

"Well, well, look what we have here." The voice yanked Bekah from her deep thoughts. She was looking directly into Alf's eyes.

Bekah glanced around the yard and her legs trembled until her knees buckled. She began to fall. Jim Bob took the back of her hair and supported her. Mister Alex's body lay on the porch. The other five slaves were piled on the ground at the edge of the porch.

"Ain't this the wench that damned nigger was sweet on?" Jim Bob queried.

"Sure is, where is your boyfriend?" Alf was smiling. Bekah shook her head. She had no control of her voice at this moment.

Alf's fist came around in a whistling arc. Bekah's eyes glazed. Hanging on to consciousness with all her might, she lowered George to arm's length and dropped him in the dirt. Jim Bob let go of her hair and Bekah collapsed besides George.

"That's a good-looking wench. Let me make her talk." Odie came off the porch.

"She don't know where he is. He's hunting her. I think we might be able to use her for bait. Set her behind the table on the porch." Alf turned to Jim Bob, "Let's get on with dividing the gold. This is the most we've got from one place."

Alf sat on one side of the table and Jim Bob on the other. The huge golden pile worked down into three smaller piles. One was twice as large as the other two.

"Too bad we have to split this," Alf commented.

"I'm not going to mess with that crazy General's share." Jim Bob shuddered at the thought.

"I was thinking of playing cards for our part." Alf tossed a deck on the table.

"Not with that deck, we ain't." Jim Bob said emphatically.

"Perhaps I shouldn't play with a professional like you." Alf noted dryly as he dropped a new deck on the table.

The game went on, with luck to one side, then the other. Luck always seems a little better on Alf's side of the table.

The men began to gather behind their commanders. Vernon glared at Odie across the table.

Alf's luck suddenly improved dramatically. He won pot after pot. Jim Bob sent Vernon to the horses for more gold. Vernon silently placed a bayonet on his rifle. The men on both sides looked to their priming.

"Friends don't cheat friends," Jim Bob stated as Alf raked in another pot.

"Are you saying I'm cheating?" Alf asked mildly.

Jim Bob rose to his feet and leaned over the table. "Yes," he screamed, reaching for the knife in his belt.

Alf's hand came from under the table with a cocked pistol in it. The pistol belched a cloud of smoke and fire. Jim Bob paled and fell sideways.

Odie shot Vernon before he could bring the bayoneted rifle into action. Vernon fell across the table, showering the porch with the golden hoard. Grabbing the rifle from Vernon's dead hand, Odie and Alf leaped into the yard.

Bekah clutched George to her breast and dashed through the cross fire. Bekah's bare feet touched the dirt at the edge of the porch. Taking deliberate aim, Odie ran George through and ripped him out of his mother's arms.

Holding the child aloft, Odie watched him struggle. Screaming, Bekah pulled at the rifle barrel. George's blood dripped in her face.

Alf shot Bekah in the back of the head. Odie watched her body until it stopped twisting. Shrugging his shoulders, he tossed the now still George into the well.

The fight on the porch had been short and deadly. All of Jim

Bob's men were down. Two of Alf's were still on their feet. Both were wounded. Alf and Odie exchanged glances.

"We'll have to take care of them." Alf said climbing the steps. One man was bleeding from the shoulder and the other leaned against a wall and tried to staunch the flow of blood from his thigh.

"Turn around so I can see where it came out." Alf ordered. The man turned. Alf nodded to Odie and shot the man in the back of the head. Odie ran his man through with such force it pinned him to the log wall.

A shot, then two more shots, followed by a ragged volley, many more random shots decreasing in intensity. Shad dropped the fat hog across his saddle and put the spurs to June Bug. Glad to be free of the smelly hog, Shad forced him to carry, June Bug leaped away and ran with a will.

Experience told Shad the shots were better than two miles away. Holding June Bug to a steady run, he closed as fast as he could.

About a quarter mile away, he leaped from the now struggling June Bug and ran as fast as his moccasin feet would carry him.

Shad came around the barn like the grim reaper. He took in the yard at a glance. Bekah lay with her head in a pool of blood. Shad's battlefield experience told him she would rise no more.

Alf and Odie were tying gold laden packs on the horses. Shad never broke stride. His moccasin feet were almost silent on the hard-packed dirt.

When he passed behind Odie, Shad placed the razor sharp steel under Odis's chin and jerked it across his throat. It was so quick Odie never realized what happened. He stared dumbly at the blood squirting onto the packhorse until he fell.

Without breaking stride, Shad descended on the still unaware Alf. Shad took Alf by the hair with such force, he tore the scalp loose from the skull. Alf screamed and reached for his weapons. Shad brushed the weapons aside without effort. Alf screamed until Shad drove the blade through his heart.

"Bekah. Bekah. Bekah." Shad moaned over and over again. Laying her body on the porch, he went to hunt George.

A thorough search took time. The hurt kept overwhelming him. He would stop and sob for a while.

"Why didn't I kill those bastards when I had them dead to rights?" Shad asked himself repeatedly. He knew this was his fault. If he'd been a man this would never have happened.

He returned to the porch at dusk, he carried Bekah to a rocker and cradled her there. There was silence. Even the wind and the crickets remained silent in deference to the terrible things that had transpired on the Scotsman's plantation.

All night Shad held Bekah and grieved. He always kept an ear open, hoping to hear the wail of an infant. With the silence, he would be able to hear a child cry, even from a long distance.

At dawn, he found a shovel and buried Mister Alex and his slaves in a common grave.

Bekah's grave, he dug deep. It was the last thing he could do for his loved one and he wanted it right. Smoothing the soil on top, he looked for something to mark the grave. But, after due consideration, he left the grave unmarked. He wanted it left alone. If he marked it, someone might desecrate it.

He left Alf, Jim Bob, and the rest of the raiders where they fell. The horses stood where they were tied the day before. They needed attention. Shad looked in the bags of the horses, Alf and Odie were finishing loading when he arrived.

Both horses were loaded with gold. Checking the other horses, he found more gold. Gold in every form, jewelry, bars, nuggets, dust, but mostly in coin. More gold than he knew existed in the world.

The horses needed attention, but he felt he must get out of here. He would water them when they crossed the creek and cater to their other needs later.

He picked the best horses and then he condensed the packs of gold as much as possible. He needed to cut the number of pack animals. He walked through the rest dumping packs and saddles on the ground. Slipping their bridles, he turned them loose.

June Bug was out there somewhere. Restlessness hit him. It was time to go. Standing in the stirrups, he surveyed the terrain. On a ridge far to the south was a short line of gray clad horsemen.

This made Shad aware of the uniform he was wearing. Tossing the cap on the ground, he slid the coat off and lowered it to his horse's feet. Taking the lead rope, he kneed his horse around the mansion and departed. With the mansion between them, he never saw the gray horsemen again.

The one armed, one legged officer sat on his horse and took in the scene. "Are you sure only one man rode out of here?"

"Yes, sir. He was leading some horses. Shall we catch him, sir?" The sergeant was also missing a hand.

CHAPTER 30

"No," the officer mused, surveying the dead soldiers in their blue uniforms. "Apparently, he's on our side. If he did all this fighting single-handed, he's a man we don't want to catch."

A cold feeling came over the officer. He shivered. Glancing at the window on the top floor of the mansion, he thought he saw a curtain move. There was no wind. An ominous foreboding settled on him.

"Pick up the gear, catch those horses, and let's get out of here." The officer backed his horse a few steps backward.

"What about the dead, sir?" The feeling had not touched the sergeant.

"They're Yankees. Let the Yanks bury them." A whoop from the porch and an enlisted man held two gold coins up to sparkle in the light. Alf and Odie failed to find all the coins.

The extra horses and gold made travel extremely difficult for Shad. It was difficult to come up with reasons for the horses. Writing passes became a chore. With the whole country hungry, it would be difficult to keep anyone from looking into a pack.

Staying off the roads and winding through the brush over the mountains was slow going. So far, it paid off. He was several days and miles north of the Scotsman's plantation and he hadn't seen anyone.

Shad found the perfect camp spot in the bottom of a steep sided little canyon. There was a meadow of perhaps ten acres with dried grass and a clear creek. Pools of water danced with the light.

The sides of the mountains were steep enough to form a fence on two sides and they pinched the meadow off at both ends. All Shad needed to do was put some poles across the openings on both ends and the horses were fenced in.

Shad and the horses were in need of rest and food. He thought it was ironic. He possessed unlimited funds and didn't dare go near a place where he could obtain the necessities of life.

Shad led the horses onto the grass. They began to fill their bellies. This made Shad's stomach growl. Taking his rifle, he left camp.

Shad was restless. This was the third day he spent in the little valley. The horses were rested and strengthened by the feed they found. Local game used the valley as a feeding ground. Without any effort Shad's rifle fed him and there were leftovers.

Shad packed. Arranging the packs and saddles, he decided to move out at dawn tomorrow.

He spent the rest of the day prowling. He had an uneasy feeling. He felt there was someone in the valley beside him and the horses.

Shad ate a cold supper and stayed out of the firelight. Occasionally, he moved in and tossed another log on the fire. He always came into the light from a different position. Letting the fire burn down to glow, Shad arranged his bed beside it. After making the bed look occupied, he tossed more wood on the fire and moved into the shadows before it blazed up.

Before midnight, one of the horses grazing close to camp snorted and shied. Shad was instantly awake. The horse moved a few feet and began to graze.

Shad carefully picked his rifle off the ground and sat holding it in his hands. A grinding of gravel and a figure seemed to grow out of the darkness. It walked a few steps and stopped.

"Hello in the camp." The deep, unexpected voice almost startled Shad into leaping to his feet. There was something familiar about the voice.

Shad held his place and remained silent.

"Hello in the camp. Are you awake?"

The voice was definitely familiar. Shad struggled to put a name or face with it.

The figure advanced to the edge of the firelight. "Hello in the camp." It repeated, leaning to stare at the bedroll.

Shad could make out a red tint to the hair. *Mickey Doon! It's Mickey Doon the store owner from Hoffman. What is he doing here?*

"Stand by the fire," Shad wanted to be sure.

Mickey jumped, looked in the direction the voice came from, looked at the bedroll by the fire and complied with the instructions.

It was Mickey, red hair, freckles and all. It surprised Shad, the sight of a familiar face could move him like it did. His spirits rose immediately.

Shad rose and moved into the firelight.

"Shad?" Mickey was staring into the darkness. "Is that you? By the leprechauns, it's good to see you." Mickey extended a hand. Shad took the hand.

Picking a hunk of roast venison from the sticks beside fire, he handed it to Mickey.

"Faith and begorra!" Mickey held the meat aloft after a bite. "It tastes better than it smells. I've been holed up downwind for two days smelling this. Starving like a dog I was."

Shad smiled at the antics of the Irishman. "What are you doing out here? I mean, why you aren't in Hoffman?"

"Well," Mickey turned reflective. "When Ennis came into my store, they started calling me a nigger lover. My business fell by half. The spit and whittle crowd began meeting elsewhere.

After the war began in earnest, I refused to join the confederate army. Rumors began to circulate that I was a union sympathizer. Later it changed to Union spy. They said I was a Union spy. My business went to nothing. I sent my wife and family north. There was no other safe place for them. Everything I owned was tied up in the store. I stayed to try to salvage something out of it. When word got out that my wife went north, the mob came for me with a rope. These were men I called friends. This hurt worse than the loss of my business. I escaped with my nightclothes on. They looked for me for a couple of days before giving up. I've been wandering since then."

"Where are you going?" Shad nibbled on a piece of the meat and waited for an answer.

Mickey pondered his answer. He couldn't see any harm in telling Shad the truth. "North, I'm going north to find my wife and kids."

"I'm going north also. Would you mind traveling with me?" Shad watched Mickey's reaction out of the corner of his eyes.

"I'd like to travel with you." Mickey seemed sincere.

"Think about it. I'm a runaway slave. I'm a deserter from the Union Army. It could cause you more trouble. They called you a nigger lover before. Think what they would call you if they knew you buddied up and traveled with a nigger." Shad laid it on thick.

"There ain't too much more they can do to me. They already have a rope with my name on it. Maybe you should be the one thinking."

"I'm beginning to get a plan that will get us both out of here alive. Finish eating and I'll be back in a minute." Shad walked out of the firelight and sat down to think.

Shad returned to the fire. "I have a little money. I've got enough to buy a coach and six. You could pretend to be a gentleman on business and I could be your slave until we got to Union controlled territory. After that you could be a Union sympathizer fleeing the South and I'd be a freedman."

"You have enough money for a coach and six?" Mickey was skeptical. "No one will take script anymore."

"Gold," Shad said softly.

They sat by the fire until daybreak, working out the details of obtaining a coach without raising undue suspicion. They also discussed the difficulty of carrying out their rolls, once they had the coach.

Shad didn't tell Mickey the other reason for getting a heavy coach was to carry the massive load of gold in his packs.

After breakfast, Shad handed Mickey a bag containing gold coins.

Untying the drawstring, Mickey took a handful and let them dribble off his fingertips into the bag. "Ohhh whee, that's a lot of money." Mickey hefted the bag.

"Do you think it's enough to keep you from coming back?" Shad queried.

Mickey sucked in his breath and seemed to grow even larger at the insinuation. "Did I give me word to this partnership?" Mickey's eyes were pools of jade beneath the straggling red brows. "When Mickey gives his word only God can stop him from keeping it."

"If you don't plan to come back, tell me now. Let me get moving instead of waiting and looking for you." Shad gave it to him straight from the shoulder.

Mickey deflated and smiled at Shad. "Don't you worry, Mickey will be back. Hit me."

"What?" Shad took a step backward.

"Hit me and don't spare the horses. If I'm going to go into town telling everyone I was set upon by highwaymen I have to look the part."

Shad hesitated. Folding his fist, he pecked Mickey on the side of the head.

Mickey growled and slapped Shad on the side of the head with a ham like hand. Shad staggered from the unexpected blow. Mickey followed, delivering, from side to side, one smacking slap after another.

Shad staggered backward. Huge stars and black spots blurred his vision. Getting his feet set, Shad hit the big

Irishman with a left hook. A straight right followed the left hook. Another straight right stopped Mickey's forward progress. Another left and a right sent the Mickey into the dirt.

Mickey rolled in the dirt, soiling his clothes thoroughly. Taking a double handful of dust, he wiped it through the sweat and blood on his face. Wiping his hands on the front of his shirt, he rose to his feet.

"Faith and begorra, you can hit." Mickey smiled and extended his right hand. "It takes a man to knock down Mickey Doon. Do I present a proper picture?"

Shad felt the side of his stinging face. He didn't know a man could slap so hard. He made a mental note not to ever let the big Irishman hit him.

"A coach shouldn't be much of a problem. Horses will be scarce, what with the military confiscation. If you can't get the horses, try to get the harness. Some of these horses we have may be broke to work and we'll break the ones that aren't." Shad watched Mickey let the stirrups way down on his saddle.

A week later Shad sat above the road, he and Mickey agreed to meet on. He chose his place well. He sat on top of a timber covered ridge on the north side of the road. He placed the horses on the opposite side of the hill to keep them from squealing at a passing horse.

From where he sat he could see a considerable distance down the road. He could also see his horses.

How far can I trust the affable Irishman? Shad pondered. *What am I going to do when I get there? What part am I going to play? What am I going to do with the fortune in gold I'm carrying?* His experience at Tendrilhoff had been in bookkeeping. Mister George did the banking and financial planning. He remembered last time and didn't want to be at loose ends this time.

While he pondered the answers to these questions, Shad spotted a cloud of dust. A red and black coach materialized from the dust. Shad rose to his feet. It wasn't Mickey, he could see three men on top of the coach. Shad settled back to watch the coach go by.

Before it reached the creek the coach halted. Shad was instantly all eyes and ears. Two of the men on top picked up rifles and dropped to the ground. The taller one opened the coach door. A well-dressed gentleman carrying a silver headed cane descended to the ground and removed his tall hat. Mickey Doon.

Shad picked up his rifle. What was Mickey trying to pull? Looking around Mickey spoke to the armed men and they took up station on each side of the coach. Mickey donned his hat and walked straight toward Shad.

"What's with the men?" Shad asked without preamble.

"Well now lad, an important man such as myself, on government business, an emissary of old Jeff himself, couldn't drive his own coach could he?" Mickey made a mock bow. "And since robbers had already set upon his person, he must have an armed guard."

Shad lay the rifle down and laughed. Mickey was one Irishman who had kissed the Blarney Stone. Mickey thrust a hand into his coat pocket and held at arm's length what appeared to be half the gold Shad had given him.

"Since I'm an important person with high connections and gold in my hand, everyone wanted to do business with me." Mickey smiled.

"Keep it. You're the gentleman around here." Shad glanced at the coach. "Get those men away from the coach until I load my gear."

"I'll have them load it."

"No."

Mickey gave Shad a long look and turned down the hill.

The trip across the South with the smooth talking name dropping Mickey was much easier than Shad anticipated.

They paid the guards and driver off and sent them home. Shad took the driver's place. His military experience helped them to find an unguarded place to cross the lines.

On the first day inside Union lines, they met a column of blue clad Cavalry led by a grizzled old Captain. It was clear this man had been military since he was strong enough to pick up one end of a rifle.

The smoother Mickey got, the more suspicious the Captain became.

"We're going to search the coach." Captain Moss announced in no uncertain terms.

"Permission to approach, sir?" Shad said out of the corner of his mouth.

The Captain looked startled. "Approach."

"Not here, sir. Not in this gentleman's presence." Shad whispered, looking straight ahead.

"Lieutenant Duckworth, take this contraband to Sergeant Hawkins. I want to know if he's the one that was in our supplies last night." Moss gave Shad a, this better be good, look.

Moments after Shad was removed from Mickey's presence, Captain Moss strode up. Shad wheeled and gave him a smart salute.

"Will the wonders never cease?" Captain Moss returned the salute.

"I have a communication from General Sherman in my boot, sir. Permission to show it to the Captain, sir?" Shad was going by protocol as much as he could remember. He knew it would impress this, by the book, man.

"Permission granted."

Shad pulled a knife from his belt and heard a rifle being cocked. Looking up, he saw Sergeant Hawkins held a steady bead on him. Bending, he split the leather on top of his boot and handed Captain Moss the papers Sherman wrote so long ago.

"Lieutenant Hoff!" This time, Captain Moss saluted. Both returned to at ease positions. Captain Moss kept staring at Shad.

"I must say Lieutenant Hoff that is the best disguise I have ever seen. For a moment there, I thought you were black. How can we assist you?"

"Take me back, kick my butt, anything, but don't give me away and get out of here."

"That was a close one." Mickey mopped his brow and watched Captain Moss lead the column away.

"It sure was. I was afraid he would question the date on those orders or hold us and check with Sherman." Shad shook his head. Mickey didn't know how close a call it really was.

"It seems we've made it to the North. What now? Where are you going? There is no reason for us to stick together now." Mickey leaned against the coach door.

CHAPTER 31

Shad looked at Mickey, turned and walked a few steps. During their time together, he developed a liking for the big Irishman and a healthy respect for his abilities and resourcefulness. He realized, he trusted Mickey. This was the deciding factor.

"Mickey would you like to go into business with me?" Shad asked.

"What kind of business? I lost everything when they burned my store. I'm broke." The thought made Mickey down cast.

"I don't know what kind of business. Don't answer me yet. Let's sit in the coach. I have a tale to tell you."

"And General Rudat will be after me." Shad finished. If you join me, he might be after you also. I'm afraid of this man. He's capable of anything."

The only thing he held back was how much gold there was.

"I knew you had something, but I didn't think it was gold. I was surprised you had the gold to buy the coach. What kind of business are you going into and how much will you pay me?" Mickey rubbed his mouth and stroked his chin.

"I don't know what I'm going to do. Look until I find something. I thought we'd be partners. We'd split what we made, fifty-fifty."

"Done!" Mickey extended a hand. "How much capital do we have to start with?"

Shad shook Mickey's hand. "I don't know."

"You don't know?" Mickey's brow furrowed.

"It's all in gold and I've not had the time or space to count it. There's something in the excess of a thousand pounds of it."

"A thousand..." Mickey's jaw dropped.

"I didn't have a way to weigh it either, but I think it weighs over a thousand pounds." Shad changed the subject." I think we ought to get rid of this coach. It was fine in the South while we were posing as bureaucrats. All it does up here is draw unwanted attention and curiosity."

"We ought to get a farm wagon." Mickey pulled the lapel of his coat. "I'll have to get different clothes, dad gum it, I was beginning to enjoy these fancy clothes. "Let's go to Washington, D.C. Get right in the middle of it. I need to write my wife and tell her I will send for them as soon as possible."

"Where is she? We'll hire a courier to hand carry the letter." Shad was feeling expansive.

The next day Mickey traded the coach and six to a Dutchman for a wide wheeled flat-bottomed wagon and a beautiful team of black Belgian horses. They were coal black with a white star on their foreheads and white stockings on the fore feet. Each of them weighed over a ton.

Building a false floor in the wagon, they secreted the gold there. Swinging north and east they avoided all parts of the country, war had touched. They rolled across a beautiful and tranquil country.

To his delight, Shad found Mickey to be a reservoir of business acumen. The quiet hours, with the black's huge feet kicking up little puffs of dust, proved to be a time Shad could round out the knowledge he picked up at Tendrilhoff.

"Foreknowledge, knowing or being able to divine what was going on behind scenes and predicting future outcomes was a topic Mickey returned to several times.

What can I do in business? Shad thought panicky. *It is a large universe and I know so little. Calm down,* he told himself. *Calm down. I remember when Mister George caught me reading. I thought it was the end of the world. The first ledger book Mister George laid in front of me was gobbledygook. I have the business and managerial knowledge gained at Tendrilhoff and the knowledge and assistance of Mickey.*

I must teach myself to think and see. Shad admonished himself. *No better place to start than right now. I need to learn the country and economy of it as we pass through. There is the railroad we are going to ride, how does it work? Who owns it and what are its potential for profit and growth?*

The farms they passed were immaculate. Fields well tilled, and buildings maintained. The latest farm implements and good working stock everywhere. War was a profitable enterprise for these farmers. Shad couldn't help but compare this with the sacrifice, starvation, death and destruction in the South.

Upon approaching the B&O Railroad, a few shots followed by several more set Shad and Mickey to looking to priming their rifles. A series of yells and whoops rent the air beyond the tree.

"What do you think that is?" Mickey watched Shad.

"Seems too far north for a Cavalry raid," Shad turned the other ear.

"Look out," Mickey warned. A rider came around the bend where the tree covered the road. His mount was running with both ears laid flat. Every few strides the rider stroked the horse with a whip. Both men instinctively got set for an onslaught.

The rider was oblivious to the danger he was in. Neither Shad nor Mickey raised a rifle as the distance between them and the rider closed. The whooping rider's hands were empty except for the whip.

"The war's over!" The rider flashed past them. "Lee surrendered!"

CHAPTER 32

Mickey and Shad stared at each other. Could this be true, the war was over? Neither realized the war was over for the North, but the poor, shattered, bleeding South faced reconstruction and was to become carpetbagger heaven.

Arriving at the B&O, Mickey booked a boxcar for the wagon and blacks. Shad and Mickey rode the same car.

Washington, D.C. was an experience Shad would never forget. Never had he seen so many people so close together. Every one of them seemed to be in a hurry. None of them recognized or even said good morning to the others.

"We need to find a good livery stable and store the wagon until we can find a bank." Mickey said.

"I'll stay and watch it." Shad volunteered.

"That might draw suspicion. I think it would be better to trust the false bottom." Mickey said.

When they unloaded the wagon at the railway station Mickey obtained directions to a livery stable. It was clean, well maintained and for the owner, it was love at first sight when the blacks pranced in.

Cal, owner of the livery stable, took his eyes off the blacks long enough to direct them to a middle class hotel.

Shad awoke to find Mickey decked out in a suit and tie. The silver headed cane in his hand.

"I'm going to find us a bank. Are you coming along?" Mickey flourished the cane.

"No, I'll check the team and wagon. I think I'll wander today. I need to think and look things over."

The blacks snorted and pranced upon his arrival. Their feed boxes still had feed in them and the water troughs were full of clean water. Shad strolled past the wagon. If there was anything wrong, he couldn't detect it.

On his way out Coaly, the largest of the blacks, stuck his head over the half door and nuzzled Shad's chest. Shad wandered along the sidewalk taking in the hustle and bustle of the city. Rounding a corner, his heart skipped a beat. The Capitol Buildings were in full sight.

The street was broad, paved, and tree lined. Two colored men operated a shoeshine stand on the east side. Shad moseyed along taking in the sights and wondering how he was going to find a way to invest the money in this large city.

Shad looked in storefronts. The amount and variety of items boggled his mind. *Where did all this stuff come from? Someone grew it, manufactured it, or imported it from someone who did grow or make it. Would the retail business be a good thing for me to go into?*

Across the street, Shad saw the shoe shine man rise from his task and reach for more shoe polish. Moses, Shad did a double take, it was Moses. He concentrated on the second man. Elias. *How did they get here?*

Shad loitered until they were through with the present customers. It was a joyful reunion. There was much hugging, backslapping and laughter as they filled one another in on the details of their escape and journey to the North. Of course, Shad made no mention of General Rudat or the gold.

Two customers approached and Shad took a seat beside the shoeshine stand.

"How is Sam coming on his efforts to raise capital for the iron works?" The bald one asked the other.

"I don't know for sure. The way his wife is passing out

favors, I'm tempted to invest in it myself." The shorter man laughed, digging a sheet of facts and figures from his pocket. They freely discussed the prospects of the iron works and the attributes and possibilities of the lady involved.

Shad listened to every word and thought about it. Moses and Elias finished the shine and the gentlemen paid, left a generous tip, and departed.

Moses turned to Shad, "Here's some money. You are going to need money to live here."

"No." Shad waved Moses off.

Moses threw a questioning glance at Elias. Receiving an affirmative nod, he continued, "We'll share the shoeshine stand with you. Maybe after a while, we can get the money together to buy another one."

"Do all your customers talk so freely?" Shad changed the subject.

"You mean about the iron works and the lady? Yeah, I'd say so." Moses scratched his head. "One thing you gotta learn is that you are the dumb nigger. Those businessmen can't see you. If someone pointed you out, they would have laughed and said you weren't smart enough to understand what they were saying.

"They live in a different world. The only place our worlds come together is when we work for them or buy something they manufacture or sell."

Shad was too preoccupied to visit longer with Moses and Elias. Giving them a promise to return on the morrow, he wandered down the street.

The shoeshine stand could be a valuable source of information. All you needed to do was get the right people in the chairs. How to do that? Perhaps you could move the stands close to the source of information.

Put in two chairs. The presence of a third party might inhibit conversation. No, put in three chairs, but only put two shoeshine boys on it. Put in two sets of three chairs with two shoeshine boys on each set. If a group of three came along, they could sit together and talk. A shoeshine boy from the other booth could assist the other two.

Perhaps if a shoeshine boy was very judicious, he could get the kind of conversation he wanted to hear started.

He was still rolling this over in his mind when he entered the hotel room.

"About time you wandered in." Mickey was out of the suit, buttoning a sleeve on his shirt.

"How did your day go?"

"Ok, yours?"

"I think I've found us a bank, the Argonne Industrial, and I found myself a job."

"A job? What kind of a job?" Shad questioned.

"You are looking at the new bartender of the Senate Club."

"Senate Club?"

"Yeah, it's where most of the lawmakers relax. What did you do today?"

"I think I found me a job." Shad grinned.

"Doing what?"

"Shoeshine boy." Shad went on to fill Mickey in on his idea.

"Sounds like it'll work. That's the reason I took this bartending job. You know how drunks like to cry on the bartender's shoulder. I'm going to check on the Argonne Industrial Bank tonight and if it checks out do you want to deposit the gold tomorrow?"

CHAPTER 33

Mickey woke Shad in the middle of the night with a gold scale in hand. They spent the rest of the night and far into the next morning counting, weighing, and tallying the gold.

The trip to the bank and Mickey's passage to the chair in the Bank President's office was uneventful. Shad guarded the wagon.

Charles Pennywell, the bank president, sat stiffly behind his desk. "You realize this is a commercial institution?"

"Yes, we understand this is a commercial institution. We've heard on good accounts this institution is a discreet commercial institution. One that never mettles in client's affairs or leaks information." Mickey leaned forward, placed his hands on the silver head of his cane, and looked Pennywell in the eye. "If it isn't, we will go elsewhere."

Pennywell nodded his head in acceptance of Mickey's statement. "How much do you intend to deposit?"

"Three hundred, fifty-eight thousand, four hundred, and twelve dollars," Mickey said slowly.

Pennywell's mouth went slack like he had been hit. "How.., how much?" He stuttered.

"Three hundred, fifty-eight thousand, four-hundred, and twelve dollars."

Pennywell gathered his wits. "What bank will the letter of credit be on?"

"No letter of credit. Gold, all gold."

"Gold? Do you jest, sir?"

"I don't jest with that kind of money." Mickey said coldly. "It's gold coin, gold bar, and some nuggets."

"When can you have it here?"

"It's already here. My partner is guarding it at the back door. Get some clerks, get it in here, and get it counted."

"Sign these papers so we have your signature on record Pennywell passed the papers over."

"Shad has to sign them also." Mickey signed and passed the papers to Shad.

"Ah, Mister Doon, do you think it good business to let a servant have access to your funds?"

"He's the man who owns these funds, he kindly gave me access." Mickey didn't bother to look up.

Pennywell reached for the water glass, he didn't think he could stand much more today. He looked at Shad with new respect in his eyes.

Mickey and Shad were shown out of the bank with the utmost courtesy. Shad carried a saddlebag containing a hefty pile of gold coins on his shoulder.

Ingrid sat staring at the water bubbling across the rocks in the front yard. After Alf and Jim Bob's raid, most of the slaves left at Tendrilhoff came to live on Albert and Ingrid's place. Ingrid was able to feed them from the food cache Shad set up. Hannibal and two house servants stayed at Tendrilhoff.

In the meantime, they built Ingrid a log house at the spring where Shad found Ennis. The slaves also erected themselves cabins at different locations on Albert and Ingrid's land.

Ingrid never liked this location as well as the one Alf and Jim Bob burned, but she didn't guess it mattered much anymore.

"What time do you expect the Judge to show up?" Ingrid shifted her swollen stomach to a more comfortable position. The child was due anytime now.

"He'll be here before your husband gets back." Sheriff Crowe said confidently. "If the Judge gets here and serves them papers before your husband gets back, it's too late. I don't care if he has the tax money in his hand. The Judge gets the place."

"He's a scalawag and carpetbagger!" Ingrid exploded. "We've got the place all cleared and in good shape. We built a new house and barn."

The Sheriff picked his teeth. "Maybe you shouldn't have done that. It made the taxes higher."

"The only thing that raised the taxes was a greedy scalawag wanting this valley. You always said you were going to be Judge. Did that carpetbagger get your job?" Ingrid taunted.

"It ain't over yet!" The Sheriff went red to the ears and brought his chair down with a thump to face a young rider who loped up to the gate.

"Who are you and what do you want?" The Sheriff growled. He wanted to take his anger out on someone. "Well, come on, state your business and get."

The young man from the saddle behind the horse, and let the horse walk out of the way. Feet spread, weight forward, the young man's hand hung dangerously close to a big pistol on his hip. Sheriff Crowe rose to his feet. He had misjudged another situation.

"Now, young man," Crowe began to bluster.

"Sit down and shut up." The young man didn't wait for the Sheriff to comply. Using his left hand, the young man pulled a saddlebag from the horse.

I'm Sam Brown, Pinkerton Agency, ma'am." The young man nodded to Ingrid and ignored the sheriff.

"Pinkerton Agency!" The sheriff exploded. "You might have told me."

"Sit down," Sam ordered again and the sheriff complied. "I'm Sam Brown of the Pinkerton Detective Agency and I'm looking for Ingrid White."

"You've found her."

"May I have a moment of your time?"

Ingrid struggled to rise. Her pregnancy was about over. "Not you, Sheriff, I told you, no further than the front porch."

"How the mighty will fall. You won't be able to tell me anything very soon now." The Sheriff looked down the road, hoping to see the Judge.

Sam and Ingrid walked to the kitchen table. Ingrid sat.

"A man named Shad sent you this." Sam unbuckled one side of the saddlebag and laid it before Ingrid. "I believe there is a letter in this one."

Curiously, Ingrid raised the flap. With a sharp intake of breath, she stared at the golden hoard.

Counting out the exact amount of taxes owed, Ingrid returned to the porch, handed the Sheriff the gold and waited until he counted it.

"Sheriff," she said. "Mister Brown, Pinkerton agent, is a witness to you collecting those taxes. You are through. The carpetbaggers won't be in power much longer. When they are gone, Albert and a hundred other men are going to be after you with a rope."

Pulling her hand from her pocket, she pushed Conrad's pistol against Crowe's forehead and drew the hammer back. A foul odor filled the air.

"Sheriff Crowe," she almost crooned. "Third time is a charm. If you ever set foot on my place again, I'm going to shoot you for the dog you are. If I let you walk, will you leave the country?"

"Yes, ma'am, I sure will!" Crowe tried to nod his head, but the pressing gun barrel held it steady.

"Git!" Ingrid shouted, stomping her foot.

Crowe leaped from the chair, fell, scuttled to the edge of the porch, and fell off it. Scratching with both feet and hands, the panicked Sheriff reached the gate. Ingrid put a bullet in the gate beside his hand. Sheriff Crowe ran past his horse and disappeared down the road.

"Wow," Sam Brown placed the hat back on his head. "I

asked Shad how to find you and he said find the strongest lady in the South. I believe him now."

Ingrid placed the still smoking pistol back in her pocket. "I would offer you some coffee, but I don't have any. I would offer you cake, but I don't have any of that either. I do have beans, peas, and cornbread." While Sam ate, Ingrid read Shad's letter.

Dearest Ingrid:

I made it to Washington, DC. I'm sending you money for your taxes. Under the guise of tax collection, carpetbaggers are stealing the South. I've paid taxes on Tendrilhoff and tied it up legally. I've found a way to obtain a deed. Tendrilhoff is now registered in your name. Divide it among the former slaves whose labor developed it. You have been teaching and dealing with the former slaves on a much freer basis than I ever saw them. Give to each according to his ambition and abilities. I realize this puts you in an undesirable position.

Tell them, it's my doing. You are just following instructions. Place a lien on each deed so they can't sell or be cheated out of the land. We will remove these as the people become more sophisticated in dealing with free life.

Give Hannibal the big house and forty acres of land. I have insured him enough income to maintain it. We are tracking the slaves Junior sold and will send those who want to come. Mickey Doon and I are in business together. The slaves who ran away from Tendrilhoff are here and working for Mickey and myself.

Mickey loves the wheeling and dealing hoopla. He does all the up front work. I keep stalling, but I can think of no easy way to tell you this. I found Bekah. She had my son with her. The very day I found her, she was killed in a fight between Alf and Jim Bob. My son disappeared without a trace.

Alf, Jim Bob, and all their men were destroyed during the fight.

Yours,

Shad Doppler Hoff

Ingrid stood in the door waving to the departing detective when the first pain hit her. Placing a hand on her side, she sucked in air. "Tamar." She yelled.

It was daybreak before Tamar placed the baby, cleaned and wrapped, in Ingrid's arms and said. "Miss Ingrid, meet your daughter. The most perfect and beautiful baby I ever delivered."

A loud banging on the door cut off the women's chuckles.

"Hand me my pistol and send whoever it is away." Ingrid listened to the rumble of voices. They were coming her way.

Tamar entered the room, followed by a shifty eyed man in a flat black hat. His clothes and weasel look marked him as one of the hangers on at Hoffman. He worked when he could find no way out of it. He carried a picnic basket in his hand.

"Are you Ingrid?" He asked before they could question him. "Yes."

A gambler gave me ten dollars to bring this to you." He plopped the basket onto the foot of her bed.

"What is it?" Ingrid raised her head to see.

"It's Junior Hoff's baby."

CHAPTER 34

"Junior's baby? What is it doing here?"

"His momma died having him in the saloon over there at Hoffman. A gambler gave me ten bucks to carry him here." With that the man walked to the door and refused to stop.

"Poor thing!" Tamar exclaimed, looking into the basket.

"Hand him to me," Ingrid requested.

"Oh my God!" Ingrid exclaimed. "He's more dead than alive. I wondered why he wasn't crying."

Ingrid held the smelly, improperly cleaned baby to a breast. No action. Milking a little milk she rubbed it in his mouth. The tiny lips moved. Again, Ingrid raised him to her breast. A tentative movement of the lips and the baby settled into a steady sucking rhythm.

Ingrid leaned forward and cuddled him. A smile curled her lips. "Tamar, no one is to know where he came from. Not even Albert. It's the only way we can repay Mister George. We will raise his grandson as our own. He will never know the circumstances of his father, mother, or birth."

Tamar shrugged, "I delivered two babies today, didn't I?"

Shad whipped the polish rag across the shoe and listened. He finished the polish job, but puttered along in order give the senators in the chairs time to finish their conversation.

"There is no way the Jacobins and Secretary Chase is going to allow the new steam battleships to be built in the Albemarle yards." The taller of the two stated.

"Right, and Seward is just as opposed to building them in the Covington yards. We need the new ships started now. Do you think I could get a compromise and award the contracts to the smaller Coalville yards?" The younger senator worried.

"I'll back it and the President will back it. He wants the battleships more than we do. Keep a lid on this for two weeks. It will take Chase and Seward that long to maneuver themselves into a stalemate." The senators tossed Shad a coin and walked away.

"The Coalville shipyards are in financial difficulties." Mickey said when Shad related the conversation.

"How bad are their troubles?" Shad was interested.

"Bad, they're facing foreclosure."

"Those contracts will make the Coalville shipyards bigger and more profitable than the Abermarle or Covington shipyards. The Coalville shipyard belongs to the Garibaldi family. John Garibaldi is president of the company and controls it all. Perhaps we should pay him a visit tomorrow?"

"It's settled then; we pay the outstanding debts and take control of fifty-one percent of the company." Mickey leaned back and relaxed.

"I stay on as company president and the family maintains forty-nine percent ownership of the company. When do you plan to send the senior vice president you are going to appoint?" John picked up a pen and the papers. He affixed his signature and looked Mickey in the eye. "Ok partner, tell me what you know about this shipyard that I don't."

The negotiations with John Garibaldi had been nip and tuck. As usual Mickey carried the verbal war. Shad sat back and listened. He and Mickey were developing a nonverbal communication only the most astute observer could discern. Most businessmen thought Shad was Mickey's servant.

Shad was tired. It had been a grueling two years since he and Mickey arrived at the Capitol. The Coalville shipyards were in full stride on the battleship contracts and were growing very profitable.

Shad and Mickey's information network kept growing, branching and mutating until it reached into every segment of business society. It reached from newspaper Hawkers to the drawing rooms of the rich.

Shad and Mickey were on the verge of joining the super rich. Shad's vast memory and analytic, reticent personality complemented Mickey's rambunctious flamboyancy. They were as close as brothers and were able to make the most out of any business opportunity.

Shad trudged up the stairs. Mickey had long since purchased a hill on the edge of the city and installed his family there in great comfort. Mickey cleared a spot near his mansion and urged Shad to build.

Without Bekah, Shad had no inclination toward a house. He purchased the middle class hotel, he and Mickey inhabited on their arrival in Washington DC and remodeled the top floor into a comfortable bachelor pad.

The loss of Bekah was in a large part responsible for Shad and Mickey's success. Shad had thrown himself into the business around the clock, trying to ease the loss of Bekah and baby George. He could think of them now in fond memory without the stinging pain of guilt and loss, he first encountered.

Shad was noticing the waitress who served his breakfast every morning. She was a winsome lass with a personality that caught his eye.

Taking his keys from his pocket, Shad spoke to a maid scrubbing the hall floor. He had noticed her before and was considering inviting her to supper when he pushed his door open.

Someone moved in his apartment. Shad stepped closer to see. Rudat! General Rudat stood and smiled at him. The General was no longer in uniform, but the little pig eyes were as sinister as ever.

"Surprised?" Rudat chuckled, his fat jowls quacking in and out. "We've been watching you since shortly after you arrived in DC and deposited the gold. We've enjoyed the lessons you taught us and the increase in our investment. But alas, the time has come for us to pull our marker in. You will sign those papers on the table and we'll all be on our way."

Shad turned to the door. Two burly men leaned against it. One held a pistol.

"What are the papers?" Shad turned back to Rudat.

"Oh, some deeds, power-of-attorney, your will, things like that."

"My will?"

"Yes, you don't think we could let you get out of this alive, do you? We considered letting you work for us. We'd been in favor of giving you a small percentage. It was decided you are too dangerous to let live."

Shad was silent. He eyed the tough looking thugs and tried to devise a way out.

"You can do it the easy way or the hard way. I hope you choose the hard way myself. If you sign, it will be a simple case of strangulation." Rudat grinned.

"What do you think my partner will think of this?" Shad stalled for time.

"We'll handle your partner. In fact, he is operating on your money. He's due to have an accident someday soon. We have forgers standing by. If we fail to get your signature, it will be ok. You won't be here to contest it and your partner won't be here either."

"I won't sign." Shad's jaw set in a stubborn line.

Rudat's face lit with a smile. "I didn't think you would. Bind one of his hands to each of you. We'll walk out of here shoulder to shoulder." Rudat turned to Shad, "Please don't make us kill you on the way out. If you do, we'll make it look like a simple robbery gone wrong."

Shad tried to think of how he could tip the maid in the hall without putting her in danger. If Rudat was the least bit suspicious, he would take her also.

Shad was still searching for a plan when the thug connected to his wrist opened the door. The maid was gone. Lock, stock, and mop. She was gone. Keep your head, he cautioned. Wait for a mistake. They are bound to make a mistake.

Stair after stair they descended. The goons either side of him were alert and he could hear the fat Rudat puffing along behind. These thugs are tied to me, Shad thought, and Rudat is a fat man. If we run into anyone who can get away, I'm going to raise a ruckus.

They reached street level and issued out onto the boardwalk in front of the hotel. A closed carriage drove to the edge of the boardwalk and the taller thug on Shad's right reached for the door latch.

"Everyone stand easy and raise your hands." The voice came from behind Shad. Before he could turn, a policeman with a weapon in his hand, stepped around the other end of the coach.

Rudat pulled his hand from his pocket and there was a blaze of fire and loud crashing noises everywhere. Shad felt a bruising shock in his ribs and the boardwalk rose to hit him in the back of the head. Blackness enveloped him.

"Sir, are you with us, sir?" Shad opened his eyes to see a blurry figure in front of him. He closed his eyes and wiped them with his fingers. Opening his eyes, he saw the face of a policeman bent over him.

"He's around." The policeman told his partner. "That was a nasty blow to the head, sir."

Shad felt for the throb in his side and found his shirt was open.

"It was a lucky hit, sir," the policeman said. "The bullet burned your ribs but didn't enter your body."

"How did you get here?" Shad queried the policeman.

"She brought us." The policeman stepped aside to reveal the maid from the hall.

"What was going on, sir?" The policeman took a notepad from his pocket. "Were they robbing you?"

Shad rose to his feet. Rudat looked crumpled, somehow smaller. The sinister quality departed with life. He was now just a dead fat man.

"Yes," Shad said. "They were in the process of robbing me."

Trying to take a step, Shad staggered. Before either policeman could react, the maid leaped to his side and steadied him.

"How did you know I was in trouble?" Shad asked the maid as he leaned on her shoulder.

"I heard voices where there should have been none and I eavesdropped." The maid confessed.

"I'm sure glad you worked late tonight," Shad was feeling stronger, but was reluctant to break contact with the maid.

"Men!" The maid exclaimed under her breath. Tilting her head back, she looked Shad in the eye. "You haven't noticed me working late, in that hall, every night for a month?"

CHAPTER 35

Bubbling from far beneath the earth the cold, clear water hurled itself over the wall. Falling, it crashed into the grasping rocks and dodged this way and that. Chucking at its escape, it dashed through a rough wooden trough under the vine-draped fence. Slamming its foaming body into a sluice gate, it became a split personality. Part of it slid quietly down a ditch to the family garden. There it spread and sacrificed itself to the plant roots. The escaping water danced and sang its way into the big river.

A light fog rose off the water and floated down the valley. The old monarchs were gone. Even their roots were ripped from the rich loamy soil. Once virgin forest converted to mighty fields, producing food for the tables of America.

Above the hazy valley rose majestic, tree haired ridges. Rank after rank they marched into the far blue distance. Once free and easy, they were now lined with fences and boundary markers.

A gentle breeze came from the indefinite far blue distance. Rustling through the trees, it stirred the leaves. Searching for fragrances it could clutch to its breast and toss across the land as it squeezed over the ridges. Peeking through the fog, it tiptoed across the valley. Rustling the vines on the fence, the breeze gently closed the door Ingrid left open.

Ingrid eased into a rocking chair on the end of the porch. Her eyes roved over the open areas close to the house and moved on to the valley. She checked all the roads across the valley. Pausing here and there. Fog or dust? Fog, she decided each time. Leaving the valley, her eyes checked the mountain passes. This was a legacy from living in dangerous and turbulent times.

It was an unnecessary habit. Peace had come to the valley. True peace. No more soldiers, Blue or Gray. Reconstruction and the carpetbaggers were on its way to becoming a bad memory. Even the hard riding, hood shrouded KKK had curtailed their activities in this area.

Ingrid turned her head to listen for sounds that never existed. Sunlight glistened on the long sun streaked blonde hair, highlighting the almost imperceptible hint of gray.

The rocker squeaked as she leaned back, truly queen of all she surveyed. Respected and admired by the white population, she was called "Miss Angel" and adored by the colored people.

Ingrid pulled a letter from her pocket and clasp it to her breast, remembering the bad good old days. Days when youth's energies knew no boundaries and faith in tomorrow carried them through today.

The twins and Alfred, Ennis's third, delivered Shad's letter on their return from Hoffman. George, with the laughing blue eyes, light complexion, and blonde hair. Tall and handsome with a mischievous curving smile, George was rambunctious and fun loving to the point of rashness. Contrasting with his dark haired, brown-eyed sister. Her English reserve looked on his shenanigans with loving, good-natured humor.

Ingrid always read Shad's letters in the quietness of the morning. It gave her time to reflect, savor the past, enjoy today, and think of tomorrow.

Dearest Ingrid,

It is with great sadness, we write to tell you we won't be vacationing at Tendrilhoff this summer. Lydia is expecting the birth of our third about the middle of this time period.

Congratulations to Albert on his successful campaign for the Senate. We need levelheaded thinking people up in the Capitol. We are hoping you will spend time with him and us here in DC.

Mickey is too busy playing Grandfather to do any more than send his love. I don't think the night riders will be as active as they have been in the past. Mickey discovered their leaders are the same group of men who destroyed his business, burned his store, tried to hang him, and hounded him out of the county. He has allotted a tremendous amount of capital to compete with their businesses and enterprises. Slow strangulation is sure to follow. This should keep them too busy to bother decent, law-abiding citizens.

Sherman has been convinced he has no political career. He has been shown the chinks in his armor. If he runs for public office, all will come out. His careless handling of requisitions will get him crucified by the North and South alike.

Your adopted son,
Shad Doppler Hoff